A NOVEL BY VONNA IVORY JOSEPH

This is a work of fiction. All names, characters, incidents, and locations are a product of the author's imagination. Any resemblance to people, living or dead, and events, true or imagined, is completely coincidental.

Published by Twelve Twenty-Six Kozart, Orlando

Cover design by Tara Mixon for Black Girl Narrative
Cover Model: Jayquan (Justice) Johnson

ISBN-10 978-0692723715
ISBN-13 0692723714

First Edition

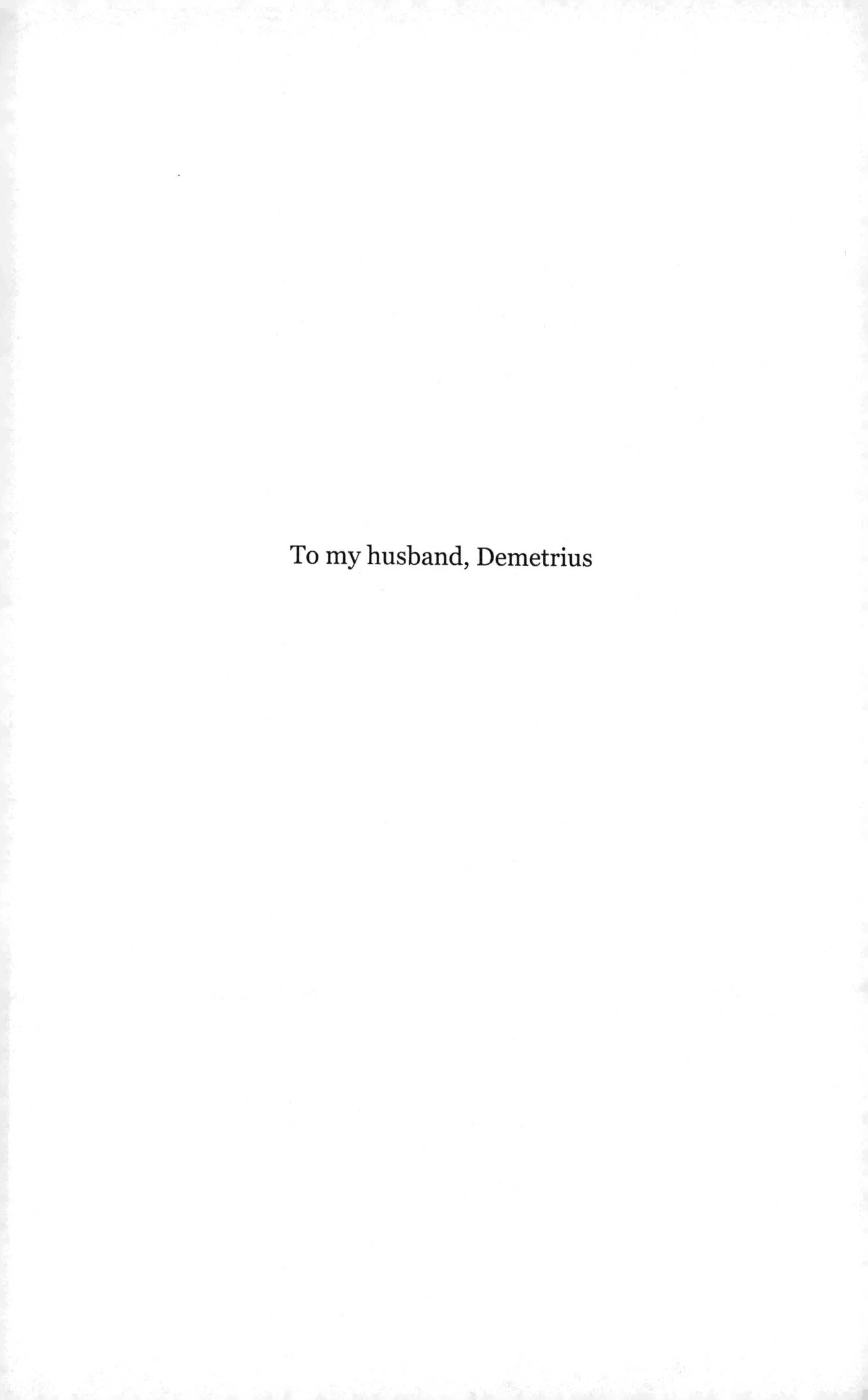

To my husband, Demetrius

CROSSED LINES

A GOOD ENOUGH NOVEL

VONNA IVORY JOSEPH

CHAPTER ONE

Back In The Day

Lacey wasn't exactly a romantic, but when he smiled, she almost forgot why she was there amongst piles of egregious carbs—cinnamon crunch bagels, cherry topped pastries and red velvet cupcakes. And two brief weeks later, there she was, in some questionable part of town, Ms. Tuskegee University 2002, lying completely nude in a studio apartment, surrounded by posters of Bob Marley and Peter Tosh and the lingering scent of smoky musk and myrrh.

"Jesus! Lace, say something," Oliver said, as he tried to suppress a nervous chuckle. "I'm feeling like I should apologize here," he whispered against her back, just between her shoulder blades. The warmth of his breath on her wet skin sent tingles racing to her thighs.

"Are you sure my car's okay out there?"

Oliver rolled onto his back and stared at the ceiling.

"I'm asking you about what just happened. Don't you have something to say about what just happened?

The annoyance in his voice was pronounced, but she was more comfortable talking about her beloved Porsche.

"Okay," she dragged out, before agreeing to play along.

Lacey couldn't bring herself to look into his eyes. Keeping her back turned relieved them both of the discomfort of making eye contact. They were practically strangers, but his cognac colored, bedroom eyes had drawn her in like a moth to a flame, and she knew on a cellular level that one of them was going to get burned.

"The second I saw you, I knew this would happen. It wasn't really anything you said or anything you did. It was just a feeling that things were going to get interesting between you and I," she explained.

Lacey had immediately caught Oliver's eye that first day she walked into his bakeshop.

"Hel-lo, how may I help you?" he cooed as he effortlessly leaned toward her.

He had an easy smile that held rows of perfectly straight, white teeth. He wore his hair in long, soft dreadlocks that were pulled neatly into a ponytail. A woman of Lacey's class wouldn't ordinarily find his type attractive. But the hair, the eyes and deep brown skin were all working together like a well thought out plot to seduce and distract her.

"For real? 'Cause I wouldn't have called this in a million years," Oliver said between more kisses to her back. Her admission seemed to put
him at ease.

"Seriously, Oliver," she said pulling away from his kisses. She needed to focus.
"It's been a really long time since..." Lacey cut her words short before divulging too much information about her fourteen years of celibacy.

"Since what?" he asked while sliding closer to her and wrapping his long, well-built arms around her waist. Lacey felt the sticky moisture pooling between her thighs again. She squirmed, wanting to avoid his question.

"So about your Boss Lady, how did you two get so close?" she asked.

It was Oliver who squirmed next.

"She's more like my sister. I just call her Boss Lady to screw with her."

He scrambled around for his shorts. Lacey turned over to face him. He looked a little surprised, but quickly replaced that look with a more pleased one.

"A sister," Lacey repeated. "How so?" she pressed, refusing to let him off the hook. She wrapped her long curvy legs around his, preventing him from leaving the bed. Feeling the wet, stickiness between her thighs squelched his resistance.

"You're a tricky one, aren't you?"

He groaned and turned to enter her again. In the throes of long, sensual hip thrusts and wet kisses, he told her that he and Cami Robbins had met as kids and had remained pretty much inseparable.

"We've been through a lot of shit together. Her and Camilla are the only family I have here—so give her a chance. Okay? For me?" he pleaded with her between clenched teeth.

It had been fourteen years since Lacey had last been with a man intimately. Her last sexual experience had resulted in her very own After School Special—produced, directed and starring Lacey Jackson Robinson.

Lacey and her older brother were very close. They'd grown up on their family's compound—just outside of Tuscaloosa, Alabama. Lennox and Lacey Robinson were home-schooled until they were old enough to enter high school. The only other children who they'd ever spent time with were their cousins. Her brother blossomed in high school. His movie star looks and natural athletic ability made for a smooth transition. Lacey's, on the other hand, was not. She was flat chested and gangly. Her thick, horn-rimmed glasses, and her light skin was too much for the liking of many Black girls growing up in Alabama. Her hazel colored eyes drew mean spirited meows and other hateful cat references whenever she was caught walking the halls without the company of her big brother. When he went away to college, it truly upended life as she'd known it. His choice to attend college on the West Coast compounded the misery of her having to attend her senior year of high school alone.

Just as the flyers announcing the Under The Sea themed Senior Prom were being plastered around the school, Lennox's friend, Tobias Bellamy, started meeting Lacey at her locker between classes. He'd walk her to class and would sit with her at lunch. Tobias was slick and beautiful. He was popular and was being scouted by all the best colleges for both his skills on the football field and his academic achievements. Most importantly, she was no longer left alone navigating the cruel hallways of Tuscaloosa Senior High. Even as an adult, Lacey still couldn't explain why she didn't tell Lennox that she was hanging out with Tobias. Whenever he called home, she mostly listened to his stories about college life and the new friends he was making. She never offered much information about how she was doing, one way or another. On some level, she knew that hanging out with Tobias wasn't a good idea. Lennox had shared stories about the guys in school making bets on unsuspecting girls, and the ugly things they'd say about them while dressing out in the musty boys locker room. Maybe that's why she neglected to mention who'd asked her to prom.

Prom night was largely uneventful, and not exactly everything she'd dreamed it would be. All of the popular girls came over to greet her and Tobias. They remarked on how pretty she looked. -

Tobias was crowned Prom King, along with one of her few friends, Kenya Armstrong. Lacey felt like a normal high school girl that night. Days earlier, Tobias had refused an offer to chip in with a few of the popular kids to rent a limousine and had decided to drive his father's Jaguar so that they could be alone. When he told her about his plans, she knew that being "alone" alluded to having sex. She wanted to have sex. She felt like having sex on prom night was something normal kids would do, and she was looking forward to losing her virginity. Her cousins had whispered and giggled about making love. They talked about how they'd do it while listening to Jodeci. They would go on about how much their boyfriends loved them. Sex seemed to make them cooler, more grown up—prettier even. Tobias had never asked her to have sex with him. They'd made out and fooled around a little and she'd let him slip his hands under her shirt in the front seat of his Ford Escort. She'd even given him an awkward hand job in his bedroom while he was recovering from an ankle sprain, but he'd never pushed for intercourse.

As the end of the dance neared, Lacey's anxiety intensified. Tobias laid out his plan over dinner; he'd perfected every detail. The plan chiefly depended on an older cousin of his renting a room for them at the Econo Lodge.

They drove along in virtual silence. Lacey quietly reviewed every piece of advice she'd ever been given about being a good lover. She fussed over her choice of underwear, and which positions she was willing to try. The silence continued through the parking lot and as they entered the dated room, she breathed in the faint smell of stale cigarettes and talcum powder. The overwhelming use of mauves and hospital blues reminded her of her parents' bedroom—striking chords of guilt within her. After all, she was sitting in a hotel room preparing to have sex. She nervously sat on the edge of one of the double beds, and watched Tobias take off his white tuxedo jacket before he sat down on the beside her on the bed.

"Are you sure you want to do this, Lacey? It's cool if you don't want to."

She was sure that she wanted to lose the un-coolness of virginity that night. She was completely sure and she let him know by kissing him on the mouth, and putting her hand down the front of his rented trousers. He stiffened instantly. After a few minutes of clumsy foreplay and kitten licks to her aroused clitoris, they were stark naked underneath the scratchy floral quilt. During his quick and jerky thrusts, she quietly wondered if this was it. It felt nothing like her cousins had described, and Tobias had forgotten to bring the boom box, so there was no Jodeci playing—there was no soundtrack for her epic moment, there was no epic-*ness* at all.

Lacey laid in silence, counting his humps. She was surprised by how long it took. When he was done, they quickly hopped up and put their clothes back on. By Monday morning, Tobias would barely look at her, and she felt like every guy in school knew that she had put out on prom night. He didn't exactly ignore her, but he sat with his friends during lunch, and left a note in her locker that read,

I have practice, so you'll need to take the bus home. -Toby

They went on that way for the next few weeks, and after a few more inelegant hook ups, the school year came to an end and after graduation, so did Tobias and Lacey.

Lacey had gone two months without a period, and she was completely freaked out. She'd never felt so afraid and alone. She remembered going into Green's Pharmacy and praying no one who knew her parents, caught her lurking around the pregnancy tests. Her stomach was always in knots, and she was as pale as a ghost. She'd lost nearly ten pounds, and her mother had become concerned. She ordered Lacey to sit for seconds at dinner on at least three occasions.

"Lacey, Baby I don't like how you're looking. You can't stand to lose any more weight, young lady."

"Tess, leave the child alone," her father said.

Lacey sat on the cold toilet seat in her bathroom and ruefully looked down at the lavender and white stick. When she saw the + sign appear, she literally fell off of the toilet seat. She stayed on the floor with her back against the cool porcelain, and both hands clasped over her mouth, stifling her sobs. When Lacey was sure her parents were asleep, she called Tobias to give him the grizzly news, she was pregnant.

Much like the days following prom, Tobias limited his communications with her. He always took her calls, but offered no assistance with figuring out what she was going to do.

"Lacey, I don't know what to tell you. I'm leaving for school in a few days. I think you should just have an abortion."

"How the hell am I going to pay for an abortion, Toby?"

"Doesn't your dad pay you for working at the cleaners?" he replied.

"What? You son of a bitch!" she shouted.

"Now, Lacey that's not ladylike," he said, admonishing her.

She laughed aloud, and repeated the absurdity.

"Ladylike! It's a fine time for you to mind my manners. You're not going to just knock me up and ride off into the horizon, Toby!"

"Of course not, Lacey. You know me better than that. Your brother's one of my best friends. We'll figure this out—together. I promise."

The mention of his loyalty to her brother, instead of to her, left her confounded.

Less than a full week later, Tobias returned with another one of his perfectly laid out plans. His cousin would take them to Birmingham for the procedure—he would borrow the $225 it cost to terminate the pregnancy. Accounting for the one-hour drive there and back, the one-hour wait, the procedure time and the precautionary one-hour recovery, they would be back home by sunset. Tobias stayed and watched *Saving Private Ryan* with her that night. It was the last time she ever saw or spoke to him again.

Three weeks after Lacey's procedure, Lennox came home for the summer. She was still feeling empty and alone. The feelings of inadequacy and abandonment were as painful as anything her eighteen-year-old self could fathom. She'd completely pulled the wool over her parents' eyes, but her brother sensed the wrong after only an hour or so in her presence.

"Hey, Lacey Baby wanna go fishing in the morning?" he asked after dinner, while they put away dishes.

"Not really," she answered solemnly.

"She's been in some kind of funk for the past few weeks," their mom yelled from the family room. "I guess she's feeling sad because her little boyfriend's leaving for Florida soon."

"Mom, please!" Lacey shouted.

"Hmph!" her mother shot back.

Lennox watched his baby sister like a hawk.

"What boyfriend?" he teased loud enough for their mom to hear, but whispered to Lacey, "Let's go for a walk, down to the docks." Something in his eyes made clear that he was not going to take no, for an answer. When they could no longer see the porch lights, he jumped right in.

"What's up with you, Lacey Baby? You're so sad. Is it really about a boy?"

She knew she couldn't lie to him; they were practically one person.

"I messed up, Lenny," she confessed. Tears overtook her will to remain unsoiled in his eyes. "I've been seeing Tobias Bellamy since just before prom. Well I *was* seeing him."

Lennox remained completely silent.

"And I'm so sorry, Lenny. I let myself get pregnant."

Lenny stopped in his tracks, took his sister by the shoulders, and hugged her hard.

"No, you didn't. You didn't do it by yourself, Lace. Is he still here, in town?"

Lacey sobbed onto her big brother's shoulder.

"Yes, but since the abortion, he won't talk to me."

Lennox's chest rose as it filled with the night air. The abortion, Lacey?" He kept ahold of her.

"Yes," she stuttered between sobs. "He and his cousin Alicia took me to Birmingham. He paid for it."

"And he just dropped you off and left?"

Lacey could hear anger rising in his voice. "No!" She pulled out of his embrace to face him. She looked into his eyes. "It wasn't like that at all, Lenny. I swear!"

He stood still, staring at her and let her go on.

"He stayed with me until I fell asleep, but the next day..." her voice trailed off with a shrug, "I don't know. I haven't heard anything from him since then," she went on explaining. "But, we'd broken up long before I found out about being pregnant. We both broke up with each other, Lenny. I promise you."

Thinking back on the confession, she didn't know why she was defending Tobias's actions so vehemently. Maybe it was her brother she wanted to protect. Maybe she wanted to prevent him from doing something that would get him into trouble, more so than she was protecting Tobias. She felt awful about her next request, but she had to ask for his silence.

"Please don't tell mom and dad, Lenny. Please, promise me," she pleaded with her brother. "I couldn't stand to break their hearts, Lenny. Please."

He hugged her again, and promised to keep her secret.

CHAPTER TWO

Not a Kid Anymore

Lacey couldn't recall ever being as happy as she was during the weekends spent with Oliver Barnett. He was an absolute surprise and delight. She'd spent much of her adult life in a fog of unrealized dreams, dashed hopes and broken promises. Lacey had built walls around her heart that scraped the sky. They kept the hurt out, but they also kept out the possibility of love. And in one autumn visit to Atlanta, a tall sinewy, dreadlock clad cashier saw straight through them.

Lacey bounced up the front steps of her parents' house effervescing. "Mom, Daddy! I'm back!" she sang out to them. She peeked into the kitchen and tossed her keys in the teak bowl on the console table that sat beside the staircase. The house was quiet. She found her parents on the back porch cuddled up, sharing a blanket. They'd been married for thirty-six years, yet they could still being caught doing God knows what under blankets. They looked like teenagers who'd been caught fooling around. Her mom, sitting with her legs in her Dad's lap, flashed a cheery smile at her. She kissed them both on their foreheads and sat across from them, folding her legs beneath her like a kindergartner. Before she could settle in her seat, her mother started in on her.

"Well, you look bright eyed and bushy tailed. Doesn't she Tommy?" She baited Lacey who offered nothing. "So, how's your big brother?" she went on.

"I wouldn't know. A Bigfoot sighting is more likely than

a Lenny sighting these days," Lacey jeered. "Little Ms. Corner Bakery keeps him under lock and key."

"Now, now, Lacey Baby," her dad gently chided.

Not one to allow a dig at her baby boy, her mother fired back on Lennox's behalf, "And my other child looks to be pleasantly occupied while in the city, too. Do tell, Dear Lacey. Are you too—being kept under lock and key?"

"I'm here," Lacey answered flatly. "Did you cook?" she said. She rolled her eyes and stood to leave.

Tess cackled at her daughter's flippant reaction. "Yes. I fixed a plate for you. It's in the fridge, marked Princess Lacey."

Lacey kissed them again and wished them goodnight. On her way out, Lacey stopped by the fridge to pick up her plate.

A feeling of loneliness swept over her as she opened the door to her dark home. The lights from the back porch were the only light in room. She'd been second-guessing her decision to decorate in shades of whites. Although everything was beautiful, the neutral palette seemed too cold, too perfect—the kind of perfection that felt isolating. Lacey recalled the time she was last at Ms. Corner Bakery's house. She instantly felt welcome amongst Cami's palette of warm caramels, golds & deep eggplants. She remembered thinking, *No wonder Lenny likes being here.* Cami's home was inviting. She shrugged off the memory and put the plate of food into the fridge. Lacey quietly showered and slipped into bed with her laptop. The phone rang with Oliver's ring tone,

"*All you've gotta do is say yes,*" Marsha Ambrosia sang and sent a smile blazing across Lacey's face. Noticing the time, she knew he'd be upset with her for not calling to let him know that she'd made it home safely.

"Hi, Sweetheart!" she sang into the line.

"So you made it home and didn't call to let me know—again."

"I'm sorry, Ollie Baby," she teased. "I stopped by my parents first, then jumped straight into the shower. I'm now just climbing into bed."

"I wish I was there—In bed with you. But, I understand that I'm still your
dirty little secret."

"You know that's not how I feel about you, Oliver.

"It doesn't matter, Babe. Really," he said, cutting her off. "One thing I've learned in this crazy life is that things have a way of working out."
Lacey loved that about him. He was so unaffected and he never pushed.

"I won't keep you, I'm sure you have empires to build in the morning. I just wanted to make sure you made it home safely."

"Thank you, Sweetie. Call me tomorrow, okay? Good night," she said, but held the line until he spoke again.

"Hang up," she urged him through a girlish smile.

She could feel his smile through the phone.

"Are you in bed?" she whispered into the phone.

"Yes."

"What are you wearing?" she asked coquettishly as she lightly thumbed at her panties.

"Just the silk boxers you bought for me."

"Why are you wearing those when I'm not there?" she whined like a child.

"So that I can feel close to you," Oliver answered in kind.

Lacey smiled and jumped out of bed. "I'll see you in a couple of hours!"

She threw on a pair yoga pants and a sweatshirt, grabbed her keys, and headed back to Atlanta. She was ringing Oliver's buzzer by 11:00 p.m. Eastern Standard Time. Halfway between Birmingham and Anniston, she called to leave a message for her mom and dad telling them she'd be in Atlanta for the rest of the week.

The weekends in Little Five Points with Oliver were a first for her. She was a thirty-plus year old woman who'd never spent the weekend with a man. Given a few hours to recap her spontaneous decision to spend an entire week with him scared her. It was an uncharacteristically bold move.

"I didn't even bother to ask if it was okay with him, and I didn't pack anything when I left; I just jumped on I-20 and headed east. What the hell, Lace?" she asked herself.

As Lacey lay beside Oliver in his full size bed listening to the menagerie of yuppies and circus freaks who populated his neighborhood, she thought it best to ask him if he minded her staying with him for an entire week.

"Oliver."

"Yes, Young Lady."

She felt her nerve leaving her, and decided to just say it. "I want to stay here with you for the whole week."

He lay there silently for much longer than she was comfortable with, and she couldn't see his face in the darkness.

"I can stay at Lenny's place. I'm sure he's holed up at Cami's," she offered in attempt to spare him the dirty business of rejecting her.

"No way, Babe. You can stay right here with me." He

wrapped his arms and legs around her, sending a huge smile across her face.

"I'm just trying to figure out how to adjust my work schedule so that I can spend as much time as possible here, booed up with you," he playfully nuzzled at her neck.

A rush a relief washed over her and she laughed out loud and rolled over on top of him.

"I don't know what you're doing to me, Oliver Darwin Barnett."

"C'mon now, I've never told anybody my government name, so keep it down," he teased. Oliver lifted her shirt over her head and buried his face between her honey-colored breasts.

"Does Mr. Perfect know about your plans for the week? he asked between kisses.

"I'm an adult," she answered. "You just keep your focus on kissing me right there," she ordered softly into his ear.

After fourteen years of self-imposed celibacy, her sexual desire was in overdrive. Oliver's lean, muscular body beneath hers, on top of hers, behind hers, inside of hers was all she could think about it. She thought to herself, "What do I really know about this man?"

The sound of Oliver moving around as he dressed for work woke her. After several rounds of lovemaking, they had gotten only about three hours of sleep.

"Jesus," she groaned as she put a pillow over her face. "How'd I get mixed up with a freaking baker?"

Bakers had to start work before the rest of the world in order to provide the morning delights people needed to kick off their days. And Lacey's new beau, was a great one. That much, she knew about him. All of the baked goods he brought home, in addition to all of the recipes he tested in his small, efficiency kitchen threatened to put twenty pounds on her easily.

"I'm sorry for waking you, Young Lady, but Poppa's gotta roll. I told Cami I'd work the first shift this week."

"Cami. Cami. Cami," she griped.

He came over to the bed and smacked her on her bare backside and playfully bit it.

"If I work the first shift, I'm back home by 2:30, licking around your hot spot—just where you want me to be." he whispered against the small of her naked back. He was right. She was a fiend for him and her desire for him was immeasurable.

"Fine! I have empires to build today anyway," she snapped imperiously.

He leaned over and kissed her. He promised he'd be back before she missed him too much.

"I left a key on the table for you," he said as he tossed it back and disappeared behind his scraping front door.

There was plenty to do to keep her busy while Oliver worked. There were emails to check, she wanted to touch base with her father, and she needed to check on Lennox. She looked over expense reports and finally allowed the lowest part of herself to lead her to snooping around Oliver's place. She combed through his drawers and rifled through his medicine cabinet. She waded through the dark corners of his closet and cabinets. Lacey found all sorts of evidence to support her suspicions that Oliver Barnett had entertained more than a few women at his place. There was a beaten up old guitar propped in the corner near an equally beat up old piano. There was also a pair of wooden African drums that stood about waist high, which rounded out his at-home juke joint. She casually banged on the drums and plucked at a few keys on the piano. She was pleasantly surprised to hear that it was well tuned.

"At least it's not just for show," she remarked.

She found boxes of condoms, new toothbrushes, and feminine scented soaps and body washes in a cabinet in his bathroom. It looked like a hotel's supply closet. A spot of jealousy tweaked at her ego, but she quickly reminded herself that they were just getting to know each other. He had left her alone in his home, with a key—not to mention he hadn't as much as batted an eye when she presumptuously invited herself to stay with him for an entire week. Surely, that all meant something. Her phone rang startling her.

"Hey, Lenny. What's up?"

"Hey, I just wanted to apologize for the way I've been out of pocket," her brother said.

"It's fine," she said, cutting him off. "We're good. No apology needed."

"Well damn, that's a 180." His voice was charged with suspicion. "What are you doing this morning? Visiting stores?" Sensing his suspicion, she spoke firmly and unassumingly.

"Not today. I'm just going over these expense reports."

She knew Lenny would avoid too much talk about the family business, so she threw in a few tedious details. "Costs seem to be rising across the board. Every store is reporting higher expenditures and I've got to figure out what's going on."

"Yeah, well I'll let you get back to it. Let's try to do lunch this weekend, if you can get to Atlanta. Deal?"

She hurriedly agreed to call him and ended the call. She hated lying to him, but she wasn't ready to tell him about her and Oliver. He'd asked her to give him time to figure things out with his little Ms. Corner Bakery, and she needed the same thing—time. And after spending the morning, snooping around Oliver's love shack, she wasn't sure this thing was anything more than a hot, sexy fling to get her back in the saddle.

Just as he'd promised, Oliver was back home by half past two, and naked underneath his mismatched bed covers with Lacey by three. Lacey had never made love in the middle of the day, and especially not during the week. She'd spent the weeks of her early twenties doing the work of a beauty queen—visiting hospitals and middle schools, giving speeches and cutting ribbons. She'd spent the weeks of her later twenties expanding her family's dry cleaning businesses across the state of Alabama, and lunching with her mother. But, never had she spent a weekday making love in a poster-clad, one room studio apartment.

The buzzing of Oliver's cell phone slightly roused her from her slumber, and his shaking of her shoulder fully woke her.

"Lace, wake up. That was Cami," Oliver grumbled and rubbed the sleep from his eyes. "Your brother's looking for you. I think he just found out that you've been here."

Lacey sprang up as if she'd been stung by a bee.

"What? What do you mean here?" she asked pointing to the mattress for clarification. "Here as in Atlanta or here as in, with you? Oh my God," she groaned and rolled her eyes. She felt like she was going to throw up.

"Hell, I don't know. She just hung up on me," Oliver answered.

She could hear the annoyance in his tone. She sat silently formulating her next words. She was sure the question on his mind. *Why the hell are you so damned afraid of your brother knowing that you dig me?* They'd exhausted that argument. She also knew that Oliver didn't want to deal with the mean girl who lived inside of her. He was much too peace loving to agitate her. His next words were cautious and measured,

"Lace, I think you're underestimating Ali."

Ali was her brother's middle name, and apparently the name he chosen to live by in his fantasy world with Oliver's best friend, Cami, who he was currently dating.

"You don't know him like I do, Oliver."

"Damn, Lace! You're a grown woman! I'm sorry, but this shit with you and your brother is weird."

He got up, pulled his pants on, and walked into the kitchen. He stood with his head in the refrigerator for what seemed like forever before emerging with a carton eggs and heavy cream.

"I'm not playing along for much longer, so you'd better put your big girl panties on and handle this shit."

Oliver was usually easygoing and lighthearted. She'd never heard him use such an austere tone, and she didn't like it. But she knew that he was right.

"Ollie Baby, please. You don't understand."

He yelled, cutting her off,

"You're goddamn right; I don't understand. What man would?" he said, as he aggressively whisked a bowl of eggs. How ironic, she thought. The vision of a manly man whisking eggs made her giggle. He turned sharply facing her.

"Lacey, I'm not going along with this charade for much longer," his voice faded away as he turned back to the oven. She heard him mumble,

"I feel like a fucking liar all the time dealing with this shit."

"OK, Oliver! That's enough. I hear you!"

She got out of bed, and wrapped his sheets around her naked body, tucking them under her arms.

"Don't talk to me like that. And I mean it!" She walked over to him and wrapped her arms around his waist. She wanted to diffuse the tension as quickly as possible.

"There are things that Lenny and I have been through," she said, stuttering over her words. "Things that I want to share with you - one day, but I'm just not ready."

She felt the tension leave his body under her touch, and took it as a cue to go on,
"He thinks he needs to protect me."

Oliver turned and lifted her face to his. "Lace you know that I'd never do anything to hurt you. Right?"

Of course she did. She kissed him lightly to assure him that she felt absolutely safe in his care.

"If you don't want this thing to get too serious, just let me know."

Oliver sincerely offered her a get out of free card. Lacey stood as still as possible and questioned herself. *What in the hell did that mean? Has my hesitance sent him that message? the wrong message?*

"Serious? Are we there?" Her face reddened.

"Do *you*? Want things to be serious, I mean?" she asked. They shared uneasy chuckles, breaking the tension.

"Lacey, you are definitely something new for me, but I know complicated, and this thing between you and Ali is complicated, Babe." He wiped at his brow and went on, "After a life filled with complications, I've carved out a pretty un-complicated life for myself. So whatever you have going on with your brother, short of incest," he laughed and she playfully slapped at him, "I can wait patiently for you to decide what we're going to be for one another. I have no interest in further complicating your life or mine." He asked if she understood his position. She did and acknowledged so with another kiss. In that moment, Lacey decided that she would tell Lenny about her and Oliver's budding romance.

"I'll tell him. I promise. Now come back to bed—and bring those silky scrambled eggs!" She slapped him on the bottom and slinked back to bed.

CHAPTER THREE

Meet MJ

Autumn had always been Lacey's favorite time of the year, but this year the season marked the finite termination of Oliver's patience with hiding their relationship from her family, and more specifically from her brother.

"I clearly understand the uncomfortable position he's in. His best friend's deeply involved with my brother—and did I tell you that they're practically living together?" Lacey explained to her cousin and closest friend, MJ over drinks in her living room.

"I think that's gonna go the distance, Lace. My mother loved her," MJ said.

"Yeah," Lacey relished the thought of her brother settling down, but she was growing to like Cami, too. "I think it's gonna go too, MJ." She crinkled her nose and took a sip of her scotch. Lacey hadn't had a night like this with her cousin in a very long time. And she missed her best friend.

"Now, back to you and how you're about to screw things up with Oliver." MJ said, redirecting her distracted cousin.

"Whenever we're all together he's forced to keep his distance, and not appear to be too familiar with me, which is completely ludicrous because we spend just about every free moment we have together."

"Girl! Thanksgiving day brought it all to a head. Cami asked one question, which *seemed* innocent enough. She found us downstairs in her basement getting ready for Oliver's first time meeting my parents. 'So, how will our little Oliver be introduced?' she asked."

She took another sip from her glass.

"Well, I obviously gave the wrong answer. I simply told her that he's mostly her friend. 'Let's go with that,' I said. That was the night Oliver made it very clear that he was done with the lying and the hiding."

MJ curled up on the couch and listened intently to her cousin's account of Oliver's ultimatum.

"Mom and Dad decided to spend Thanksgiving at Cami's house in Atlanta—of all places. As you already know, they had instantly fallen in love with her when he brought her home to meet everyone. He'd never brought anyone home before, and of course Tess Anne's perfect son would only bring home a perfect mate," Lacey sarcastically mocked her mother.

"Cami's a lot like Ma. She's down to earth, hardworking and domestic. She bakes—works outside of the home. She's a "self-made" woman. No one had given her anything, according to our gushing mother."

MJ pursed her lips, admonishing Lacey's salty attitude.

"Sorry," Lacey apologized flatly. "Well, when they met Oliver on Thanksgiving Day, they loved him too, just as I knew they would. And Cami made sure to sing his praises at every opportunity. 'My best friend, Oliver did this.' 'Oliver did that!' 'Oliver cooked it.'"

"He cooks, too? Damn, Girl." MJ said, interrupting Lacey's tirade.

"I know right?" Lacey blushed.

"At any rate, Cami really laid it on thick and they ate it up. At one point, your mother whispered to me, 'You'd better snatch that one up. Cami says he's single.'

My mom was on high alert, too. She was all over me with

questions and suspicion.

'So, I take it you've already met Oliver.' 'He seems like a real catch.' 'You should get his number.'"

Lacey and MJ laughed at Lacey's impersonation of both their mothers.

"She's a crafty one!" MJ said.

"She thinks so anyway, but I gave up nothing." Lacey bragged. "After dinner, when I'd gotten everybody situated at the hotel, I slipped away to Oliver's. The reception I expected was not the one I received, at all!"

-"Oliver opened the front door and turned his back to me without as much as a hello," she recalled. That night his place smelled of sweet orange and frankincense.

"I walked in and closed the door behind me. 'Well, Hello Mr. Barnett,' I said. And he lost it! He jumped all in my case." 'Hello? We've just spent the whole night together, pretending to not know each other. Or are we still pretending?'" he yelled at me.

She looked out onto the lake and recalled the way he walked into the bathroom, tying his waist length locks into a topknot. There was a marked bitterness in his tone, and it hurt.

"He's typically so laid back, and this was a new side to him so I stayed quiet, and left the first words to him. He told me that it was the worst Thanksgiving he'd ever spent with Cami and Camilla!"

"Who's Camilla?" MJ asked.

"Cami's mom. She lives with her."

"She lives with her mother and now so does Lenny?" MJ asked with a puzzled look.

"Not exactly. But that's a story for another time." Laced

sighed dramatically. "MJ! Focus on me! Me! Me! Me! Stop interrupting and listen," Lacey ordered her cousin. "So, Oliver says to me, 'Tonight shouldn't have been this way, Lacey. Damn it! I'm mostly her friend? Then what the fuck are we doing here?'

'What are you doing here?' I recoiled.

"I have never been so humiliated. I am a grown damn man. And you and Cami wanted to send me skulking around like some kind of low class, no account secret!"

"What?" M.J. gasped.

"Yes! I had to stop him at that point. I said to him, 'I've never treated you like a low class, no account anything.' Then the kicker... 'Cami loves you!' I said. She praised your every move all night.' "

Lacey slumped in her seat and covered her face with her hands, trying to shake the pain in Oliver's face from her memory. MJ placed a hand on her cousin's thigh, encouraging her to continue.

"His voice dropped to nearly a whisper. 'She asked me to go around the back, to enter the house. All for you, Lacey,' he said. 'My best friend wanted to sneak me into her damned house for you—to save face!' The hurt in his eyes almost broke me in two," Lacey said, clutching at her heart.

MJ sat completely still for a moment and then she took ahold of her younger cousin's hand. "What'd you say to him?"

"What could I say?" she snapped. "I told him I was sorry. What else was there to say, Mary-Anthony? He was right about everything."

Warm salty tears streamed down Lacey's face as she recalled just how close she was to losing him. MJ handed her cousin a wadded paper towel and cautiously asked,

"How'd you leave things?"

"I reached out to him, and he pulled away from me." she whimpered, while recalling the pain she felt when Oliver rebuffed her apology. The sound shocked and embarrassed her.

"I begged him, 'Oliver, please. Don't be like this. I'm so sorry.' And it felt as if I was being remotely controlled, because I fell to my hands and knees on the pine floor in his kitchen and sunk into my remorse. I asked myself, what had I done?"

MJ moved closer to her cousin and hugged her.

"I love being with Oliver. But, I've been so afraid to let him in." Lacey cried into her cousin's lap, and fell asleep there on the couch.

Lacey's head was pounding when she woke up and found MJ sprawled across the floor at her feet. She carefully stepped over her sleeping cousin, and crept to her bedroom for a pillow and blanket to make her more comfortable. Lacey covered MJ and kissed her on the forehead before wrapping a cashmere throw around her own shoulders and walking out to the lakeside. She sat alongside the damp lakeshore and stretched her legs, reliving the rest of the Thanksgiving night fight between her and Oliver.

That pivotal fall night, Lacey sat on Oliver's kitchen floor and shared her deepest secret with him.

"Oliver I love being with you," she said through body shaking sobs. "But Toby hurt me to my core before my core was even fully developed. I trusted him and he scraped my insides out and left me. I was just a child! And I know that you didn't do it, but," she drew in a deep cleansing breath, "you're the first man I've been with in fourteen years, and I'm just so scared,

Oliver. I'm just so afraid of everything."

She couldn't bring herself to look at him, but she felt him slide onto the floor beside her. He put an arm around her and pulled her close.

"I don't know what the hell you're talking about or who the hell Toby is, but I've got you, Lace," his sincerity was clear and it was touching. His tone made her giggle through her sobs. "But, it stops right now. I won't hide our relationship any longer, okay?"

Lacey nodded in agreement. Oliver lifted her from the floor and carried her to the bathroom.

"You take a shower and I'll warm up some of your mother's pie for you."

"You have my mommy's apple pie?" she mumbled like a sulking child.

Oliver squeezed her and nodded. As Lacey showered, the hot water ran down her back and she relived the scene—her on the floor, the words she said to Oliver. She instantly regretted it all.

Oh my God! Had I told him that I loved him or that I loved BEING with him, I couldn't recall what I'd said out there! And had I said that Toby scraped my insides? How can I face him again? How long can I stay in his tiny ass bathroom?

She didn't wait for long to have her questions answered. Oliver drummed on the bathroom door, calling out to her.

"You OK in there? Don't be embarrassed now, Crazy Lady!" he laughed through the cracked and peeling door, putting her at ease and giving her the confidence to dry off and face him.

That fall night, Oliver and Lacey lied in bed eating her mother's apple pie. They talked straight through daybreak, and he told him everything. She told him about her first time having sex, the abortion, telling Lennox about it, and her self-imposed celibacy. To which, Oliver coolly replied,

"So what you're telling me is—the kitty is mine?" he laughed, as he mounted her. He lowered is long lean body onto hers and asked again,

"This kitty is mine?"

He fingered at the wetness between her thighs and kissed her.

"No wonder it feels like home," he whispered as he entered her.

The next morning, Lacey woke up at least an hour before Oliver and washed up. She cooked breakfast and put on a pot of coffee for her man.

"Mommy would be proud," she thought to herself. She could hardly wait for him to wake up, she had so many questions she wanted to ask him. She'd opened up and made herself vulnerable - now, it was his turn.

Oliver stretched like a tomcat and rolled over looking for Lacey. He smiled when his eyes fell on her fiery hazel ones,

"Good morning, Young Lady. This is a first," he said as he sat up, stretching his long legs. "What got into you?" he smiled and answered his own question, "Oh yeah. I did!"

Lacey turned up her lip at his crass remark and carried a TV tray over to his bedside. He didn't have one real table in his entire place. She made a plate of scrambled eggs and filled a cup with coffee and carried it over to him. Scrambled eggs were just about all she could cook. She sat beside him and watched him eat the meager breakfast she'd prepared, before starting her own questioning.

"Babe," she cautiously started. "Now that I've spilled, I think it's only fair for you to let me know more about you."

"Do you now?" he teased.

"Yes, I do."

He chuckled, but didn't face her.

"Ok. What do you want to know?"

He turned with the cup of coffee and stretched his long legs across hers, and pulled her closer. She started innocently.

"Do you play all of these instruments?"

"Yes. But I'm still learning the Djembe."

"Is that the proper name for the African drums? They're beautiful."

"Yes, Ma'am. They're West African goblet drums," he chuckled. "Now, let's get to the real questions, Lace. Shoot! I have nothing to hide."

She found his openness refreshing and followed suit.

"Ok. Why do you have so many condoms and feminine cleansing supplies?"

He laughed heartily about her wording and repeated her.

"Feminine cleansing supplies?"

He nervously twisted at a lock of hair. "Lacey, I am a bachelor and I have enjoyed the company of a lady or two. But it's only been you since you walked through that door," he said, pointing to his front door. "Of that I can assure you." His eyes never shifted. He had a way of delivering a line that left Lacey feeling completely settled.

"OK," was all she could muster in the face of such sincerity. "Tell me about your family. And not Cami and Camillia. I want to know about your family," she said firmly.

His quick laughter didn't show up with that question. Instead, a solemn expression took residence on his face.

"My family," he slowly repeated. "Well, there's my mother, the crack head—she's recovering now, or so she says. And there are my two drug dealing older brothers. Izzy's serving ten to fifteen years in federal prison for trafficking. He's really a sweet guy. He was just put in a very tough position. I mean, he was head of the household when he was only twelve." He took a sip from his cup. "And then there is Benjamin—we call him Benji. He's probably still in Ohio slanging dope and running women. I don't talk to them much. Well, not to Benji or my mother, but I do talk to Izzy. He's here, serving time in Atlanta. He was transferred here about two or three years ago."

Lacey listened quietly before she continued.

"How'd you escape that life?"

"I just left," he answered flatly.

"Just left, huh? Did you come here for college?" Lacey didn't actually think that a man as free spirited and artistic as Oliver had really gone to college, well at least not finished college, but, she didn't know what to say.

"Not exactly, Young Lady."

There was another long pause before he continued. "When I was thirteen, the Drug Task force came busting into our house. I had just gotten home from the Boys Club. I grabbed a couple of stacks from Izzy's stash and went out the window. I ran back to the Boy's club where I hid out until it was dark. When I went back home, the place was wide open. It was ransacked, and nobody was there. So I sat down to try to figure out my next move. I saw this copy of Ebony Magazine on the floor. I don't know why I took time to flip through the pages, but I did and I came across an article about, believe or not—Freak Nik in Atlanta," he said, chuckling at the memory. "And I knew that's where I was going," he finished with a shrug.

"And you were only thirteen? How did you work that out?"

"I wrote myself a note giving instructions to go to Atlanta to my imaginary grandparents, and forged my mother's name to it. I took five one hundred dollar bills, and left the rest of Izzy's stash tucked in a TV stand. I walked to the Greyhound station, handed the note to the attendant, and bought a one-way ticket to Atlanta. That simple. No one cares about a teenage black boy travelling alone, so no one bothered me at all."

Lacey was glued to his every word. It was as if he were one of those volunteer storytellers at the library where her mom used to take her and Lennox to hear stories read aloud every week.

"Go on. Where'd you go when you got here?" she urged him.

"That's where things got interesting. I felt duped, because there was no Freak-Nik partying going on," he laughed.

Lacey loved that his smile brightened his face, even during a tough reliving of such a painful experience. His smile was a stark contrast to her blubbering when she'd shared my past hurt. She felt petty and was embarrassed.

"You OK, Lace?" he asked, noting the shame that registered on her face.

"Are you kidding? Don't worry about me. Go on," she said, patting his hand.

"Well, a valet at the Magic City strip club that was across

the street from the dingy bus station pointed me to a nearby extended stay motel, where I naively went only to find out that a thirteen-year-old boy could not rent a room on his own. So I went back to the bus station and fell asleep in the lobby. After I don't know how many hours, I was awakened by a police officer, who asked me tons of questions. I wouldn't answer any of them, so he assumed I was retarded or mute, I guess. He took me a to a group home for women and children - true story- I swear to God," he said, raising his right hand above his head. "And long story short, that's where I met Cami and Camilla." He ended abruptly with the mention of Cami and Camilla. Lacey noticed the shift in his mood and thought it best to let it go without further discussion. She teased him, in an attempt to bring his smile back.

"Wow, Oliver Barnett. That is some story. It's like the Odyssey. You're like my very own Odysseus."

It worked. He flashed a flirty smile and replied, "So you've got a throne waiting for me in one of those empires you build throughout the week?"

She loved that he got the Odyssey reference. It turned her on, and they were back under the bedcovers before he finished the eggs.

Oliver's story had left Lacey with so many more questions about him—his relationship with Cami and Camilla, and the likelihood of a future for them. There were also some concerns about his sex life, and just how long he'd be satisfied with just one woman. And what were his aspirations? He seemed to dabble in several things. He was a musician, and played with a rock band, played the African drums for a dance troupe. He also played piano for the ballet studio down the alley from his apartment. Oliver was really rooted in his community. He was attending culinary arts school and working full time for Cami at The Corner Bakery. And even with all of his endeavors, he still seemed aimless, which was a major concern for Lacey, in light of his upbringing.

The newly cemented couple joined Lennox, Cami and her mother Camilla on Black Friday to deliver gifts to the women and children at the very group home where Oliver and Cami had met as children. Lacey was pleased to spend the day with her brother. She couldn't recall a time in my brother's adult life, when he looked as happy and free as he looked that day, playing with the kids at the group home. As much as she hated to admit it, Cami really brought something pleasant out of her brother, who was all too often, rigid and aloof. After leaving the shelter, they all went Christmas shopping - as two openly affectionate couples. Once again, Oliver had been right. Lennox was very accepting of their new status, and treated Oliver like an old friend throughout the entire day.

CHAPTER FOUR

Family Ties

The holidays brought with it a proposal of marriage from Lennox to his little Ms. Corner Bakery, who Lacey had grown to like very much. She loved who her big brother was when he was with Cami. And God knows Oliver loved Cami and she loved him - they were all one big, happy family. By the time Spring had arrived, Oliver and Lacey were tossing around cutesy idioms for those three little words: "I'm so into you, you know that I'm head over heels for you, you're everything to me," and so on.

They'd become quite an item. They spent evenings with Cami and Lenny in their new backyard, as he'd practically moved in with her. She'd introduced him to a few girlfriends and to MJ, so when he proposed that she accompany him for a visit with his brother, the felon, she shouldn't have been so taken aback, but she was. *Lacey Robinson had never been to a prison!* she thought to herself. *I've never imagined my life being on track for a prison visit. Do I even know a felon?"* Her apprehension was written all over her face.

"You don't have to be afraid, Lacey. The killers and rapists won't be running around grabbing and cat calling at you."

He chuckled a little, but there was something in his tone she couldn't quite make out. She'd nearly forgotten that he had a biological family brimming with felonious characters. She'd never heard him on the phone with his mother or his brothers--not even for Thanksgiving or Christmas, and she told him so.

"Don't be condescending, Oliver. I'm not that naive. I'm

just surprised. I mean, you never mention your biological family and you never hear from them."

"That's not true! I spoke to my mother on Christmas Day," he said, convincingly. It was a lie.

"And I visit Izzy at least once every few months. I only missed Thanksgiving and Christmas visits because I was playing house with you and your family!" he snapped, cutting her off.

His accusatory tone angered her and she snapped back. "Who the hell asked you to, Oliver?" Lacey wanted to stop there, but indignation urged her on. "You left them long before I came into the picture and replaced them, I might add. So don't you dare try to blame me for your lack of allegiance to your family?"

Oliver calmly stood from the piano bench where he'd been playing and walked to the door.

"Lacey, I think we'd better see each other later."

"Excuse me?" His reaction shocked her. She couldn't believe what she was hearing.

"I mean it, Lacey. I want you to leave, right now." His tone was stern and even; his cognac brown eyes were seething.

"I'm not dressed, and I will not be kicked out of anywhere, so closed the damned door and get over yourself." She said, mirroring his demeanor. She locked eyes with him.

He stood there at the door for another few seconds before slamming the door and sending his guitar crashing to the floor.

"Now look at what you've done," she pushed. "And I'd bet that's my fault, too."

"Lacey, don't push me. Get dressed and leave. I have to get ready to visit my criminal brother," he snapped. He snatched the guitar from the floor and propped it back against the corner. Lacey seemed completely unaffected by his anger, but her eyes showed that she was sorry for upsetting him.

"I'm coming with you, so I'll get dressed, but I won't be leaving without you."

He rolled his eyes and smirked. "Man, you're a real punk! You're so spoiled!"

"And how long have you known that colorful little factoid, Mr. Barnett?"

She showered and got dressed in what she deemed appropriate attire for a prison visit. She wore a white V-neck t-shirt and a gray and lavender, printed knee length cardigan with a pair of dark skinny jeans. She tied a silk scarf around her neck and pulled on her favorite wine colored wedge ankle boots. She swiped a wine colored lip stain over her plump lips and put her horn rimmed, cat eye glasses on. A tinge of worry crept up again. She looked pretty. *Maybe too pretty*? she worried.

"You must want a pen pal going to a prison looking that good, Lace," Oliver said jokingly, confirming her fear.

"I don't have anything more appropriate, according to the requirements I read online," Lacey whined.

"You went online to check the dress code?"

"Of course I did. I wouldn't want to be turned away or anything."

He held his arms open to her, and she walked into them and laid her head on his shoulder.

"I know this is important to you, and I'm honored that you want me to meet your brother," she quietly admitted.

He smiled down at her and kissed her on the mouth. "I love that you did that." He kissed her again. "And guess what, Lace? Cami has never met him, so that's two for you. She doesn't know my middle name and she's never met my brother," he said, teasing her. He was always accusing her of competing with Cami for his favor. And if Lacey were to be completely honest, she'd admit it too.

The prison was literally minutes away from Little Five Points, but the neighborhood was distinctively different. The area surrounding the U.S. Penitentiary was a mosh of abandoned factories and rail yards alongside newly constructed high rent townhomes and mixed-use complexes. There were two grand stone walls marking the entrance of the prison. There were no sky-high barbed wire fences, like the shows she'd seen on TV. There were no weary looking inmates dressed in dirty striped pajamas breaking rocks, nor were there body any armor clad, armed guards perched high on steel towers with assault rifles. It was nothing like Lacey had imagined, not at all. Instead, the prison was housed in a stately, grey stoned building that looked very much like a distinguished historic library. Once Oliver and Lacey were cleared for the visit, they entered the visitor's area, which did look like the prison she'd seen on TV. They sat side by side at a small, pentagon shaped metal table with six little metal chairs that were bolted to the table. The walls were painted with a mural featuring an underwater theme, complete with mermaids and scuba divers. It reminded Lacey of her senior prom. She shuttered at the unflattering likeness. The harsh overhead lighting buzzed and flickered making the room feel like a carnival funhouse, without the fun. They sat quietly waiting for Isaac to show up. Oliver put a hand on her jumpy thigh.

"Are you nervous?"

"I don't think I'm nervous. I'm more so, anxious. Do you think he'll like me? I'm sort of an acquired taste," she giggled nervously.

"He'd better not acquire a taste for you, or we'll be sharing a room again." He joked and reassuringly patted her thigh again. "He's going to love you, too." Oliver's use of the word, "too" covered them like fog.

They sat quietly avoiding each other's eyes when his brother approached them wearing a huge smile that looked exactly like Oliver's. He spread his tattooed arms wide, awaiting his brother's embrace. Oliver nearly jumped from his seat, and greeted his big brother with an equally big smile, and a long hug that made it clear just how much he loved his brother - felon or not.

"You need to cut this damned hair, Short Stuff!" Isaac boomed. Isaac Barnett stood at six feet five inches tall - about three inches taller than Oliver, with a lean muscular physique, much like Oliver's, but more rugged. He boasted a rich, dark mahogany skin tone, thick shiny hair that he wore cut closely to his head and slanted brown eyes. He was a strikingly handsome man. Had he taken another path to support his family, he could've easily been a model or a Hollywood actor. The brothers let each other go and turned their attentions to Lacey. She stood quietly behind the stainless steel table, enjoying the sight of their reunion. She extended a delicate and trembling hand across the table to Isaac. He graciously took it in both his hands.

"Whoa, little brother! Atlanta looks good on you." He smiled proudly at Oliver. "You must be Lacey. I'm the felon brother, Isaac, but you can call me Ike."

"Awww, come on Izzy. The felon?" Oliver chastised his brother. Ike and Lacey both laughed.

"Little bro, I think she may have noticed that I live in a United States Federal Penitentiary. I am, right Lacey?"

Ike was charming and forthright. Lacey liked him right away. She smiled and nodded.

"The pat down was kind of telling."

He laughed and slapped Oliver on the back.

"I like her, O!"

Oliver and Ike laughed and chatted about childhood memories, the holidays and how their mother was doing, when the light-hearted banter took on a more somber tone. Ike motioned in Lacey's direction and spoke in a hushed tone.

"Does she know about Momma?"

Oliver glanced at her and nodded. "For the most part; yeah."

Having the OK to speak freely, he asked if Oliver had laid eyes on her, to which Oliver hung his head and shamefully answered, no. Ike slipped into the big brother role effortlessly.

"O, look man, I know she's messed up, but she's the only mother we have. And you know we can't depend on Benji. Please, go check on her. Go put your arms around her—for me."

Oliver didn't exactly agree to his brother's request, but he dutifully nodded and shook his brother's extended hand. And just as swiftly, Ike turned the conversation back to Lacey.

"So, Ms. Lacey what exactly are your intentions for our little O.D.B.?"

The Old Dirty Bastard reference nearly knocked her out of her seat with laughter.

"Really, Isaac Edison? You want to go there?" Oliver's capricious manner had returned as he verbally sparred with his big brother.

"Well woman, answer the man!"

Lacey straightened in the little metal chair and took Oliver's hand in hers.
"I have a few plans in mind, starting with getting him up to Ohio to check on his mother."

Ike howled and threw his hands in the air. "Oh yeah! Marry her or I will, O! I swear, I will, Short Stuff!"

And just like that, the visit was over. They both stood to hug Ike one more time before he was escorted back behind the big steel door. He turned to give them a final wave goodbye, his eyes bright with gratitude.

"Oh my God, Ollie. I love your brother!"

"Yeah he's the charismatic one of the Barnett boys." He was quiet and obviously in a pensive mood. "Lace, I'm not going to Ohio." His tone was curt and final. "I was thirteen and I called her for at least one year straight with not a single call back. I left messages with neighbors for her, with old teachers and the counselors from the Boys Club, and she never called me back."

He drove along without looking at her. "I don't know how Camilla got in touch with her, but one day the phone rang at their house, and it was my mom. She asked me for money. I was fifteen years old by then and working with Cami at Checker's. I asked her how much and where to send it. I didn't speak to her again until I was grown." Lacey lovingly patted his shoulder as he repeated, "I'm not going to Ohio."

CHAPTER FIVE

Dear Mama

Summer time burgeoned with promise. Lacey had been working closely with both her mother and Oliver on the plans for Lennox and Cami's fall wedding. The three of them were like the three musketeers of wedding planning. Lacey beamed whenever she found her mother chatting on the phone with Oliver. She loved talking openly to her parents about her time with him, although she had yet to mention their romantic involvement.

"That Oliver is unreal!" Tess Robinson exclaimed. "He's picked out a couple of cake flavors for us to try when we're in town. And he invited your Dad and I to some kind of cooking expo he's putting on during the Atlanta Food and Wine Festival." Tess gushed and so did Lacey.

"Yeah, he told me he wanted to invite you guys." Lacey beamed, but replied as casually as she could as she scavenged around in her mom's refrigerator.

"Lacey, cut the crap! You like him. Come on, tell me. I'm your mom!"

Lacey's face turned beet red.

"I do! I like him so much, Mommy!" she squealed like a little girl

"I knew it!" Tess exclaimed, slapping her thigh. "So does he know? Or are you guys already," Tess searched for the right words. "Seeing each other?"

Lacey had only a few seconds to answer her mother's

question honestly without revealing more than she was ready to share.

"I guess you can say that. We hang out whenever we can find the time," she quickly answered, turning her back to the refrigerator. Tess leaned against the kitchen counter and crossed her arms.

"Hmph. Is that it?" she pressed.

"Is what it, Mommy?" Lacey was feeling pressed and it made her defensive.

"Don't get short with me, Lacey Jackson Robinson. I won't stand for it," her mother warned. "We're just standing here having a pleasant conversation about your new beau, so why are your feathers getting all ruffled?"

Lacey relented, because she knew her mother was right. She propped herself on the counter facing her mother full on.

"Fire away, Mommy. What do you want to know?"

"You know what, Ms. High and Mighty, forget I asked. I'm sorry to have bothered you," Tess shot back.

Lacey could see that she'd hurt her mother's feelings. That was truly not her intention.

"Mommy, I'm sorry."

Lacey hopped down and went over to hug her mother. Tess was as tall as Lacey, but curvier. She and Lacey shared the same hazel eyes and pillowy, full lips. By any measure, Tess was a very attractive woman with a home-spun manner that made everyone feel welcomed and cared for. She wore her sparkling silver hair in loose, shoulder grazing waves with the front and sides pinned back highlighting her high cheeks and exquisite bone structure, both of which Lacey had also inherited.

Tess hugged her daughter back. She'd missed being so close to her and held on for as long as Lacey allowed. They stood there holding one another until Tommy Robinson walked in.

"How can I get a ticket to this hug-in?" he laughed and wrapped his long, muscular arms around both of the women.

Lacey had forgotten how nice it was to be embraced by both of her parents. She wondered how many women her age were afforded such a luxury. Lacey spent the evening having dinner with her parents and catching them up on her blossoming romance with Oliver.

"Mommy, we've got to go!" Lacey yelled from the first step of her parent's lakeside cottage. "What are you girls doing in there?" It tickled her to witness her mom make such a fuss about how she wanted to look for Oliver's cooking demonstration.

Tess had wasted no time inviting her sister, Katherine Beatrice, who the family affectionately called, Katy B when Tommy said he had, "no interest" in going to a cooking show. Lacey had also invited her cousin MJ, who jumped at the opportunity to see Oliver in action and to spend a mother daughter weekend with her family.

"We haven't done this since we were kids," MJ noted with a giant smile.

"I am so excited!" Katy B and Tess sang.

"Me, too! My baby has a man, Honey! And he cooks!"

The singing sisters slapped high fives in the back seat of the Lacey's beloved white on white Porsche Panamera. Lacey and MJ exchanged sardonic glances and snickered at their mothers.

"Keep it down back their girls, and make sure to keep those seat belts fastened," Lacey said, taunting her mom and aunt.

"So Lacey, what should we expect?"

"What do you mean, Auntie?"

"What should we expect at a Wine and Food Festival? Is Oliver going to be on a stage? Will we be standing or sitting?"

"Will there be cameras there?" Tess interjected her own inquiry.

Lacey dramatically inhaled and shook her head. "Yes, he'll be on stage. And yes there will be cameras. He'll be sort of teaching while he bakes."

"Bakes?" MJ repeated her cousin.

"Yes, Ma'am. He's a pastry chef," Lacey boasted.

MJ trailed off, "Oh my goodness. Does he have a brother?" she quietly remarked.

The question struck Lacey, putting a lump in her throat. She had deliberately left out all discussion regarding Oliver's family when telling her family about their courtship. The Robinson-Jackson family put on their best efforts to present themselves as "common folk," but they were quite elitist when it came to lineage and legacy. Tess was known all over town for touting her lineage and carrying on about the land her ancestors amassed and passed on to her generation.

"He has brothers, but they're not in the South."

"Oliver's from Ohio," Tess informed her sister and niece.

"Oh, I can't do Ohio, it's too cold up there," MJ said, dismissing the Barnett brothers with an animated headshake. The women chattered without cease until they reached the Loews Hotel.

"Wow, this is really fancy, Lace!" Tess took it all in with childlike wonder. "I thought we'd be outdoors."

"Well, we'll go over to the tasting tents later, but the classes and demonstrations will be in the hotel."

Lacey was filled with pride. She had impertinently relegated Oliver to his duties as a cashier and barista at the Corner Bakery. But her mom had said it. This was all "really fancy". Lacey rifled through her designer handbag, and presented her ID to the young blonde woman stationed at the Will Call counter.

"We have four passes for you, Ms. Robinson. Enjoy your day." She handed Lacey four laminated cards on black plastic cords, tasting tent wristbands and festival maps for everyone.

Lacey handed the passes, wristbands and maps to her family and put her own pass over her head, minding to not muss her freshly trimmed bangs. She laced arms with MJ, and nudged her cousin who had been pretty quiet since they'd parked.

"You OK, MJ?"

"Yes, I'm just so happy for you, Cuz," she smiled and nudged her cousin back.

Oliver was surrounded by grinning men and women who were hanging on his every quip and witticism. His entire demeanor changed when he caught a glimpse of Lacey. She stood out in the bustling crowd of white faces. At nearly six feet tall, with hazel eyes and caramel colored skin, she was in no danger of blending in any setting. Lacey was dressed in her uniform of sophisticated neutrals and her trademark cat-eye glasses. She seemed to glow in Oliver's eyes. He politely excused himself, and stepped down to meet her, when he noticed her entourage. He adjusted the Nehru collar of his chef's jacket, and warmly greeted Lacey's family. He hugged Lacey and kissed her lightly on the cheek. He hugged Tess and Katy B, and MJ.

"Double Duty, MJ, the cousin and the best friend. It's good to see you again." MJ blushed and thanked him for inviting her. Oliver looked every bit the leading man. He was breathtakingly dressed in all white with his hair in a high bun. He wore a short-sleeved chef's jacket with one button open to expose the tattooed sunrays at the top of his chest and the brilliantly etched sleeves on his forearms.

"I've never seen you dressed like a professional," Lacey flirtatiously fingered at the collar of his jacket. A boyish grin spread across his face. "Is that good thing or bad?" he responded.

"It's just an observation," she said. She stood on her toes and whispered in his ear, "I prefer you undressed."

"I heard that, Lacey Jackson Robinson!" Tess and Katy B laughed.

Oliver chuckled and escorted them to their seats.

"I'll be the brother up there with the mic," he winked and pointed to a highly stylized makeshift kitchen, situated on stage.

"What are you making?" MJ asked.

Oliver immediately lit up like a Christmas tree. His enthusiasm reminded Lacey of the day she met him. He lit up then too, as he told her about a blend of Hawaiian and Jamaican coffee beans he'd concocted for Cami.

"I'm making a Kaffir lime and coconut panna cotta. I'm putting a modern, island twist on a classic Italian dessert. I'll see you guys afterwards and we'll hit the tasting tents. I have a little surprise planned for y'all."

With another peck for Lacey, he jumped on stage and got mic'd up.

Oliver was truly in his element in the kitchen. He floated around as if he were on roller skates. His presentation was laced with comical anecdotes, culinary tips and shortcuts. He really knew his stuff. Lacey was hooked and she knew it.

"Hey Lenny!" Tess cried. "Where's my future daughter in law?" she asked before seeing Cami approach. Lenny affectionately hugged his mother, eliciting an eye roll from his baby sister. Lennox and Cami had entered into the artful choreography of hugs and "good to see you agains," when Oliver joined the fray. The group applauded and praised his demonstration.

"You looked good up there, Brother," Lennox said, as he pulled him into a half hug, half chest bump.

Cami embraced him.

"I'll never get used to watching that skinny kid from Oh-HI-Oh, up there whipping out panna cottas and chocolate soufflés." She was very proud of him and it showed.

Cami was a classic beauty, with delicate features and soulful brown eyes. She was very reserved, but astute and accessible. Her deep umber brown complexion seemed to lend a rich, ethereal glow that lit her from her core. She wore her raven black hair in an easy long bob with long layers that framed her heart shaped face, making her look every part the angel Lennox thought she was.

True to her no fuss, no muss, all American style, Cami was dressed in a fitted white V-neck tee and slim ankle length khakis with a small cross body tan leather handbag. Her relaxed look was a stark contrast to Lennox's designer short sleeved safari shirt and high-end navy, ripped jeans, but somehow they worked—and beautifully so.

Lacey stood patiently allowing Oliver to soak up all of the accolades being heaped upon him. He seductively smiled in her direction from time to time, his eyes filled with a longing to reach her. The look filled her with anticipation and happiness. Tess and Katy B linked arms with Oliver and whisked him to the head of the group.

"Lead the way!" Katy B sang.

Tess opened her map and held it up to better see it. "I want to head straight to Bourbon row."

"And then to the Sweet Home Alabama tents!" Katy B added.

Oliver, always the gentleman, included MJ and Lacey. "Where do you ladies want to go?"

"To Little Five Points," Lacey retorted. Cami burst into laughter and Oliver joined in.

Tess inquisitively eyed the map, looking for the "Little Five Points" tent.

"That's where Oliver lives," Lacey leaned in and clued MJ.

MJ laughed and taunted her cousin. Keep your panties on! In due time, Cuzzo."

Lacey petulantly rolled her eyes, but complied.

After a few hours of polite introductions and tastings, Lacey handed the keys to her car to MJ, and asked her to follow she and Oliver. Lennox smiled, overhearing his sister, and offered to take their family off her hands.

"I'll see to them getting to the hotel, Lacey Baby." Oliver motioned for an audience with Lennox.

"Ali man, I have VIP tickets for them at Rathburn's

Watchlist."

"Rathburn's what?" Lennox asked.

Oliver chuckled and ran a hand over his locks. "Cami will explain it to you. Hey! Why don't you and Cam take our tickets," he gestured in Lacey's direction.

"Cami would love it, besides, I haven't seen Lace in two weeks, prepping for this weekend."

The pleading in Oliver's voice made Lennox chuckle. He shook Oliver's hand and took the tickets. "I got you, Brother."

"Man, I owe you!" Oliver exclaimed and gratefully hugged him.

"Chef Boyardee just dumped you ladies!" Lennox playfully proclaimed as he walked away from Oliver. "And once again, it's Lennox Ali to the rescue."

Oliver gallantly bowed to them. "My sincerest apology, but I am wiped," he said, kissing Tess and Katy B on the cheeks. He gave Cami and MJ big hugs.

"I really appreciate you all coming down here to show a brother some love."

Lacey didn't bother with the goodbyes; she waited near Oliver's truck with her arms crossed and her foot tapping impatiently.

Oliver directed the Jeep Grand Cherokee into the dark alley that ran along the rear of his apartment while Lacey snoozed.

"Lacey Baby, we're home," he cooed in her ear and put soft kisses down her neck.

"It's about time. Carry me."

Oliver laughed and shook his head. "As you wish, Your Highness," he said, carrying Lacey into the courtyard.

"How do you propose I unlock the door?" he asked.

“Teamwork makes the dream work, Baby,” Lacey quipped. She took the key from his hand, unlocked the door, and ordered him out of his clothes.

“Can I shower first?” Oliver smiled.

“Do you want this or not?”

Lacey slipped her top over her head and unfastened her bra. She slipped her jeans off and then her lacy underwear. She stood before Oliver completely naked with her hands on her womanly hips and seductively tilted her head.

“Young Lady, there is absolutely no other human activity I’d rather do than make love to you right now.”

He took her in his arms and headed to his bed.

“No,” she stopped him. “I want you right here. You work so well in the kitchen,” she purred.

Oliver’s eyes widened along with his mouth. He sat her on the stainless steel countertop and unzipped his pants in one effortless motion. He took his erect cock in his hand. “Is this what you wanted so badly that you gave over the keys to your precious Porsche?”

Lacey smiled wantonly and her fiery hazel eyes glistened at the sight of Oliver’s fully nude, tight and tattooed body.

“Exactly.” She pulled him between her thighs using only her legs, and kissed him.

“Hmmm, she’s throbbing for me,” Oliver playfully bait-ed and entered Lacey right there on the kitchen counter. Lacey tightened her grasp around his waist holding him firmly against the raging waterworks at the meeting of her thighs. She pressed her whole body to his and thrust lecherously against his stiff-ness.

“I think I love you.” The words escaped, snapping her

from her carnal enchantment. She squeezed her eyes shut.

"Yeah? Me too," Oliver bit her bottom lip and said. He picked her up and carried her to the bed where he flipped her on all fours and entered her from behind.

"'Me too means I think I love you, too," Lacey pondered. And that was that. Those three little words were out there, in the sexually charged atmosphere, with no sign of regret on either of their parts.

Oliver was fast asleep lying horizontally across the bed, when the phone rang. Lacey glanced at it and rolled out of bed. She gently kissed the space between his shoulders and brushed a lock of hair away from his face.

"Ollie, your phone's ringing. You want to make something or do you want to go out for food?"

Oliver groggily rolled onto his back and rubbed his eyes; his curly eyelashes were always falling into his eyes.

"Can you make that warm Brussels sprout and bacon salad?"

"Oh really? Ms. I don't eat Brussels sprouts," he jeered. "Anything for you." He pulled her back onto the bed and kissed her.

"Good answer, Mr. Barnett. I'm going to jump in the shower first."

Oliver sat up and pushed himself against the dark gray wall. He didn't have a headboard, but had been considering building one to appease Lacey.

He didn't recognize the number on the missed call log. He dialed it back.

"Hello," a vaguely familiar voice answered.

"Hi, I think someone from this number called. This is

Oliver Barnett."

After a long pause the voice on the other end spoke again. "Hey, Baby boy."

Now the silence was on Oliver's end of the line. He looked to the closed bathroom door.

"Momma?"

"Yes, it's me, Baby Boy." Her voice broke. "How are you?"

He breathed in deeply and ordered himself to get it together. "I'm good. How are you?"

His chilly reaction made her second-guess her decision to call.

"I got your number from Camilla. I spoke to her last week."

Oliver could feel gall building in his throat. *Why wouldn't Camilla tell me that she talked to my Momma?* he thought. He repeated his question.

"How are you, Momma?" He could hear quiet sobs on her end.

"I'm doing well, O. Really good." She sounded sincere. "I don't want to keep you. I hear you're doing really well, too. I just wanted to let you know that I'll be coming to Atlanta to speak at a fundraiser for my Women's Recovery Center," she said, stammering like a nervous child.

Oliver recalled what he thought he'd heard her say. Had she said "her" Women's Recovery Center?

"Oh? So are you clean now?"

His directness took her by surprise. "Yes."

Her elongated pause made Oliver feel sorry for his accusation veiled as a question.

"Seven years clean now."

"And you're just calling me?" His tone turned cold. He scoffed at her nerve. "What the hell, Ma?" he said.

"I'm sorry, O. I'm sorry for so much. I needed to get myself together so that I could come to you boys whole and ready to be a Momma to y'all." Her sobs steadily built. "I want to see you, Son," she begged.

The construction of his outrage was cut short as Lacey rose from behind the bathroom door through a cloud of steam.

"Look, I'm going to have to call you back. I'm in the middle of something right now," he said as he ended the call without saying goodbye. "Hey, I think I need a red onion. You want to run out to grab one while I start shredding Brussels sprouts?" he said to Lacey.

Lacey agreed and headed out as soon as she dressed. Oliver used Lacey's run to the market to call Camilla. He wanted to privately rip her for not telling him about his Momma.

"What's up Oli-Nerd?" Camilla answered in her usual fashion.

"Why didn't you tell me that you've been talking to my Momma?"

"Excuse me, Boy?" Her response made clear that this call was going to be contemptuous.

"Who the fuck you talking to like that? I'ma hang up and let yo ungrateful ass try again. Bye!" Camilla said, as she abruptly ended the call.

If he weren't so angry he would've laughed. Camilla Robinson was nobody's pushover. She was the mother of his best friend, and Lacey's soon to be sister in law, Cami. Camilla was hands down, one of the toughest and most cantankerous people he'd ever known. He knew that he'd approached the call in the worst way, especially in dealing with a firecracker like, Camilla. He dialed her again.

"Hello," Camilla sang into the phone, as if she didn't know it was Oliver again.

"Hi, Camilla—Woman I love like my own mother."

"Now, that's what I'm talking about," she boasted. "Now you listen, you fucking brat! Yo Momma needed time and someone who would keep her up on her child—someone who would not judge her. And someone who she didn't owe shit, and who don't want nothing from her. That's what a recovering addict needs—especially one who is a Momma." She took a breath and went on. "She was real 'shamed about asking you for money when you was a kid. She never forgot that shit. So I promised her, fucked up Momma to fucked up Momma, that I'd see 'bout you until she could do it for herself."

Oliver sat quietly posted against the kitchen counter.

"Now you talk!"

Oliver laughed again and fingered at his locks.

"I'm sorry about talking to you like that earlier. And thank you for being there for her."

"That's all?" She snapped.

"I think so," Oliver chuckled.

"Well, Bye! I got shit going on over here."

And like that the conversation was over, leaving Oliver to process everything Camilla had laid on him.

The key in the door brought him back from his private thoughts. He forced a smile and greeted Lacey with a passionate French kiss. She tossed the bag and keys onto the counter and pulled at the shorts Oliver was wearing.

"I thought you were hungry," he asked between gasps for

air as Lacey kissed and licked his chest and abs.

She stopped abruptly and stood. "Oh. Yeah. Rain check?" She smacked him on the bottom and started unpacking the plastic bags. Not seeing the shredded Brussels sprouts or a mandolin slicer, she asked, "Babe, what have you been doing? Where are the sprouts, Man?

He took a few seconds to decide whether or not he was ready to have the *Mom* conversation with Lacey. He wasn't.

"I was talking to Camilla. I'll have everything done in a minute," he said, disarming her with humor. "Didn't you catch my demonstration woman? I'm one to watch!"

"True. True. I read that somewhere," she joked. "Well, I'll be over here with a giant glass of white wine."

*****

"Lace, I've been invited to participate in a Master Class at the Savannah Food and Wine Festival in Tybee Island. It's a whole week in November," he said as he glanced over at her while she tapped away on her laptop.

"That's awesome, Babe!" She gave a fist pump in the air, but kept working. Oliver hesitated before continuing.

"I want you to come with me," he kicked in to sell her on the benefits. "We'll be staying at a Bed and Breakfast called the," he leafed through the pages for the name of the place they'd be staying. "Olde Savannah Inn. It looks up to your standards." He handed her a large manila envelope he'd pulled from underneath his bed. Lacey placed her laptop aside and perused the information Oliver had handed her. She filled with joy when she saw the dates in writing, *NOVEMBER 9 through 15*. November was about four months away. The dates spoke to his commitment to be with her four months in the future and she was moved.

"I would love to go with you, Ollie!" Lacey's eyes filled with tears. She removed her glasses and wrapped both arms around his neck. He hadn't expected such a visceral response, but he was thrilled to have made her so happy.

Lacey intensely examined the paperwork using her keen business eye. "Ollie, not that it matters to me, but how much are you paid for these Master Classes?" She could sense his discomfort with her question, and she quickly elaborated. "I mean you'll be off from your job for a week, including that weekend and they are charging $99 per person for a one-day class with you and as much as $600 for an ALL CLASS PASS for an entire week of watching you whip cream."

"Watching me whip cream," Oliver slowly repeated her put down.

"Babe, I don't mean it like that. Really, does what you make cover the loss you take from not working that week?"

Oliver knew that Lacey was a shrewd businesswoman and he knew that she'd grown her family's business from one small town dry cleaners to a successful franchise of drycleaners that spanned the entire of state of Alabama, but he wasn't ready to have her "grow" him. Oliver liked the idea of having more than one iron in the fire. His work at The Corner Bakery sustained his day-to-day expenses. His work at the dance studio and with the band, sustained him spiritually, and his after-hours work on Atlanta's culinary scene sustained his ego and challenged him creatively. They were all equally meaningful to his well-being. And she seemed to want him to choose just one on which to focus all of his energies—to ultimately build his own brand and empire, neither of which interested him.

"They pay me well. And I get per diem, lodging and invaluable exposure."

"Exposure for what, though? To what end? Do you even have goals, Babe?"

Oliver found her tone condescending and it read on his face.

"I don't mean to offend you, Babe," she climbed into his lap and straddled him.

"I just have never seen you check a schedule or even wear a watch. The only electronic device you own is your cell phone." She thought it was a fair question.

Oliver kissed Lacey on her pillow soft lips and lifted her off of his lap.

"Lacey Love, everyone doesn't have to live by a hard and fast business plan for their lives. I do just fine. Have I ever had to depend on you for anything?" With that, Oliver was done with the conversation and Lacey knew it. She couldn't for the life of her understand why he didn't want to cash in on his culinary skills. *He could make a fortune, she thought to herself.*

CHAPTER SIX

R.I.P

The tail end of summer brought with it more than just the change of season. Lacey learned a lot about herself in a public restroom on a balmy August night, as she sat slouched with half of her bare ass hanging off the stool. The day Lacey found out she was pregnant as an unwed, seventeen-year-old high school senior, she thought her life was over. She hadn't been bred to be "that kind of girl." She had been raised and groomed to marry an accomplished, highly educated and pedigreed Black man after she'd completed at least, her Bachelor's degree. The recollection of the humiliation she felt as she scurried into the town's only drugstore to buy the pregnancy test was as fresh and relevant fourteen years later, as it was that very day. She walked into the Walgreens in a complete daze. She felt the remnants of the day's late lunch and early dinner slowly churning and lurching into her throat with every step. She looked towards the overhead sign that read, *Feminine Products/Family Planning*. She hadn't allowed the thought of children to ever take up residence in her mind after the procedure.

She'd watched the Hallmark commercial where the little boy baked the Valentine's day cake for his mom, and the Baby Magic commercial with the mom bathing a sudsy little blue-eyed baby girl come across the screen. Her mother would tear up amidst ohhs and ahhs, but Lacey would only remark, "That'll never be me. No thank you," to her mother's great dismay.

But, seeing the words, "NOT PREGNANT" appear on that

stick, broke her heart, which confused her immensely. *Had she wanted to be pregnant? Did she want a baby with Oliver? Did she want a future with Oliver? Hell, did Oliver want kids or a future with her?* The questions swirled around her head so quickly; her brain couldn't command her legs to lift her from the toilet seat. She wasn't sure how long she'd been in there staring at that stick, when someone knocked on the bathroom stall door.

"You OK in there, Honey?" an unfamiliar voice asked through the door, snapping Lacey back to reality. She wiped herself and answered,

"I'm fine, thanks. I'll be right out."

"Don't hurry yourself on my account. I was checking on you. Take whatever time you need, Honey." The unfamiliar voice reassured her.

Lacey left the parking lot of the store and headed home to Alabama. She couldn't bring herself to face Oliver until she'd made heads or tails of the grand disappointment she was feeling about not being pregnant. She called him at the shop and told him something had come up and she had to go home. He was disappointed. He'd planned on further discussing the trip to Savannah when he got home. He'd grown accustomed to her being in his space when he got home on the weekends, and immediately missed her. Lacey merged onto East Ponce De Leon and dialed MJ.

"Hey, MJ."

"Hi, Lace. What's the matter?"

She could never keep anything from MJ and the confirmation made her cry.

Lace, what's going on? Where are you?"

Lacey tried to pull herself together. The tears in her eyes

were making the cars around her blur together.

"I'm on my way home. Please come over."

"How far out are you?" MJ asked.

"I should be home in about two hours," she said as she sobbed.

"I'll stay on the line with you."

"OK." Lacey whimpered.

As Lacey turned into the clearing, she could see MJ's car at her house and the kitchen lights on. MJ was very much like her mother; she was a born nurturer. MJ was a year or two older than Lacey. She was Lacey's rock. The weeks following Tobias's disappearing act, MJ gently said to her, "You never have to tell me what's going on with you, but know that I've got you no matter what." And those simple words cemented the women as not only blood relatives, but as best friends.

"Mary-Anthony Jackson Jones, I love you."

Lacey fell into her cousin's open arms as she walked through the front door of her home.

MJ had two glasses filled with wine and two pints of chocolate ice cream with spoons. "You go shower and get comfortable, and I'll meet you on the porch."

Lacey did as she was told and was wrapped up on the porch with MJ in under twenty minutes.

"So, what's going on? You've got me freaking out, Lacey Baby."

Lacey took a sip from her glass. A single tear rolled down her cheek. She wiped at it with the back of her hand. "I thought I was pregnant."

Her answer hung between them in the dark still of the country night air.

"You thought?" MJ was cautious in her speech.

"Yeah, but I'm not," Lacey answered and wiped at another tear before going on. "I didn't think I wanted to be, but I'm hurting so bad right now, MJ."

"Have you talked to Oliver about it?"

Lacey pulled her legs onto the chair and laid her face between her knees.

"No."

The tears came back aggressively.

"I don't know what to tell him. I don't know what he'll say. And what if he's happy about it? Or what if he's sad?"

MJ could barely understand her cousin's incoherent speech.

"MJ, what if I can't have babies after the abortion?"

Lacey stopped talking. Hearing those words aloud again threatened to send her back in time. It had been fourteen years since she'd vocalized the word, *abortion*. The last time she said it was when she'd told Lennox her dark, ugly secret. MJ sat paralyzed with her mouth agape. Lacey wouldn't look up to face her cousin. MJ moved to sit next to Lacey and wrapped her arms around Lacey's rounded shoulders.

"It was Tobias, wasn't it?"

"Yes." Lacey's shoulders shook uncontrollably.

MJ kept ahold of her cousin and stared out onto the lake.

"I'm sure you're fine. People have abortions all the time and go on to have healthy children." MJ tried reassuring her. "And your gyne would have found something by now if there were something to find. Lace, when you're ready to start a family, you'll see that everything's in absolute working order down there." She nudged her cousin, trying to lighten her mood.

Having the unique ability to know and give Lacey exactly what she needed, MJ hugged her cousin, freeing a little chuckle from Lacey.

MJ was the only child of Lacey and Lennox's Aunt Katy B. Aunty Katy B was a loveable character and her quirky ways were as equally loveable. MJ, was short for her full Catholic name, Mary-Anthony Jackson Jones. The Joneses weren't Catholics, but Lennox and Lacey's Aunt Katy B had always liked the way nuns took the Mother of God's name as a first name and a male saint's name as their second name. And all of the female Jackson descendants were given the name, Jackson as an homage to the family name of their mothers.

"You really do love me, don't you?" Lacey joked.

"Without a doubt. I've told you before - I've got you. No matter what, Little Miss Perfect." The two sat quietly side by side as they ate their ice cream. There was no further mention of procedures or babies.

*****

Oliver dialed her number again. And like the previous times, she didn't answer. He left another message.

"It's me, Oliver again. I'm not sure what's up with you," he stopped and rethought his word. "With us, but just be a woman for once and talk to me."

He started to end the call, but he had more to say. It had been almost two full weeks since he'd last heard from Lacey, and he was hurt and angry about her dismissal of him. "Lace, I never asked anything of you. I've been nothing but honest with you about who I am and this is what you have for me? I guess you've had your fun slumming around with the help." He took a deep breath. He was beginning to yell into the phone again.

"You know what, Princess Lacey - Have a nice life!" And with that, he was done.

It was less than a half hour later when Oliver's phone rang. He ran his hands over his head and picked up the phone from the kitchen counter. He saw Cami's name on the display, and couldn't conceal his disappointment. He'd hoped it was Lacey.

"What's up Cam?" Oliver answered flatly.

"Hey, Man. This is Ali. There's been an accident. Cami needs you."

"Where are you? Is she okay?" Oliver's mind raced as quickly as his feet did. He ran to find his keys and get to wherever his best friend was.

When Oliver reached the Grady Hospital Emergency Room, he was a wreck. Ali had informed him that Camilla had been in a car accident, and had been brought to Grady. The Emergency Room whirled with activity, scents and sounds, which completely overloaded Oliver's senses. The adrenaline coursing through his body seemed to heighten every one of them. The screams and moans of the injured meshed together with the stench of urine and cigarette smoke making him nauseous. The sight of Cami and Ali were a welcomed respite. He rushed over to them and took Cami into his arms.

"Have you seen her? How's she doing? How are you holding up?" He fired questions at her. She looked pleadingly into his eyes, and laboriously shrugged her shoulders. He held onto his friend and felt the weight of her fear in his arms.

He turned to Ali. Speaking over Cami's bowed head, he asked, "Has a doctor talked to you guys?"

Ali nodded, and kept his eyes glued to his fiancé.

"Um, yes. His name is Dr. Cousins and he's getting her settled in a private room. But we won't be able to see her for a while."

Oliver walked Cami to an empty chair and sat her down. He gestured for Ali to join him just outside of the ER. Ali looked to the door and back to Cami sitting slumped in the worn fiberglass chair, and reluctantly followed Oliver outside.

"How bad it is?" Oliver asked.

"It sounds pretty bad, Man. She was run over by the car and dragged some ways. She's heading into surgery tonight."

"Thanks for calling, Ali," Oliver said as he fist bumped him and gave him a little bro hug.

Ali accepted the gesture and quickly returned to Cami's side, leaving Oliver alone and wishing for a joint.

It was the longest night of Oliver's life since he'd arrived in Atlanta as a boy, only to find out a thirteen-year-old boy could not rent a hotel room without a parent or guardian. He and Ali took turns getting food and water for Cami, and for each other. Camilla came through surgery in true Camilla fashion, but she was bruised and swollen beyond recognition. Seeing her lying lifeless and bandaged up like a mummy broke Oliver's heart. Feelings of helplessness consumed him. He'd always been the fixer between Cami and her mother. There had never been a spat or slight that he couldn't smooth between the two of them and now watching Camilla hooked up to all of the machines and tubing and Cami slowly losing grip of her usual cool and collected persona was gnawing away at him. He wanted so badly for Lacey to be there with him.

Oliver spent every free moment he had at Camilla's bedside, sitting vigil with Cami. After day three, Cami sent him back to work. He knew she wanted to be alone with her mother, so he didn't protest. Oliver headed home to shower and dress for work. He sat on the edge of his bed and checked his voicemail for a message from Lacey, but instead heard his mother's voice.

"Hi, Baby Boy. It's me, Valentina. Your mother." He giggled at her clarification of her relationship to him. "I just wanted to remind you that, I'll be coming to Atlanta in a few days," she fell silent for what seemed like a full minute or maybe even two. "And I'd really like to see you." Oliver could hear the tears in her voice and felt guilty. "Please Son, call me." He played the rest of his messages and dressed for work. There was still no call from Lacey.

Oliver was completely ineffectual at the shop. He baked a few bear claws and muffins, but he opted to limit his interaction with the customers. The entire staff was accommodating. They sent their well wishes for Cami's family. His mind was teeming with *what if?* and *then what*? scenarios regarding Camilla and Cami, but the thoughts that kept shoving their way to the forefront of his psyche were the *what ifs?* and *then whats*? regarding Lacey's sudden departure from his life. *What if she was just as shallow as she seemed and he'd simply reached his usefulness with her? Or what if she thought he was just too beneath her and had decided it was best to end the relationship? Or the scariest of all the scenarios, what if she was pregnant or something and was deciding how to handle it on her own - then what?* Oliver was a wreck and had to know what was going on, one way or another.

Oliver had just turned the key to his small studio apartment that once seemed perfect, but was now immature and inadequate in the wake of Princess Lacey, when Cami called and delivered the biggest blow he'd ever received in his thirty-two years of life.

"She's gone. There was a blood clot. I've got to make a few more calls. Love you," was all she offered. The room started spinning around Oliver—his hair seemed to weigh a ton in that moment. Lacey's absence was more pronounced than ever. The silence in his apartment was only penetrated by the bickering of his neighbors below. He sank to the bed and remembered his last conversation with Camilla. He was glad he'd told her that he loved her and instantly ached for his own mother.

Oliver woke the next morning to an excruciating headache and hunger pangs. He jumped from his bed looking for his phone. He had every intention of going over to be with Cami, but had somehow fallen asleep. He drove to Cami's, racked with guilt for leaving her alone. When he arrived to find Ali's car parked in what used to be his space, a wave of relief washed over him. He thanked God aloud. "Thank You! She wasn't alone." He used his key to let himself in and announced himself.

"Cam, it's me," he said as he looked around the still kitchen. He ached to hear Camilla yell from the basement, *Boy, stop that yelling in here!*

"I'm going to put on some coffee and fix breakfast." He yelled down the dark hallway.

Ali arose from the dark hall just as Oliver was putting the last pancake on a platter.

"What's up, Oliver. Thanks for cooking."

"No problem, Man. How is she?" Oliver gestured down the hall to where he assumed Cami was still in bed.

"She's not good," Ali answered as he mounted a bar

stool across from where Oliver was fixing plates of pancakes and bacon. He took the steaming cup of coffee Oliver offered him. "It's like she on auto pilot. She's not crying or anything, but she's," he paused looking for the right words and couldn't find them, so he simply shook his head in confusion. "Man, I don't know. I've never seen her like this."

Oliver leaned against the kitchen sink and searched his mind for a way to help his friend.

"Do you mind if I go back?" he asked Ali.

"Please, do whatever you think will help. I'm stomped."

He nodded and headed to Cami's bedroom. He'd never actually been in her bedroom - with her in it and with Ali down the hall he felt weird about it, so he left the door open. Cami was laying across the bed on top of the covers typing away on her laptop.

"Knock. Knock. Boss Lady," he said as he cautiously entered the room and sat on the tufted bench that was situated at the foot of the bed.

"Hey, Ollie. How are you holding up?" she asked without looking up from her computer screen.

"I'm holding up. How are you?" he asked ironically.

"I'm good. I'm just trying to get a service put together for her," Cami said matter of factly. "I've always hated when people kept their folks' bodies out for too long before burying them. And with all the wedding planning," she stopped abruptly. "I don't want her out for too long. She deserves some dignity."

Oliver had known Camisha for all of his adult life and much of his childhood. He knew all too well about the coat of armor she was donning. He'd seen it when Camilla didn't make it home in the morning by school time, on a weekday. He'd seen it when they got off of the school bus to find all of their household goods piled on the street corner, because Camilla had failed to pay the rent. He'd last seen it at her college graduation when Camilla showed up late, stinking of gin and weed, wearing a sequin mini dress and too much red lipstick. He too had donned the very same coat of armor, a time or two and respectfully went along with her efforts to regain some sense of normalcy. It was their way - they sucked it up and pressed on.

Cami planned a tasteful and dignified graveside service for her mother. A young, good-looking pastor read from Psalms 23 and sang a hymn. Oliver couldn't help but think that Camilla would have appreciated the pastor's rugged good looks and he laughed out loud, triggering Cami to laugh, too. They always got each other. There was no doubt in his mind that Cami laughed at the very same thought he'd had. In Cami's grief she'd neglected to plan a repast for Camilla, so he left ahead of the processional to prepare something for the guests. All of the Robinsons, including Lacey, had made the trip from Alabama. A few friends of Camilla's from job had attended as well.

Oliver was putting whole chickens into the oven when he saw Lacey's sleek Porsche Panamera turn onto the parking pad of at the rear of Cami's house. He held his breath and took off the apron he was wearing when he saw only her rise from the car. He met her at the back door. She hugged him tightly before he could say a word.

"Oliver, I'm so sorry for your loss. I swear I just heard about it last night," she said, defending herself.

Oliver coldly took her arms from his neck. "You didn't call. Did you at least call Cami?" His curtness took her aback. She squinted to recognize the man who stood before her.

"I did. I'm not a monster, Oliver."

He didn't reply. He turned back to the cutting board where he'd been trimming green beans. Lacey guardedly stepped past him in the kitchen, and asked if she could help him.

"Help me with what exactly, Lacey? What can you do in here?" he said, dramatically swinging the knife he was holding in the air? Sensing his anger, Lacey adjusted herself accordingly.

"Oliver I'm sorry. I know that this has to be hard for you, but I just want to be here for Cami."

Her exclusion of him stung like hell and he put on his coat of armor that matched Cami's.

"You're right. I'm sorry," Oliver flatly replied. He pointed toward a sack of red potatoes and ordered her to scrub and chop them.

Oliver's return to work kept him busy. He'd been promoted to Cami's old job as store manager after she took on her new position as District Manager. Oliver found the challenge of managing the shop, while perusing his culinary after hours work, fulfilling. It kept him from thinking of what had happened between he and Lacey, although he couldn't shake the fear that she was sitting in Alabama with his child growing in her womb. Cami's phone call came right on time.

"Hey, Ollie Dollie! Can you talk?" She sounded like her old self, which gave him great comfort.

"Hell yeah! I'm the boss up in here," he boasted jokingly.

She laughed, and told him all about how she'd found peace with her mother's death.

They talked for at least an hour. They chatted like old

times, riffing off of each other and completing each other's thoughts and sentences. Oliver had to take a documented lunch break to hear all of the news Cami had to share. He was so happy to have her back that he would have taken an entire day off to hear whatever she wanted to tell him. In true Camisha Ann Robbins style, she turned the conversation to him and how he was feeling.

"Enough about my craziness. What's going on with you? And don't lie, because I hear it in your voice. So spill!"

Oliver squeezed his eye shut and led with the heavy. "Cam, I think Lacey's pregnant."

They both sat in complete silence allowing the gravity of his announcement to set in.

Cami stuttered, "Why? Would you think that, Oliver Barnett?"

Her measured tone screamed disappointment. He could practically read her mind, and her thoughts were not nearly as measured. They were screaming, "What the F**k!" But, she remained calm and let him explain.

"Everything had been going so good between us and then all of a sudden, she's not taking my calls, she's not coming here, and at Camilla's repast, she acted as though we'd never met—as though we'd never," he sighed before continuing on. "Never felt anything for each other."

"Felt for each other, huh?" Cami asked thoughtfully.

He went on, "She made all of the rules of engagement between us. God forbid I try to make plans beyond the next weekend, she'd give me the, 'we're just having fun' speech." His end of the line went silent, but then he spoke again, having read Cami's mind again, "We stopped using protection about 3 months ago, but I was always careful." Cami sat speechless. Oliver went into defense mode.

"Cami, she'd stay with me even when she was on her cycle, so it's not just about the sex, damn it! And now she's gone M.I.A. on me."

He paused to let Cami have her say.

"I'm sure it's not that, Oliver," was all Cami came up with.

"I don't know, Cam. Can you try calling her? Isn't she helping with the wedding on that end?" Oliver pleaded.

Hearing the desperation in his voice was unfamiliar and unsettling for Cami. She had only known Oliver to date a certain type of girl, and Lacey was surely a deviation, but so was the consistency in which he was seeing her. Most of his girls didn't even have names. He'd referred to them by distinguishing characteristics, like her skin tone: *Yella Girl* or where he met her: *Indian Hill*, and after a few months or so, he was on to the next one. This thing with Lacey had progressed beyond his typical expiration date, and had obviously crossed some lines. Cami and Lacey weren't exactly girlfriends, but her best friend needed her and she promised to call Lacey on his behalf.

CHAPTER SEVEN

Recovery

Thursdays were typically pretty non-descript days of the week for Oliver, but this Thursday was the Thursday he'd be seeing his mom for the first time in eighteen years. He was as nervous as a long tailed cat in a room full of rocking chairs. He'd twisted and knotted his locks in every imaginable configuration known to man. He'd changed clothes at least four times and he had even brought a watch, in an effort to look more grown up for her. Cami had agreed to accompany him to his mother's speaking engagement, which turned out to be just down the street from Cami's house. When Oliver arrived to Cami's house to pick her up, they were dressed alike. They were both wearing gingham button down shirts and navy blue jackets with suede elbow patches, but he wore khakis and she opted for dark skinny jeans and riding boots. They laughed at the coincidence. Cami picked up on his energy like a magnet.

"Look at you in grown up clothes!" she teased him. "Don't worry, Ollie. You're going to be fine. She loves you. Remember what you told me about Camilla being a hurt person hurting people?" Cami asked pointedly.

Oliver nodded.

"Well ditto, My Brother. Ditto."

Cami smacked him on his back and locked the door behind her. She jumped into the passenger seat of his Jeep Cherokee and directed him to the Recovery Center where Valentina was scheduled to be the keynote speaker.

They rode along silently, both of them imagining how Oliver and Valentina would greet each other. *Would they rush to one another? Would they hug and hold on to each other? Or would they awkwardly shake hands?* Cami was the first to speak breaking the awkward silence.

"Do you look like your mother?"

"Yes. We all do. Well, Izzy and I do. Benji must look like his dad, and he's kind of short. We're all tall—me, my brother Izzy and her."

"What?" Cami exclaimed. "You've never told me that you had brothers! What's up with that, Oliver?"

Oliver shrugged. He felt ashamed and thought about what Lacey had said about him replacing his family with Cami and Camilla.

"Those weren't the best of times, Cam. I just didn't want to go into all of that with you. You had your own problems."

"For the past eighteen years, Oliver? You've seen me through some pretty tough times. No?" she pressed.

He could feel her glaring at him, but refused to face her. "I know. I don't have a good reason. I just didn't. Okay? Can we just drop it for now?"

"For now," she pointed angrily at him.

Before they knew it, the GPS was informing them that their destination was on the right—a mere 4.2 miles from Cami's neighborhood. The recovery center was nestled in a lush garden, deep in the woods of South Fulton County. The parking lot was filled with exotic luxury cars and a valet station had been setup at the entrance. The oddity drew the obvious question.

"What the hell kind of rehab is this?" Oliver asked, prompting wild laughter between the best friends again, breaking the ice.

Valentina Barnett was remarkably beautiful. She was regal and statuesque at six feet tall, with a youthful lean and toned body. Her rich dark brown complexion along with her svelte and well-defined arms, gave her the look of an obsidian sculpture. She wore long, thin silver dreadlocks French braided down her back, and was dressed in a white pencil skirt with a black leather halter-top and pointy toes pumps. She looked chic and rich. Cami couldn't reconcile the crackhead Oliver had described with this powerful and wealthy looking woman who stood before them. By the look of absolute shock on his face, neither could he. Valentina spotted Oliver from across the room and opted for the outstretched arms approach. She grabbed her son and held on to him tightly. When she finally let go of Oliver, she turned to Cami and hugged her.

"Cami, I am so sorry for your loss, Baby Girl. Your mother was an angel to me. I can't say enough about the way Camilla cared for me and my son." Her words that were meant to comfort, sent Cami sobbing to nearest restroom. She turned and apologized to Oliver. "Oh my God, I didn't mean to upset her."

Oliver assured her Cami would be fine. "That's a breakthrough and a much needed affirmation," Oliver plainly explained his best friend's tears.

Valentina showed him to their seats, which were marked, *Reserved.*

Oliver looked suspiciously and asked her how'd she know he would show up. She patted his arm. "I only hoped, Baby Boy. I only hoped," she said as she left for the restroom.

Minutes later, she returned with a pulled together Cami before excusing herself, and taking her place at the corner of the makeshift stage.

Oliver's mother spoke honestly and poignantly about her battle with addiction. She spoke about losing all of her sons, and the shame she felt about it. She spoke about the people who helped her right her life again, and how she'd dedicated the rest of her life to helping others beat drug and alcohol addiction. Oliver learned a lot he'd never known about his mother that day—including the fact that she was married. Valentina invited Cami and Oliver to dinner at the hotel where she and her husband were staying. Cami politely declined, and Oliver took her home on his way to his mother's hotel.

When Oliver reached the Atlanta Airport Hilton, his mother was already seated with a distinguished looking white man. They both stood as he approached the table.

"Oliver, this is my husband, Dr. Mikkel Johannessen." She squirmed a bit. It was hardly noticeable, but her husband put a hand on her back, comforting her. He came around the table extending a warm welcome to Oliver.

"It's truly a pleasure to finally meet you, Oliver. Please, call me Mix." His accent was thick, and reminded Oliver of the cartoon Count Dracula's he'd watched on Scooby Doo as a child. His gesture toward Oliver pleased her greatly and it showed on her face. Oliver shook Mikkel's hand and pulled out the chair for his mother. Valentina beamed. The night went along seamlessly, until Valentina asked about his brothers. She had no idea where Benji was living, nor did she know that Isaac was there in Atlanta. Oliver felt a strong tinge of resentment, and took a moment to analyze it. Among the clinking of wine glasses and silverware, Oliver reached the source of the belligerence. She'd gotten clean and gone about her life, collecting accolades and praise for overcoming the addiction that stole it and triumphantly rebuilding it. She'd married her wealthy, Norwegian doctor who she'd met while working with the rehabilitation program that helped her get clean, but had taken seven years to reach out to her sons. His anger spiked when he thought about how worried Izzy had been about her. He was sitting in prison because she couldn't take care of them, and she was out giving speeches about how she'd been born again through the wonder of the Twelve Steps. Well what about the, Making Amends step? Had she needed seven whole years to get around to making amends to the people who she'd hurt the most? Oliver's emotions raged and he lit into his mom.

"Izzy's been worried sick about you. He begged me to go to Ohio to find you and *put my arms around you* for him," Oliver's voice was escalating. "He's probably spent countless nights in there worrying that you were strung out in some crack house being abused," he chided her. "All the while you were off driving your fancy ass car, in your designer clothes with your white doctor!"

"Oliver! That's not okay!" Valentina yelled at him.

"Now, you want to discipline me, Tina? Man, fuck you!" Oliver pushed away from the table a stormed out of the restaurant, with Valentina hot on his trail.

"You wait just a minute, O!" She pulled the tail of Oliver's sport coat, spinning him around to face her. "I know I messed up! I know! I know!" she cried. "But, I needed to come to you boys whole. You deserved that and I owed it to you."

Oliver couldn't look at his mother. No matter how angry he was with her, he couldn't stand to see her cry. "I'm here now, and I want to make things right." She held on to his hand tightly with both of her hands. Mix stood watch just outside of the rotating door.

"Oliver, please let me earn your forgiveness. All's I'm asking is for a chance. Please?" Her pleading melted him a bit, and he took her in his arms.

"Momma, I'm sorry. I know that you were sick. I know that, but I need some time to process all of this. And I need to talk to Izzy. And apparently find Benji!"

She tearfully nodded against his shoulder and kissed him on the cheek.

"When you go to see Isaac, may I come with you? I'm staying here for as long as it takes."

"How does the good doctor feel about that?" Oliver asked, waving Mikkel over.

He came over and took Valentina's outstretched hand.

"Mix knows that getting my family back is my number one priority."

He nodded in agreement and endorsed his wife.

"It's the sole reason she is here, Oliver. There is nothing more important to your mother than getting you guys back, and that makes it of the utmost importance to me."

Mix's declaration was as sincere as any Oliver had ever heard, and he truly appreciated his new stepfather's commitment to helping his mother rebuild her family.

Oliver called Cami as soon as he opened his eyes the next morning to tell her all about his new rich, foreign and very Caucasian stepfather. She loved every detail and was happy for her best friend. She knew better than anyone, how much he'd missed his mother. As far as the brother in prison, just down the street, who she'd known nothing about—she decided to take that up with him at a later date.

Oliver dressed and waited for his mother to pick him up for the visit with Izzy. Just as they'd agreed, she arrived sharply at eight a.m. Valentina arrived in a pristine Aston Martin. "It's a rental!" She quickly explained, to which, Oliver laughed.

"Is it an exact replica of your own, back at home?"

Just as witty as her son, Valentina retorted, "Not exactly. Mine is a convertible." The two of them laughed easily.

On the short drive to the prison, Valentina was visibly nervous. She fiddled with her silver locks. She smoothed her hands over her slacks and patted Oliver's hand more than a few times. He chuckled a little and assured her that Izzy was as cheerful and loving as he'd always been, and that he was going to love seeing her healthy.

"I promise you, there will be no more F-bombs dropped. He was raised better than I was."

His joke put her at ease, until they turned onto the gray, prison yard. There was the usual awkwardness during the visitor search and pat down, and before they could settle in the cold metal seats, Izzy was coming through the door, practically trotting. Tears streamed effortlessly down his face.

"Thank you, O! Thank you, Little Bro! Thank you!" Isaac exclaimed as he warmly embraced their mother. "I knew you'd come through for me." He held her away from him to get a good look at her. "Momma," he cried. "You look so healthy and pretty." He embraced her again, until a burly guard ordered him to take a seat and calm down. Isaac couldn't take his eyes off of Valentina.

"How'd this happen? I don't have long so just hit me with the highlights and write me with the rest." He said to their mother.

She giggled girlishly and repeated his instructions.

"It's so good to see you, Isaac," she cried and patted his smiling face. "Ok, Ok. just the highlights. I've been clean for seven years now. I'm working with rehabilitation programs all over the country. And I'm married," she ended with a light hearted shrug. Isaac shook his head from side to side.

"Dang," was all he could think to say. "Is dude nice? Is he good to you? Was he a crackhead, too?"

They all laughed at his bluntness.

"No. He's one of the doctors who worked at the recovery center where I got clean."

"Is that allowed? Aren't there some kind rules against hooking up with the addicts in those programs?" Isaac asked, with a furrowed brow.

"Isaac! We didn't start dating until I began working for the program. I'd been clean for well over five years by then."

Oliver was so pleased by her openness; he put a hand on top of hers. She was really a captivating figure. She stood out among the dreariness of the prison's visitor room. And all of the other inmates and visitors openly watched them.

"Izzy, she's being modest. She done very well for herself. And her husband's nice, and rich, and white!" Oliver said with a nudge to their mother's shoulder.

"White!" He yelled, which garnered a final warning from the guard.

"And he talks like Count Dracula!" Oliver teased.

Isaac sat shaking his head from side to side again. "Wow!" He said quietly. Then he turned on the big brother, first-born role."So where's Benji?"

The joviality ceased with the mention of their middle brother, Benjamin. Valentina hung her head and answered truthfully again, "I don't know."

"You ain't heard nothing from him?" Isaac's tone was stern and she squirmed again.

"No, but I've heard that he has about three or four kids around the old neighborhood. I've got feelers out for him, Isaac."

"Feelers?" he repeated her. He had a distinctive way of communicating tons of emotion through one-word questions. He turned his attention to Oliver.

"O, you stay on this deal. Okay?"

Oliver was clear on his orders, and dutifully nodded. Valentina stared at the distressed metal table and traced their names on it with a manicured fingernail.

"We've hired a private investigator, too!" she added. It appeased her sons.

"Good. Good. That's real good. But no cops! Okay?"

In the presence of her firstborn, Valentina seemed docile, greatly diminished from the powerhouse keynote speaker Oliver had saw speak just the day before. She behaved like a small, shamefaced child. And as only Isaac Barnett could, he switched back to a charming, fun loving rascal with his next breath.

"Where's that long legged, beauty of yours, Short Stuff?"

Oliver shook his head furiously trying to discourage his big brother from that particular line of questioning in front of Valentina. Lacey was definitely not someone he wanted to talk about in the presence of his mother, if at all. Isaac waved him off.

"Man, I don't care about whatever you talking about, I

was looking forward to seeing her fine ass!" Isaac grimaced and quickly apologized for swearing. "Sorry, Momma."

"O, you have a lady friend? It's not Cami is it?"

"Nope!" Isaac snapped. He was getting great pleasure from seeing his baby brother nervously wiggle in his chair. It was like they were kids again.

"That didn't work out," Oliver answered crossly. He shot a look at Isaac that clearly conveyed his irritation with him. His older brother was unbothered.

"So, you messed up. Or did she come to her senses?" He kept at his baby brother.

Valentina, sensing Oliver's sincere discourse, interjected.

"That's enough Isaac. Come on now. Leave him alone. I'm sure he'll write you all about it. Now behave." Her tone was motherly and unfamiliar to both her boys.

"Behave?" Isaac repeated in his condescending, Isaac Barnett way.

They all felt the iciness and insolence in his tone. The guard stood and announced the end of visitor's hour, breaking the uneasy silence at their little family reunion. Isaac snapped up and grabbed Oliver into a tight embrace. He hugged their mother and kissed her hands.

"I love you Momma, but we've got a long way to go. I hope you think we're worth it this time around." The mistrust in his voice brought tears to her eyes. She held him tightly.

"You are so worth it, Isaac. You'll see! I'm going to get you back—all of you." She held out her free hand signaling Oliver to join them. He did. "You'll see!" Her voice was barely audible beneath her sobs.

Valentina and Dr. Johannessen had taken up temporary

residence in Atlanta. And just as she had promised, Valentina spent her evenings getting to know Oliver, Cami, and Ali. Oliver thoroughly enjoyed getting to know his mother. Unlike Lacey, she truly championed his culinary dreams, and his commitment to his community and his loyalty to Cami and Camilla. She didn't share Lacey's opinion that he should commit himself to the highest bidder. She advised him to take every opportunity that allowed him enlightenment and joy. Oliver loved the way Valentina spoke; the words she chose and the cadence in which she delivered them were poetic. He tried fervently to recall if she'd always spoke that way. When he shared his thoughts with Cami, she summed it up with a know it all shrug.

"You were only a little kid when you last knew her. She was sick; she wouldn't have been the same and you wouldn't have been the same. Things work out. Don't they, Ollie Dollie?" Oliver smiled and winked at his friend. Valentina was pursuing an online Bachelor's degree in Psychology and Addiction Counseling, which kept her busy during the day, studying and writing papers. She visited with Isaac every Sunday and really seemed to enjoy reconnecting with her firstborn. They were very much alike. They were both formidable antagonists when provoked, but equally as warm, engaging and loving - fiercely so.

CHAPTER EIGHT

Wedding Make-Up

The days leading up to Lennox and Cami's wedding were a whirlwind of appointments, keeping Lacey and her mother in Atlanta going to the bakery, dress shop and florist. Lacey spent much of the week trying not to crawl out of her skin. Atlanta wasn't the same city for her, since she'd fallen for Oliver and subsequently dumped him. She'd once loved the city. It offered the creature comforts Alabama sorely missed. There were many high-end shops and boutiques, world-class restaurants and a vibrant nightlife filled with young ambitious, upper and comers. But, since the ending of her time with Oliver the city seemed to burst with ghosts of memories past and dashed hopes.

Cami had relinquished much of the wedding planning to Lacey and Tess and had been pretty much, out of the loop. But she had picked out her own gown and looked stunning as she stood in the three-way mirror on a lighted pedestal in front of her soon to be mother and sister in law. Cami chose a full-length gown. It was a white, lace A-line gown by Marchesa with lace elbow length sleeves and a beaded bodice. Lacey couldn't recall a more beautiful bride and felt guilt pull at her heart. Cami had just lost her mother and Oliver was the only family she had left—they'd shared just about every big moment of their lives together. And she was sure that the only reason Oliver wasn't there to share this experience with Cami was to avoid seeing her. The last time she'd been alone with Oliver was awfully uncomfortable. She'd gone to Cami's house with the noblest of intentions and when faced with Oliver's piercing brown eyes and devilishly good looks, she crumbled and kicked into defense mode. She'd said all the wrongs things and allowed her notoriously foolish pride to prevent her from apologizing and begging his forgiveness. She spent every day of their week in Atlanta hoping to run into Oliver and dreading it at the same time.

Cami and Lacey had shared a brief moment of warmth, signaling Cami to speak up for Oliver and she wasted no words. "Lacey, I don't exactly know how to tactfully ask this, but is there something you should be sharing with Oliver?"

Lacey straightened her back, crossed her long legs at the ankles and smoothed her skirt with both of her hands, making it clear to see that the cold Lacey was back.

"What are you asking, exactly Camisha?"

Cami adjusted herself to face Lacey confidently and commenced to speak on the behalf of her best friend.

"Lacey, I've never known Oliver to," she took a moment to find the right word and settled on care. "I've never known Oliver to care for someone the way he cares for you. So, if you're expecting, he has the right to know."

Cami's accusation visibly shook Lacey. She briefly lost her usual poise and snapped her head up to meet Cami's gaze, but before she could light into Cami, Cami soldiered on and offered a less life altering scenario.

"Or if you've simply had your fun with the boy from the wrong side of the tracks, you could at least show him the decency of a proper goodbye."

Cami's second scenario seemed to mollify Lacey a tad,

and she smoothly responded in classic Lacey style.

"Are you done?"

"I am," she said, but then added a sharp warning, "You talk to him, or you'll deal with me."

And this time Lacey was the first to look away. Like her mother, Lacey was not one to allow the last word to be had by another.

"I'm not pregnant. So please, don't be ridiculous," she willfully noted.

Tess came out with her dress over her forearm ending the brief tête-à-tête.

Lacey could have kicked herself for allowing her pride to hijack another opportunity to right the mess she'd started between her and Oliver. Cami offered the perfect pathway back to the man she was sure she'd fallen for, and she'd stupidly blown it.

The cake Oliver chose was a perfect combination for both Cami and Ali. It was Ali's favorite cake flavor: chocolate with Cami's favorite accompaniment to chocolate, raspberry filling.

"That Oliver knows he has good taste, Honey!" Tess exclaimed while swirling her fork in the air, with a mouthful of cake. "Lacey, girl you'd better snap him up and stop stringing that man along," Ms. Tess warned.

Cami nearly choked! Tess laughed and admitted that she'd figured it out the moment Oliver bounced up the basement stairs behind Lacey at Thanksgiving.

"Mom!" Lacey shrieked like a moody teenaged girl and looked at Cami, for her reaction, who quietly excused herself leaving them to talk.

"Do you like him as much as it seems?"

Ms. Tess wasted no time getting to the point.

"How much does it seem, Madame Cleo?"

"Well, you've been handling all of this wedding business from home, when just a few weeks ago we couldn't keep you out of Atlanta. You've been brooding down there in your house just looking for a fight with anybody. So I'm guessing y'all having some kind of disagreement. How am I doing?" Ms. Tess playfully asked.

Lacey's answer was barely audible. "You're right about one thing, I like him. I like him a lot. The second I saw him, I knew that it would happen. It's not really anything he said or anything he did. It was just a feeling that this was going to get interesting. He smiled at me and I could've sworn he was an angel," Lacey paused as if she wanted to savor the memory before she went on. "Mommy, his eyes rivaled my own and I knew I was in trouble," she quietly giggled. "But his were drawing me in," she nodded to her mother, reflectively. "And I knew, that it wasn't going to end well." Something brought her back from her own personal heaven and she cooled again. "But, there was no disagreement. It's just over. It could have never worked—so that's that." Lacey ran her hands over her skirt again, straightened her glasses and continued once she'd recouped. "Mommy let's be real. My life is in Alabama, running the cleaners. Oliver is doing well here, and he has his own goals that don't include running drycleaners, in Alabama. We can't have a weekend-only relationship forever. So what's the point?" She hurled the last question at her mother who sat quietly, stuffing cake into her mouth.

"Lacey, you have to know that your happiness is what's most important to your daddy and me. If this city and that man is where life leads you, so be it. Baby, fly."

Ms. Tess moved her chair closer to Lacey's, put her arm around her daughter, and kissed her at her temple.

Lacey laid her head into her mother's embrace. "I love you, Momma," she said.

Cami barely made it through the rest of the day with the news. She wanted to call Oliver so badly, to put her buddy's mind at ease and give him some peace, just as he's always done for her. In Lacey's not-so-private conversation with her mom, there had been no mention of pregnancy, and it sounded like Lacey was simply afraid and trying to protect herself from what she thought was an inevitable break up. With the information Cami had provided, Oliver had a renewed sense of confidence and committed to winning Lacey's trust.

"The days of 'Oliver and Cami: Against the World', were quickly drawing to a close." Oliver thought to himself as he and Cami idly chatted about music and the news as he steered his truck onto I-20 West towards Birmingham, Alabama. As Cami and Ali's wedding neared, Oliver suffered mixed feelings about his best friend's burgeoning womanhood. Of course he loved her and was very proud and happy for her, but he couldn't ignore the pangs of loss that tugged at him. For much of their lives, he'd been the man in her life. He was the brother, he best friend, the confidant. And in less than a full year, she'd gotten a boyfriend and a dad. And in three days, she'd have a husband—a husband who didn't much like him and who was the brother to Lacey, the force of nature who had completely uprooted his comfortable bachelorhood. The thought of seeing Lacey in her natural habitat both excited and nauseated Oliver.

"So how do you think Lacey will be?"

Cami shrugged. "Who knows how the Ice Princess will behave? She's a mess, Ollie and I still don't understand your deal with her."

Oliver knew that she was right, but he had lost control over his emotions for Lacey Robinson. "Cam," He almost whined. "You think I don't know that? Do you think that I want to be all messed up about her? This shit's not fun for me. It's not a walk in the park for me. Damn!" he concluded and Cami gave him a reprieve.

"Let's just figure out how we'll deal with her. Let's play offense and not give her the damn ball at all." They both burst into laughter.

"What do you know about playing offense?" Oliver teased his friend.

Cami shrugged again. "I pick up odds and ends. Ali watches football all the freaking time." She laughed at herself, too.

"So we'll just walk in there, as cool as polar bears, and if she plays it cool, then that's it." Oliver offered up.

"But, what if she doesn't?" Cami rebutted.

Oliver hadn't considered any other scenario, given that they were dealing with the Ice Princess. She only played one way—cool.

"She will," was all he answered.

Cami pointed out where to make a left between the simple white fence posts. Oliver's heart leapt into his throat. He commanded his cool to step up. As the truck reached the top of the bend, Ali was standing on the front steps waving to them. He was too tall and athletic, to be a desk jockey, as Oliver called him. He practically stretched the full height of the bead board porch ceiling, and he was dressed in fancy sweatpants and a Stanford hoodie with a nearly full beard. The four-car garage was filled, and Ali directed Oliver to park a few feet farther away, down a winding hill.

"This is Lacey's place," Cami pointed out to Oliver.

He didn't respond. Cami jumped from the truck before Oliver had it in park. Ali had bounded down the hill and swept Cami up into a bear hug, swinging her around like a ragdoll.

"We're doing this, Cam! We're getting married, Woman!" he exclaimed. His enthusiasm to marry Cami cheered Oliver greatly. Ali carried her all the way up the stone path to the main house. About half way there, he turned and thanked Oliver.

"Hey, man! Thanks for getting my lady here in one piece." Oliver nodded.

"He's turned to stone because he's really not sure what to expect from your crazy baby sister," Cami whispered into Ali's ear.

Ali grinned and kissed her. "A wise woman once told me, 'They're adults', so they'll figure it out."

Ali effortlessly carried Cami into the house and yelled out, "My lady's here!"

Oliver quietly followed with his arms filled with bags and boxes.

The Robinsons' home was beautiful. It looked like a house he dreamed of as a child, on freezing cold nights in Ohio—nights that he and his brother spent huddled together on the bare, concrete floor in front of the old floor model T.V. Izzy had brought home from the community dumpster, nights that they'd share a tattered old comforter in order to stay warm, while their mom was God knows where, doing God knows what. Freezing cold winter nights, when they'd share the last of the Captain Crunch cereal for dinner and shiver themselves to sleep, alone and afraid. Oliver couldn't imagine any freezing cold nights in the Robinson home. The view of the lake was breathtaking, and perfectly framed by the floor to ceiling wall of windows that was situated directly across from their front door. The house was filled with family and friends and probably always was.

"There's even a fireplace in the dining room!" Oliver whispered just over Cami's shoulder, just as she was whisked into a whirlwind hugs and handshakes.

The handshaking and hugging strangers were Ali and Lacey's cousins, aunts and uncles. A few were introduced, and a tall white man with tan skin and blonde hair was introduced to Cami and Oliver. Kai Beltram was Ali's best friend from college. Shortly after the bustling introductions, Mr. Robinson and Ali led Oliver outside where the rest of the men had congregated.

Mr. Thomas Robinson was an imposing, but gentle figure. Both Mr. and Mrs. Robinson were tall, just as both Lacey and Ali were. Although, Mr. Robinson stood just a half-inch or so shorter than Oliver, his broad shoulders, massive hands and gravelly voice made him appear to tower over most men he encountered. Over Thanksgiving dinner the previous year, the Robinsons talked about Mr. Robinson's early years as a boxer, and Oliver shivered at the thought of being pounded by his gigantic hands, if he'd not taken the news about he and Lacey dating very well.

"Oliver!" Mr. Robinson's booming voice snapped Oliver's head into the present. "Welcome, Son. Welcome!" Mr.

Robinson met Oliver with a bear hug and a hearty smack on the back. He handed Oliver a cigar and ordered a cousin to make him a drink. "What are you having, Son?"

"A coke or something is fine, Sir." Oliver nervously took the cigar and nodded hellos to the other on-looking men who were sitting on the back porch.

"Not today, Oliver. My only son's getting married. Today we're drinking!"

Mr. Robinson laughed robustly and the others joined in with a chorus of Yeahs!

"Fix this man a Hennessey and Coke. You look like a Hennessey man, Oliver."

"That sounds good, Sir." Oliver politely accepted. Mr. Robinson looked pleased and introduced Oliver to the host of uncles, cousins and colleagues. Oliver found it interesting that he was introduced as Lacey's friend instead of Cami's and wondered how long Mr. Robinson had known, and what exactly he knew. Just as Oliver settled down in front of yet another fireplace and lit his cigar, she appeared from the French doors –a heart stopping vision amongst the thick air of machismo and cigar smoke. Lacey was wearing a ruffled apron, and the tortoise shell, cat-eye glasses Oliver loved to see her in. He felt his crotch stiffen and adjusted himself in the wicker chair in which he was sitting. Lacey said nothing; she simply curled her finger in his direction, for him to follow her. Oliver took a cursory glance around the back porch, and dutifully followed Lacey around the side of the house and down the same stone path he'd recently walked up with Cami and Ali. She took him by the hand. "I want to show you my house."

He let her hold his hand and quietly followed her.

Lacey's home was as beautiful as she was. It fell completely in line with her white Porsche Panamera and her predominantly white wardrobe.

"It's a great place, Lace, but, we need to talk."

She put a finger to his mouth.

"Thank you."

She took him by both of his hands. Walking backwards and keeping her eyes on his, she led him behind a large pair of distressed sliding, barn doors, that appeared to hang from the ceiling. Oliver was dumbfounded by Lacey's forwardness, but simultaneously pleased. Part of him wanted to hold on to his indignation, but the southern parts of him wanted to hold on to her cocoa colored waist and hips. Her come-hither hazel eyes were blazing and she'd began unbuttoning the fitted white jeans she was wearing. Oliver stepped out of his shoes, untied the apron, and lifted her blouse over her head. He lifted her into his arms, and tossed her onto her four-poster bed.

"I'm sorry," Lacey whispered breathlessly between wet kisses.

"You should be," Oliver winced petulantly.

Lacey flirtatiously turned over onto her stomach and smiled back at Oliver.

"Oh, you'd like that. Wouldn't you?" Oliver cooed, knowing exactly what she wanted.

"I deserve it. I've been a really bad girl. I've been mean to you."

He agreed and smacked her curvy bare ass. He followed the slap with his tongue. Lacey writhed beneath the warmth of his mouth and bit down hard on her bottom lip. He entered her dripping womanhood and whispered in her ear, "We're going to talk, Lacey."

Lacey wept in surrender, "OK."

She'd missed him so much. Her lady parts seemed to quiver of their own volition long after they'd made love. Lacey drew the linen drapes that surrounded her bed and climbed under the covers where Oliver laid. She wrapped her arms around his thin waist and covered his muscular shoulders in wet kisses.

"I've missed you so much, Oliver Barnett."

"Hmm."

"Babe, please don't be like this. I know I messed up. I was afraid."

"You. Afraid? Come again with that one, Lacey."

Lacey sat up to face him. "Look, Oliver. I'm trying to apologize!" The Ice Princess had reappeared and Oliver didn't want to lose the opportunity to have an open and honest conversation with her, so he sat up with her.

"I know you are and I appreciate it. I know it's not easy for someone like you to apologize."

Lacey furrowed her brow and Oliver quickly moved to extinguish the fire building behind the look. "I just want to understand what the hell happened, Lace."

He kissed her, and the embers in her hazel eyes softened again.

"Before you, Oliver. I hadn't been with a man in fourteen years." She paused to let that sink in. Oliver seemed unshaken. She went on, "When I was seventeen years old, I got pregnant from the first and only guy I'd ever been with. He took me Birmingham for an abortion and I never heard from him again." Oliver sat completely silent, taking in all of Lacey's story, trying to make sense of all of it. He felt for her, but couldn't understand where he fell into all of it and his confusion registered on his face.

"I'm sorry that that happened to you, Lace, but, what happened between us?"

She loved that he was so steady and easy to talk to.

"I thought I was pregnant."

Oliver's eyes widened with surprise.

"But, I wasn't!" Lacey exclaimed. "But that's where things got wonky for me."

"Wonky?" Oliver repeated the absurd word choice.

"Yes. Wonky," she laughed and swatted at him. "Ollie, when I saw that minus sign on the pregnancy test, I got so sad. I mean, I was really sad."

It was Oliver's brow the furrowed with her last words. "You," he carefully dragged out, "wanted to be pregnant? From me?"

Lacey didn't know what to make of Oliver's response, and felt her temper rise. Oliver noticed it too and offered clarification.

"I mean, that surprises me, Lace. I didn't know that we were there. That's all."

He took her delicate hands and kissed them.

"I'm good with that," he kissed her between her breasts. "I'm very good with that."

Lacey's body relaxed at his touch and then tensed again.

"You're good with what, exactly?" she asked. "I don't want a baby! Well, not right now. That's not what you're talking about, are you?"

It wasn't what Oliver meant at all. He shook his head. "No. I just mean, that I'm good with you being okay with having my baby—someday, any day in the future—near or far."

His words surprised him and he wanted so badly to end the whole baby conversation, and so did Lacey. She wrapped her long legs around him and guided him back inside of her. They made love again, well into sunset.

"I love having you here," Lacey purred into Oliver's ear as she stood behind him with her arms wrapped around his waist.

"I love being here, but, I'm trying to cook," he playfully responded while trying to free himself from her grasp, in order to move around her well-appointed gourmet kitchen.

"Lacey Babe, for the life of me, I'll never understand why people like you, who don't cook, put so much design into your kitchens. It's criminal!"

"I guess the fates knew I'd fall for a Master Chef."

"Fall for, huh?" Oliver sarcastically chided her. Which was not lost on her, but she didn't want to go another round with him. She was all too happy to have him there, with her in her space and with her family—openly together.

"Ollie, I've apologized more than once,"

Sensing the iciness in her tone, he interjected with a kiss. "I know. I'm just giving you a hard time, Babe."

Lacey was completely disarmed, and leapt into his arms, straddling him. Oliver lifted her onto the kitchen counter and kissed her, gently at first, and more and more passionately with their every breath. A knock on the door came just as Lacey began unbuttoning his jeans again. She covered his mouth with a hand and they both giggled.

"Lace!"

It was her cousin, MJ. Lacey hushed Oliver and kept her hand over his mouth, trying to quiet his laughter.

"Babe, come on now. Where the hell else would we

be? We're in the middle of nowhere," Oliver laughed out loud.

"Really, Lacey. I can hear you in there! Are y'all screwing around in the damned kitchen! We're having breakfast in there tomorrow!" MJ yelled and kicked at the door.

Lacey and Oliver laughed hysterically. Oliver adjusted his bent and twisted crotch as he went to open the door for MJ. Lacey stayed perched atop the kitchen counter.

"What's good, Mary-Anthony?" Oliver said, greeting MJ with a hug. "Nice to see you again."

MJ frowned at him and teased, "I hope that's a rolling pin down there, Nasty Man."

Oliver smiled and replied, "Wow."

He stood aside to let her through the door.

"Classy, MJ," Lacey scoffed at her cousin's remark.

"Says, Ms. Tuskegee University, who's getting boinked on the kitchen counter." MJ lifted the lid of one the steaming pots. "Hmm, that smells so good! What are you cooking down here, Oliver?"

Oliver shook his head and left the room to find his shirt. "Dirty rice." He answered before returning fully dressed.

MJ was a firecracker and Oliver really liked her. She and Lacey were physically, total opposites. Where Lacey stood nearly five feet ten inches tall, MJ barely broke five feet. Lacey was busty with a lean, but hourglass figure and MJ was pleasingly plump and hippy, like her mother, Tess. But they both shared the signature, Jackson family high cheekbones, bright smiles and hazel eyes, but MJ's were more emerald than were Lacey's cat-like ones. The two were quite the pair, verbally sparring and one upping each other. They finished each other's sentences and seemed to speak fluently through facial expressions and body language.

Exhibited as soon as MJ closed the pot lid. Lacey sat perched on the counter and eyed the lid from MJ's chubby fingers back to the lid's resting place atop the pot. She didn't utter a word, but her look elicited a fiery counter from her cousin.

"Damn, Lacey! There's enough food in that pot for everybody up in here and up there, too." MJ motioned towards the main house.

"You wouldn't," Lacey warned. The two remained locked at their matching eyes.

"I didn't say I would," MJ didn't back down. Instead, she straightened her back, put her hands on her wide hips, and shifted her weight to one foot.

"I'll give you a call when it's done, Mary-Anthony Jackson Jones." Lacey over enunciated each of her cousin's names.

MJ stood unmoved for another few seconds before they both erupted in laughter.

Oliver stood against the sliding barn doors of the bedroom and quietly watched the standoff. Their laughter signaled for him to breathe again.

"You're such a B!" MJ hurled at Lacey between belly laughs.

"It takes one to know one, Mary-Anthony Jackson Jones!" Lacey chuckled and added, "With your greedy behind!"

"You are two very scary women," Oliver sighed and returned to his dirty rice. He playfully smacked one of Lacey's thighs and she grabbed him for a kiss. He obliged her before heading out to his truck to get his things.

Once she'd watched Oliver walk out of earshot, MJ whipped around to face her cousin.

"He does know that Uncle Tommy ain't having him staying down here with you, doesn't he?" The girls chuckled.

"Trust, Lennox will be down here shortly. Besides, Cami's staying down here with me." Lacey surmised.

"Cuz, I am so happy for you. You've got a good one out there."

MJ took three glasses from the cupboard indicating her intention to stay. Lacey laughed and hopped down from her post and took a bottle of Riesling from the refrigerator.

"Yeah. I just hope I don't mess it up. I feel like a teenager all over again—unprepared and misinformed," Lacey confessed, but was interrupted when Oliver rejoined them with Cami, Kai and Lennox in tow. Lacey rolled her eyes and audibly growled.

"Looks like it's a party, Babe," she whispered to Oliver and slapped him on the behind. Oliver returned to his pots, winked at her, and blew a kiss in her direction.

Cami and Ali's wedding was a rousing success and Oliver's plans for their reception were full steam ahead. The two married in the Robinson's family church in Alabama, and planned to host a reception at Cami's in Atlanta the following week. Although Lacey had done much of the ceremony planning, Oliver took the helm for the reception. He was wholly committed to celebrating his best friend's nuptials in grand style. At the insistence of his mother and wealthy new stepfather, he spared no expense. Oliver personally oversaw every detail. There were so many personal touches—poster size pictures highlighting Cami and Ali's childhoods, their up and down courtship, and intimate shots of their wedding day were artistically displayed throughout the backyard. Oliver and Valentina made a great team, as shown in the music and menu choices they'd made for the celebration.

"He turned this backyard into Tuscany!" Cami squealed with delight as she took in all of the loving details Oliver had appointed throughout the reception. Ali walked around the yard marveling at its transformation.

"The man is truly talented. I've gotta give it to him," he said, shaking his head in amazement.

Yellow up lighting cast a golden glow all over the back-yard, globe string lights lit the carport and the pergola, both of which were draped with white tulle. Oliver used the ribbons and wooden dowels from the church to line the driveway. There were tall, modern patio heaters and two long tables with white Chiavari chairs. There was a DJ, a string quartet, valets and servers all dressed in white coats. He'd thought of everything—a coat check, dinner music, passed hors d'oeuvres, a three-course meal, buckets of champagne on ice and two dance floors. His mother and her husband were among the guests and so were Cami's newly discovered father, James DaCosta and his wife, Evangeline. Lacey and Oliver made a striking couple that night. He wore a double-breasted navy blue suit with a baby blue and navy striped bow tie. His locks were French braided down his back and he'd grown out a handsomely trimmed goatee and mustache. Lacey's knee length body hugging dress perfectly complimented her man's suit. It looked as if the coastal blue duchess satin and lace dress was cut especially for her long legs, tiny waist and ample bosom.

"Aren't you a vision, Baby Sister," Ali complimented his sister with a kiss and hug.

"Thank you, Big Brother." Lacey smiled as she turned to hug her new sister in law.

"Cami, you're glowing." The women hugged.

"I'm so happy for you and Lenny. I truly am."

"Thank you, Lacey. You have no idea what hearing you say that means to me."

"Welcome to the family." Lacey said, hugging Cami once more.

"Have you had a chance to chat with Valentina?" Something flashed in Lacey's eyes with Cami's question about Oliver's mother. Ali noticed it too. He gave Cami a curious glance.

"Not exactly," Lacey dragged out. "I don't think she likes me."

"How could she not like you, you've just met?" Ali asked with a discernable amount of concern in his tone. Lacey shrugged. Oliver joined the threesome, putting Ali's question on hold.

"Are you happy, Boss Lady?" he asked.

Cami warmly embraced her best friend. "Oliver, words can't express how happy I am. I can hardly believe this is my house—heck, my life!" Cami squealed and hugged Oliver again. She turned and kissed Ali square on the mouth, to an eruption of applause and clinking of glasses. Their guests gleefully applauded each time the newly married Mr. and Mrs. Robinson shared a kiss.

"Own it, Cam, because you deserve it more than anyone else I know on this Earth."

"Awww, Oliver. Lacey is really softening you up, Old Boy." Cami teased.

Lacey wrapped an arm around Oliver's slim waist and laid her head on his shoulder with a loving pat to his chest.

"See, I'm good for you, Mr. Barnett."

"Yes, you are, Ms. Robinson." The two shared a light kiss

as Ali and Cami looked on smiling.

"Ahem!" Valentina butted in as she joined the group of friends.

"Cami you look beautiful. I only wish Camille could be here to see you so happy."

The group nodded their heads in agreement.

"She was so proud of you, and so am I for what it's worth."

"Thanks, Valentina. It's worth a lot," Cami beamed.

"And Ali, it's been truly a pleasure meeting you. Mix and I are going to head out."

"Oh, Mrs. Johannessen, I wanted to formally introduce you to our parents," Lacey piped up.

Valentina stiffened. "We were introduced while you were primping, Lacey." Valentina's curt retort visibly struck Lacey. Oliver pulled her closer to him, and coldly stared at his mother.

"You don't know what she was doing, Tina." Oliver warned in the lowest register of his voice. Sensing Oliver's defenses rise, Valentina wished them all a goodnight and kissed her son on the cheek.

"What the hell was that about?" Ali demanded. Cami swiftly moved to diffuse the situation with a hand to her husband's chest. "Let's just enjoy the rest of the night, Love."

Ali's posture relaxed and he leaned over to kiss his wife again, to another round of boisterous applause.

CHAPTER NINE

She Hates Me

"Are we going to talk about why your mother hates me and she only met me like two breaths ago?" Lacey asked, kicking off her nude stilettos as soon as the door to Oliver's apartment closed behind them. Oliver flinched at the question. She hadn't mentioned the awkward exchange on the ride from Cami's, and he fervently hoped she'd forgotten about his mother's bristly reception. He tossed his keys on the kitchen counter and laid his jacket across the piano bench on his way to the restroom.

"I don't know, Lace. I wouldn't worry too much about it," he answered from behind the restroom door. Oliver washed his hands and stood looking at his reflection in the tiny bathroom mirror. He mentally readied himself for the barrage of questions that were surely waiting for him on the other side of the restroom door. He wondered how much he'd share with Lacey regarding the conversations he'd had with his mother about her. They were in a rough place when his mother returned to him. She'd been the one who disappeared on him without any warning. What was he supposed to tell his mother about her? At that point, she was a she-devil in his eyes, and he'd painted her as such to Valentina. He mustered up his resolve and left the security of his little tub-less bathroom.

"You bad mouthed me to her, didn't you?" Lacey hurled the accusation at Oliver from across the room. She stood beside the bed with her hands on her hips. "Didn't you, Oliver?' she demanded.

"Lacey, you left me! I was confused as hell and mad."

"And hurt," Lacey quietly added.

"Yeah. And hurt," Oliver walked over to her with his hands outstretched.

Lacey accepted the gesture and let him lower her onto the bed.

"I'm sorry, Babe. I'll straighten it all out," Oliver promised Lacey between kisses.

"I'm the one who should be sorry," she breathlessly relented. "And I am. And I just have to show Mrs. Doctor Johannessen that I am not the monster her precious son has painted me out to be."

"Yeah. Yeah. You looked shook, tough guy!" Oliver jeered as he unzipped Lacey's dress.

"Heck yeah. She is a former crackhead. I hear they're pretty scrappy."

"You better know it, Has Been Beauty Queen," Oliver fired back and tossed the satin and lace dress across the room before burying his face between her legs.

Lacey giggled and closed her eyes against the pleasure shooting up from her hot center.

The buzzing of Oliver's cell phone on the wrought iron nightstand sent it crashing against knotty pine hardwood floor, slicing through the haze of lovemaking. He stretched his long body to reach the phone, while staying firmly planted inside of Lacey.

"Oh my God! Really, Oliver?" Lacey yelled and slapped him across his bare back.

"Sorry, Babe. It's six in the morning. It must be important. It could be Cam!"

"Effing Cami," Lacey mumbled under her breath.

"Can't she even honeymoon without consulting you?" She grumbled on and writhed beneath him.

"Hello."

"Hey, O! It's me."

It was Valentina. Hearing his mother's voice shrunk his cock. He rolled over and grabbed his boxers to slide on, turning his back to Lacey.

"Hey, Ma. What's up? Everything okay?"

"Yes. Everything is great! I have news about Benji! Good news! I'm coming over."

"No! Let's just meet for breakfast somewhere."

Lacey punched him in his back. "Or brunch," he coughed and chuckled at Lacey.

"Are you trying to catch a cold, O?" Valentina asked in a motherly tone.

"No," he answered between chuckles and kicks to his back from Lacey.

"Well, take some Vitamin C anyway and I'll see you for breakfast, not brunch."

"Ma, I can't make breakfast," he protested. "I'm in the middle of something," he chuckled as he put a finger into Lacey's wetness. She threshed and slapped him against the back again.

"Oliver Darwin Barnett, it's about your brother, so I'll see you at eight a.m. Bring Ms. High and Mighty with you!" Valentina added before giving her son the location of the place he was to meet her.

Oliver snarled and rolled back onto Lacey, where his erection returned as quickly as it had disappeared.

Valentina Rose Barnett-Johannessen stood underneath a forest green vinyl awning waving as Lacey's Porsche turned into the parking lot. She was a splendid sight in the early morning light. Her long silver locks were pulled high on her head in a chic bun highlighting her exquisite bone structure and long graceful neck. Lacey ran a nervous hand over her cranberry red cashmere sweater and straightened her glasses, before Oliver made it around to her door. Oliver helped her out of the car and held on to her hand. "You look beautiful, Lace," he assured her.

Valentina greeted her son with an affectionate embrace.

"You look nice, Ma."

"Thanks, Baby Boy." She shot an icy glance at Lacey.

"Good morning, Lindsey."

"It's Lacey," Lacey politely corrected Valentina and shook her outstretched hand.

"Of course, it is. My apologies."

Oliver gave Lacey's back a reassuring pat as he escorted the ladies inside.

A cheerful server breezed by to take their drink orders and vanished leaving the kitchen doors swinging behind him. Murphy's was already in full swing by 8:30 a.m. The small restaurant was vibrating with energy. There were young hipster couples with babies and bicycles cozied up at small tables along the patio and half marathon runners bellied up to the bar. The scent of freshly baked breads and rich coffee brewing filled the air and made Oliver feel at home. He stretched his long legs across the booth and interlocked his fingers with Lacey's.

"So what's the news about Benji, Ma?'

"Let's just order first and then we'll get into that. Is that OK with you?"

Oliver shrugged.

"Ok, with me. They have the best eggs benedict in the city here!"

"My little O, eating eggs benedict." Valentina gushed.

"My little Valentina Rose, knowing what they are," Oliver jeered and immediately regretted the slight. Lacey struggled to stifle a giggle and Valentina noticed.

"Sorry, Ma," he quickly apologized.

"You don't owe me anything."

Lacey gasped and stood. "Please excuse me."

Oliver stood to let her pass. "I'll be right back."

Once Lacey was out of sight, Valentina cast her eyes downward and nervously asked, "Have you told her about me? About my past," she stopped and chose other words. "About my drug addiction?"

A lump rose in Oliver's throat. He nodded. Valentina twisted her mouth a little and nodded back.

"OK. Thanks for your honesty."

She and Oliver sat in silence until the cheerful young man reappeared with a tray of coffee cups and a carafe of orange juice.

"I'll be right back with glasses and I'll take your orders then."

"OK, thanks." Oliver almost whispered. He grappled with the lump in his throat and looked out onto the street until Lacey was back.

The server returned with her. They ordered the eggs benedict, the sausage and spinach breakfast meatloaf, and a basket of honey butter corn muffins.

"So, O tells me you're quite the business woman." Valentina was the first to speak.

Lacey gave a small smile. “It’s my family’s business, so I’m properly motivated to do a good job.”

“She’s being modest. Her daddy credits her for single handedly growing his business. Lacey can be dogged when properly motivated,” Oliver teased and raised her hand to his lips.

“Is growing Oliver a part of your business plan?” Valentina’s question was loaded with sarcasm. Oliver shifted uncomfortably in his seat, but Lacey was unmoved.

“If he wants to be.” Lacey lifted her hand back to Oliver’s lips and answered as equally as sarcastically.

Oliver sensed the contempt between the ladies and searched his mind for an exit strategy.

“Ma, tell me about Benji.” His strategy worked like magic. The light in Valentina’s eyes returned.

“We found him! And he’s doing well. He’s in North Dakota of all places!”

“North Dakota!” Oliver exclaimed. “How the hell did he get out there?”

“Probably with the Oil fields,” Lacey interjected. Oliver and Valentina both looked at her as if they’d forgotten she was there with them.

“Lindsey’s right,” Valentina said as she rolled her eyes.

“Lacey, Ma! Her name is Lacey.”

Oliver was growing more and more irritated with the both of them. “Her name is Lacey, and you know it. So please, let’s all just be civil.”

“Let’s, as in Let Us? because I’ve been nothing but civil to her!” Lacey snapped.

"Why is she even here, Oliver? I told you I wanted to talk about family business."

Valentina countered, without looking at Lacey. Lacey pointed a perfectly manicured nail at herself. "Why am I here? Me?" Why are you here?" Lacey laughed.

"I'm your mother? What the hell kind of question is that?" Valentina snapped at Oliver, refusing to address Lacey directly.

Lacey pushed her glasses on her nose as the server returned with their food, allowing fresh air to cool the heated atmosphere. Sensing the discord, the once cheery server quickly placed the plates and baskets in front of them and darted off.

"Please, chill out. I love you both and I want y'all to just try to get to know each other." Oliver pleaded.

Lacey sat dumbstruck by Oliver's declaration of love for her. He had never told her that he loved her. She figured he did when he readily forgave her at Lennox and Cami's wedding. Furthermore, she'd reconciled, during their separation that she loved him too.

"You love me?" Lacey asked. Oliver sat stunned by his words and slowly answered.

"Yeah, Lace. I do." He turned to face her full on.

Her hazel eyes sparkled and a bright smile spread across her face. She blushed and said,

"I do too."

Valentina cleared her throat, snapping the lovebirds from each other's gazes. "Oliver, you have to be careful with your heart, Son."

Lacey scoffed. "Will you shut up already? Your son disappeared at thirteen years old and where were you then—when he needed you? Huh, Missus Doctor Johannessen? Where were you then?"

"How dare you, you stuck up little bitch?" Valentina seethed.

"How dare me? How dare you, showing up here after he's raised his damned self, trying to play mommy knows best! Get the hell out of here with that. You're a day late and a dollar short, Tina!" Lacey had had her say and stuffed a bite of she and Oliver's eggs benedict into her mouth.

Jarred by Lacey's outburst, Oliver stuttered. "Really, Lacey? So you're pleased with yourself now?"

His anger was palpable.

"Me?" Lacey whined full of petulance. Valentina sat across the table, her eyes filled with tears. She slowly stood up and smoothed the burnt orange cape she was wearing over cream riding pants.

"Oliver, I'll talk to you later."

Oliver jumped up knocking over the carafe of orange juice, sending the sticky liquid spilling over the entire table and onto his mother's pants. The chill of the juice stiffened Valentina. She calmly dabbed at her pants with a napkin and their server rushed over with more napkins and towels. She stepped out of the booth and looked down at Lacey, who had not moved to help either of them throughout the commotion.

"I'm here now, Lacey Robinson. And I'm going to be here."

With that, she blew a kiss to Oliver and left the restaurant.

Oliver spent the ten-minute car ride back to his place with Lacey in complete silence. He was so pissed at Lacey, he thought it best to not open his mouth until he'd cooled. Lacey didn't push. She turned the car down the alley to the rear of Oliver's apartment and parked. He stood from the car and headed upstairs without opening her door as he usually did. She knew instinctively that it was not the time for any dissent, so she humbly let herself out and followed him upstairs in silence. Oliver tossed his keys on the counter, and sat at his piano. He slid over and patted the empty spot beside him. Lacey obediently sat with him. He played a few notes and she joined in. They sat exchanging no words, playing a lighthearted riff on Heart and Soul.

"You infuriate me, Lacey."

"I know I do."

"You can be such a snobby brat," he said, shaking his head. "I don't know what I see in you."

"Neither do I." She put her hand over his, stopping the music. "But I'm glad you see it. I love you, Oliver Barnett. And I didn't even think my heart worked."

Oliver took her face in both his hands and kissed her. "You've got to give her a chance. And so do I. She's trying, and that's all I've wanted from her all of my life, Lace."

Lacey knew she'd gone too far. She knew how important a relationship with his mother was to Oliver. Chastened, Lacey grimaced. "I know. I know. I'll call her to apologize, but, I'm going to need another kiss first."

Oliver kissed her passionately and playfully nudged her glasses up her nose. "Thank you, Lacey Baby. I really appreciate it," he laughed and remarked, "How about that? I love Lacey and Lacey loves me. But, you know if Tina was anything like Camilla, shit would have been very different this morning."

Lacey nodded and joined his boisterous laughter.

"Camilla would have kicked your ass. You know that, right?"

They laughed at the thought, because they both knew it was true.

The big slice of humble pie didn't go down easily for Lacey. Her stomach turned as she dialed the numbers to call Valentina, with Oliver anxiously looking over her shoulder. Mix answered in his musical Norwegian accent, warmly greeting Lacey.

"Hello, Dear."

Lacey was surprised by his easy familiarity. "Hi, Dr. Johannessen. Is Valentina available?"

"Yes, she's coming. And please, call me Mix."

She turned to Oliver and mouthed to him, "She has my number saved in her phone."

He whispered back, "How do you know?"

"Mix just answered." The sound of Tina's voice stopped Lacey's explanation mid-sentence. Lacey took a deep breath and forced a smile onto her face.

"Hello, Tina—I mean, Valentina. I owe you an apology."

The line was silent.

"Hello?" Lacey said again.

"Yes. I'm here." Valentina's voice was even and not at all musical like Mix's.

Lacey gritted her teeth and soldiered on. "OK. I was out of line and I hope you can forgive my behavior." Lacey tried to curb the irritation in her tone. "It's very important to Oliver for us to get to know each other, and Oliver's very important to me."

"Is he? I mean, is he important to you? Just the way he

is."

Lacey was rattled by Valentina's accusation. She felt her temper elevating and turned to Oliver, who noticed the familiar flash in her fiery, hazel eyes. He grabbed the phone from Lacey's hands. "Mom, please. She's trying to tell you she's sorry."

"No, she's trying to placate you, O. Ask her to call when she's ready to apologize." Her response was finite.

"Are we going to see your brother together tomorrow? Mix is coming."

Oliver relinquished. "Yes. Eight o'clock. I guess I'm driving since Mix is coming. See you then." Oliver ended the call.

"Is that it?" Lacey yelled as she jumped to her feet.

"Lace, you really went off this morning! She's not ready. Damn! What can I do about that? You were wrong," Oliver fired back.

Lacey grabbed her lapis blue Kate Spade weekender bag and locked herself in the bathroom. She pulled her stained cashmere sweater over her head and yelled at the door.

"Eight O'clock, Mommy! I'll drive, Mommy."

Oliver lightly drummed on the closed door. "Lace, don't be a baby. Come out of there. What are you doing?"

"Why not? You're acting like a baby! Baby O, precious Little O." she mocked.

She listened for his come back, but there wasn't one. She pressed her ear against the door, and heard the front door close and lock. Lacey swung the bathroom door open to find the dimly lit apartment still and empty.

Oliver sped off towards East Ponce De Leon Ave. He was nearly blinded by rage—a contemptible and insolent rage that lived deep inside of him. At times it churned and toiled just beneath the surface of Oliver's well-rehearsed happy-go-lucky countenance, and at other times, it laid inactive for months at a time, giving Oliver a false sense of self-control. Oliver was almost surprised by the cold, silence that greeted him as he entered Cami's empty kitchen through the basement door. A strange sadness joined the rage as it hit him. Cami was on the other side of the country on her honeymoon with her new husband, and Camilla was dead. In that moment, he realized that the basement just behind him would no longer be his and Camilla's home away from home. He was sure that Ali would ask for his key and revoke his liberal privileges to come and go as he pleased. The newly married couple would undoubtedly make Cami's much larger home their primary residence, as it was more appropriate than Ali's small, stainless steel bachelorette pad. Everything was changing so quickly and decisively. Oliver felt lightheaded. He opened the refrigerator door and pulled out a bunch of fresh spinach.

"Why would she leave fresh spinach in here?" he wondered aloud. He shook his head and took out a carton of heavy cream and eggs. He rifled thru her cupboards for spices and any other inspiring ingredients. Cooking always righted Oliver. It was the one thing that was sure to satisfy him in multiple ways. A great dish, be it sweet or savory, would lull several of his senses; he would be intellectually challenged by measures and figures, he would be sensually engaged by scents and flavors, and lastly his ego will be adequately stroked by a perfectly executed meal. As Oliver poured the mixture of cardamom, cream and eggs over the hot, wilted spinach, which lined the Pyrex baking dish, he could feel his rage dissipate. He put the dish into the oven, and popped open and bottle of craft beer that he was sure belonged to Ali.

"Bougie ass negro. Just like his stuck up ass sister." Oliver hoisted himself onto the kitchen counter. As if she was cued, Lacey's sparkling white Porsche turned onto Cami's rear parking pad.

"Fuck!" Oliver exclaimed. He felt the rage slither back into his chest, but he didn't move.

Lacey sat in the car watching him through the window. She wasn't familiar with this side of Oliver and took another few minutes to assess his face through the kitchen window. She'd planned and ranted all the way over to Cami's house, where she was sure he'd gone. And as she sat within thirty feet of him, she was paralyzed by uncertainty and remorse for her behavior, once again. She wondered how many more of her outbursts would he take, and the answers she came up with unnerved her. Lacey conjured up the courage to get out of the car, after what seemed like hours of the standoff –he didn't move from his spot atop the kitchen counter and neither did she from the luxurious leather racing seat of her Panamera. Lacey expected Oliver to meet her at the door, but he didn't. She knocked lightly. He didn't answer. She knocked again, her humility fading.

"Really Oliver!"

"What do you want, Lacey?"

"I want to come in."

"Lacey, I left because I don't want to see you." Oliver yelled. "Damn, you're a college graduate, aren't you?" He snapped.

"Oliver, trust me. This is not what you want," she warned, her voice filled with ire.

"Oh, now you're threatening me? You messed up, and I'm done. That's it. So, yeah, Lace, it's exactly what I want." Oliver turned and walked away from the back door, but not before Lacey kicked the door.

"You bastard! How dare you walk out on me!" Lacey cried. "You pursued me! And now you want to walk out on me for being exactly who you knew I was."

Oliver stood frozen by the harsh truth Lacey flung through the locked door.

"To hell with you, Oliver Barnett!"

He heard the click of her heels as she stormed off. Just as she started the car, Oliver walked out onto the carport. Lacey turned off the engine, and let the driver side window down. Oliver didn't move towards the car, but he didn't move towards the door either.

"Lace, come on now."

She opened the car door and slowly followed him back into the house.

"How'd you know I'd be here?" Oliver asked without facing her.

"I just took a chance. Did you forget she wasn't here?" She regretted the smart remark as soon as it left her mouth.

"Did you come here to fight? 'Cause I'm tapped out, Kid."

She hadn't. She'd come there to humble herself and beg him to not give up on her.

"Something smells good."

"It's the cardamom. I'm making a spinach pie."

Lacey chuckled. "What a man. Sexy, talented—and forgiving?"

"Keep going," Oliver smirked.

"Loving and patient and kind."

"Quoting the Good Book, huh?"

"I'll quote whatever it takes to get you to not give up on me, Mr. Barnett." Lacey slinked over and linked her arms around his waist. She closed her eyes and took in his scent. She was so madly in love with this man. Her heart sunk at the revelation.

"Lacey, you've got to chill with the tantrums. They only ignite a part of me that I don't like, a part of me that I'm not proud of. So when I leave, you have to let me. Okay?"
She didn't understand, but she agreed to just trust him.

"Where does Ms. Corner Bakery keep the wine stashed?" Lacey asked, lightening the mood.

"It's not even noon, Lacey."

"I deserve a glass of wine after the start to this day. Don't I?"

"Point taken. But, at least add some sparkling water or orange juice to it." Oliver pointed out a small wine cooler next to the custom built, floor to ceiling pantry. He took down a glass for Lacey.

"I'm drinking some fruity ass beer of your brother's."

"Don't even start in on my big brother. He has refined tastes, Oliver." She teased.

Oliver pulled her close with one arm and kissed her.

"How did I get here?" he asked aloud.

"I can't say, but I'm glad you did." Lacey kissed Oliver and lifted the Bob Marley t-shirt he was wearing over his head. She loved to see his long locks cascade over his tattooed shoulders and chest.

"Babe, here?' he asked breathlessly between kisses.

"What about the pie? It's almost done," he laughed, as Lacey effortlessly unzipped his cargo shorts.

She took his hard cock into her hands as he shuffled backwards with his shorts down around his ankles.

"Lacey Baby, just let me take it out." He pleaded.

"It is out." She looked him in his eyes and licked his chest.

"I mean, the pie. Oh my God," he grunted and braced himself against the oven.

Lacey dropped to one knee and then to the other. She took him into her mouth and ran her tongue along the underside of Oliver's manhood. His knees weakened and he could smell the acrid scent of the spinach pie burning.

"What would your precious big brother think of what you just did in his kitchen?" Oliver taunted as a naked Lacey lay across his bare chest, tracing his tattoos.

"Have you ever considered waxing your chest?" She asked as she fingered at the curly tufts of hair on Oliver chest.

"Hell no! And don't you get any crazy ideas about it either. Stop trying to change me!"
His sharp reaction stunned her.

"I just asked. And what's this about me trying to change you?"

She sat up to look him in his face. "I don't want to change you. Change you how?"

There was something in his tone that she didn't like, but she couldn't quite identify the nuisance. She had a sneaking suspicion that it was something planted by his Johnny-come-lately mother, Valentina.

"Oliver, why would you say that I'm trying to change

you?"

Oliver knew that when Lacey pressed, she wouldn't relent. "I mean, you started with the trip to Ohio, to find my mother,"

Lacey groaned, but Oliver ignored the gesture and kept on, "And then it was the Wine and Food Festival paperwork. 'Babe, do you have goals?'" he mimicked her voice. "And now you want me to get my chest waxed."

She interrupted again. "I never asked you to get your chest waxed! It was just a question, an innocent question!"

"Yeah right, Lace," Oliver retorted. "What's next? Tattoo removals? Italian loafers? Matching Porsches?"

Lacey sensed his growing agitation. She was getting good at that. "You're right. You're right. Calm down. I'm sorry." She apologized but went on to plead the merits of her suggestions. She sat up in the full size bed and folded her long legs Indian style. "I just want the best for you. I think you undervalue your talent, that's all, Babe. And I don't even like Italian loafers!"

He laughed a little and kissed her. He took her perfectly heart shaped face in his hands and whispered to her,

"I appreciate your faith in me, but I've made it just fine without your coaching."

He was right, but Lacey grew enterprises and she had every intention on growing the Barnett brand. The possibilities absolutely thrilled her. Changing the subject, she asked.
"So what are we eating since you've burned the spinach pie?"

Oliver swung his long legs out of the bed and pulled his underwear on.

"I guess we're going out again. We never did finish breakfast. And we should probably clean up Cami's kitchen."

Lacey corrected him, "Lenny and Cami's kitchen."

CHAPTER TEN

North Dakota's Cold

"So let me get this straight. His mom is living Atlanta?"

"Yes, Mommy. Well, temporarily." Lacey tried to explain for the third time.

"Temporarily?" Lacey's Aunt Katy B interjected.

"Jesus, Ma! Yes, temporarily. She's trying to reconnect with her boys. How many times does she have to say it?" MJ was exasperated with her mother and her Aunt Tess's incessant questions.

"And Oliver has a brother in prison? In Atlanta?" Lacey's father, Thomas walked into the kitchen with his own question.

Yes, and another brother who's in North Dakota."

Thomas Robinson slowly rubbed his hand over his thick, salt and pepper hair.

"A son in prison and another in the frozen tundra. I'll just be damned."

"Hush, Tommy! Let the child finish." Ms. Tess ordered her husband with a wave of her hand. Lacey took a bite of apple pie from her mother's plate and continued.

"As I was saying, her name is Valentina Rose—can you believe that - and she married some rich, white Scandinavian doctor from Norway or Denmark somewhere."

"Hush yo' mouth!" Katy B exclaimed and turned to her baby sister.

"And she was a drug addict?" Tess shook her head in disbelief and stuffed a forkful of apple pie into her mouth.

"Well, she's fully recovered now and all too high and mighty."

"And she fails to see the charm in my lovely daughter?" Tess taunted Lacey. "Those drugs must have fried her brain!" she added and exploded in laughter with her sister and niece.

Tommy quickly scorned the women for poking fun at Lacey while she was so obviously upset.

"Oh lighten up, Tommy. Lace is a big girl. She knows we're just teasing!"

Lacey patted her father on the arm and assured him that she was fine. She'd grown up with those audacious broads and had dished her fair share of taunting in their directions over the years. If there was one thing she was certain of, was the love they all had for her.

"Lace, tell them how she looks and about her fine white man," MJ requested.

Lacey didn't want to sing Valentina's praises, but she acquiesced under the pressure of their eager gazes.

"She truly is a commanding presence. She's at least six feet tall—give an inch or two. And she's very pretty. She's reminds me of one of those ancient Mayan statues made of obsidian that Lenny and I saw in Guatemala."

"Wow. So she's dark skinned woman?" Tess asked.

"Yes, very. And her hair's the color of yours, Mommy—pure silver. But, she has locks like Oliver, and just as long. She wears them pinned up in sophisticated chignons or wrapped scarves." She recalled the last time she'd seen Valentina, when she insulted her. "And she's very stylish. Money has served her well."

"So what does she do?" Thomas asked.

"She's some kind of motivational speaker for other addicts. And it sounds like she and Mix, that's her husband's name—they run a recovery center of their own in Ohio. I don't really know. Oliver's still getting to know her."

The phone rang with Oliver's ring tone, "*Say Yes*," lighting Lacey's green eyes.

"I've gotta take this, it's Oliver."

Lacey took the call outside on the back porch.

"Hey, Sweetie. How'd the visit go?"

Oliver could feel the smile on her face, which warmed him. "I don't think it went so well. She didn't say what happened, but Mix told me that she'd found a meeting to attend in Midtown."

"What kind of meeting?" Lacey asked, and instantly felt stupid. "I'm sorry, I know what kind of meeting."

Oliver chuckled.

"Babe, you don't have to tiptoe around the fact that she's an addict. She doesn't. Hell, she makes a living talking about it."

Lacey loved the way he took care of her. "Okay," Lacey smiled. "Well, did she say if he's going to come here or if you guys are going to try to get together soon?"

"I really don't know, Lace. I figure, I'll give her some time to process whatever the hell happened up there. Benji can be a real dick. He's always been like that."

And with that, Oliver was done talking about his family.

"What are you wearing? He said, slipping into a seductive tone.

"Save it, Sexy! I'm at my parent's house with my nosey

family staring at me through the window." Lacey smiled a wide grin and waved at the onlookers.

"I was just telling them about your supermodel ass Mommy, who hates me!"

"She doesn't hate you."

"Yes, she does!"

Oliver laughed loudly and agreed. "Yeah, she does."

Lacey pouted like a sulking child.

"But, you'll win her over, just like you won Cami over and Camilla over and me," Oliver said in attempt to stroked the ego of his sulking lady.

"Maybe you can spend some girl time with her," Oliver paused. "In Savannah, if you come with me."

"What! They're going, too?" Lacey shrilled.
"Damn! Doesn't Dr. Prince Charming have to get back to work at some point?"

Oliver chuckled again, because he'd wondered the same thing. "I guess he is working. I don't know how rich white people roll?"

"Don't forget foreign! He's probably a prince back in, wherever he's from,"
the couple laughed in unison.

"Well, Lace. You still haven't answered me. Will you come with me?"

"Of course I will. I just need to move some things around here, at work."

Oliver smiled and wished Lacey a goodnight.

"I love you, Lace."

"I love you back, Ollie," Lacey purred. She marveled at how nice it felt to hear those words from someone other than a blood relative and how good it felt to say them.

The bright sun provided much needed warmth through the dusty metal blinds of Oliver's primarily one room home. He found it hard to shake the haze of his late night at the after-hours restaurant turned club, Little Big Trouble, where he served as sous chef and partygoer after the kitchen closed. He was confused by the sound of knocking at his door at such an early hour. He reached for his cell phone to check the time.

"Are you kidding me right now?" Oliver checked himself for underwear, and rolled out of bed. He shook his locks and stretched his long limbs. "Yeah!" Oliver yelled at his front door.

"Oliver, it's me, Mix."

"Mix?"

"Yes. I'm sorry to wake you. It's about your mother."

The mention of his mother rang through his hangover. Oliver opened the door and directed Mix to the small table Lacey had bought for his place. He went to wash up and quickly rejoined Mix. Oliver set about putting on a pot of coffee. The mix of late nights and early mornings was unforgiving and he needed his faculties to deal with news about his mother.

"The visit with Benjamin was bad for your mother."

"I figured as much. Have you guys talked to Izzy? He can deal with Benji."

"Yes." Mix took the cup of coffee from Oliver and went on.

"He said he would handle Benji." Mix laughed and admitted he didn't understand the use of the word, handle, but Isaac explained it to him.

"Isaac is a very good person. I want to help him in any way I can." The sincerity in Mix's declaration was clear and meant a lot to Oliver.

"How is she?"

"She's a very strong woman, but she's not open with me about you all. She thinks she has to rebuild trust with you all, on her own. She won't let me help."

Oliver nodded. He understood the stubborn streak. He shared the trait, and so did Izzy and Benji. "It's a family trait," he said.

Mix frowned, obviously confused.

"We're all stubborn. Me, Izz, and Benji. I guess we learned it from her."

Mix laughed and went on, "She was very quiet on the flight from Fargo and took a car to a meeting from the airport. She talked to Isaac when he called, but she took the call outside."

"So you met Benji?" Oliver asked.

"Yes."

"How was he? How'd he look?"

"He wasn't very talkative. He looked well. He was shorter than I expected."

Oliver let out a boisterous laugh. "Yeah, he missed out on the height. I've always suspected it's why he's so mad all the time."

Mix laughed too, but his expression turned solemn.

"Well, she's going on with the work, but I can tell she's really affected," he took a deep breath. "I'm worried she'll suffer a setback in her recovery."

Mix's words hit Oliver like a blow.

"You think she'll use again? What the hell did he say to her?"

"I don't understand."

The language barrier between he and Mix was beginning to irritate Oliver. "Do you think she will use drugs again?"

"No! No!" Mix answered definitively, but backed off. "I hope not. I don't think she will."

"Where is she now?"

"I left her sleeping. I'm picking up breakfast when I leave here."

"Thanks for coming to me, Mix. I'll stop by in a few hours to see her."

"Thank you, Oliver. Please don't mention my concerns to your mother."

"No worries, Man," Oliver said as he thanked his stepfather again, and walked him to the door. The cold air slammed against Oliver's bare chest, cutting his farewell short.

"I'll see you later, Mix."

Oliver wanted to talk to Cami and picked up the phone to dial her. The sound of Ali's voice startled him.

"Hey, Man. What's up?'

"Not much, Oliver. It's eight in the morning. Cami's in the bathroom."

Ali and Oliver were still working out their new roles in Cami's life and respectfully danced around one another.

"Yeah, I'm sorry Man. It's early as hell. I just wanted to bounce some family stuff off of her. She makes sense of stuff for me. You know?"

Ali's tone softened. "Yeah, she's special that way, that wife of mine. I'll have her call you when she gets out. Cool?"

"Cool. I appreciate it, Bro."

"So, I hear you and Lace have a big trip coming up."

Ali's statement caught Oliver off guard. "Um, yeah. She just agreed to come with me to Savannah. I'll be working and my mom will be there," Oliver said.

Why did I just tell him about my mom coming? He thought. The statement caused him to shudder. He sounded like a teenager, assuring his prom date's father that they'd be chaperoned. He didn't know why Ali made him so nervous. He made him more nervous than their father did. Mr. Robinson loved him, but Ali still seemed to only tolerate him because of his relationship with Cami.

"That's cool. If Cam can make it work, we may come down, too. She loves those Wine and Food Festivals. But, of course you know that."

Oliver couldn't make out Ali's intent. His tone always seemed to convey several things, good and bad.

"Yeah, I'll put together some good stuff for us. I'll make sure Cami has a good time."

"I'll handle Cami's good time. You just handle the tickets and stuff," Ali replied.

"Will do. Besides, I'll have my hands full juggling work and Lacey. You know how much attention your sister requires," Oliver batted back.

The silence on the line was bracing.

"Babe, it's Oliver."

Cami's cheery voice relieved Oliver like a warm hug.

"Hey, Boss Lady."

"Hey, Ollie Dollie! I feel like I haven't heard your voice in forever. I miss you, Man!" "I've missed you, too. How was California?"

"Oh, please. You didn't call me this time of morning to

ask about my honeymoon. What's going on? You want to come over?"

"I don't want to intrude."

"Oliver, stop it. You can never be an intruder here. You're my brother. So, are you coming?"

"Yeah. I'll be through in a few."

"Bring coffee. And eggs! I don't know what happened to mine."

Isaac sat sternly listening to his mother and stepfather's account of their trip to North Dakota. He sat still with his large, dark hands neatly folded atop the cold steel table, only nodding and rubbing at his furrowed brow from time to time. His disappointment and rising anger registered clearly on his face. Oliver shifted in his seat and shared darting glances with his big brother, as their sobbing mother told them how disrespectfully her second born had treated her. Isaac reached across the table and held his mother's hand. Oliver followed suit and rested a hand on her bouncing knee.

"I know I wasn't Claire Huxtable. I know that. But I want to make things right with you boys—I mean, my sons."

Her correction stood out like a sore thumb. For she was absolutely right, she'd long ago left the Barnett boys alone to navigate their childhoods into manhood.

"Ma, you don't have to keep apologizing to us. We forgive you and love you," Oliver said.

"And we know that you were sick. Momma. If there's one thing I know for sure, it's that addiction is a sickness. No one in their right minds would choose to be a damned drug addict. So make that your last time apologizing to us - any of us."

As if he'd been coached by Valentina herself, Tommy's

cease and desist order was finite.

"Do you have a mailing address for Benji?"

"Yes. I have it here somewhere." She set about rambling through her purse.

"Dear, you can't give it to him here," Mix gently reminded her.

"Pops is rights. You'll have to send it to me in the mail."

The group erupted in laughter.

"What? I've always wanted to call somebody Pops. And now I've got a rich, white one!" Isaac laughed. "Who sounds like Count Dracula!" Oliver added between belly laughs.

Mix had taken to the Barnett boys like a fish to water.

"I'll make sure you get the address, Son," Mix tossed back and stood to dap up Isaac, which sent the group into another round of wild laughter.

Isaac wished everyone a good week and thanked them for visiting, but asked to speak to Oliver alone. Once he was sure Mix and Valentina were out of earshot, he wrapped an arm around Oliver's shoulders.

"O, I want you to get in touch with that sawed off little shit, and set his ass straight. You got me? If I could, you know I would. So it's up to you. She needs all of us, even him."

Oliver always hated getting caught in between his two older brothers. When they were kids, Isaac and Benji would get into bloody fights over the simplest of things: Who would eat the last of the Lucky Charms, who would be Batman and who would be Robin. If Benji won at Donkey Kong, Isaac would put him in a headlock until he got weak at the knees. Isaac had always been the bigger, stronger brother and he wielded his physical superiority over his younger brothers with ruthless regard. Even as adults, Oliver stood nearly eye-to-eye with his brother, but felt like the seven-year-old baby brother of their youth, pressed against the corner between his feuding older brothers.

"I'll call him," was all he answered.

The sun was high and washing the abandoned, gray buildings that surrounded the federal prison, in its glorious light. Valentina drove along admiring the beauty of the city, when a tune on the radio caught her attention. She turned the volume up and sang along,

"Know it sounds funny but, I just can't stand the pain."

Mix smiled at his wife and rested a hand on the nape of her neck.

Oliver joined his mother at the chorus,

"That's why I am easy. I'm easy like Sunday morning. That's why I'm easy; I'm easy like Sunday morn-orn-orn-orning."

The two swayed and snapped their fingers in unison.

"Mix, my man, we've got to get you up on the classics!"

"I'm very familiar with the Lionel Richie and the Commodores. Thank you, very much Oliver."

Valentina smiled into the rearview mirror at her son, and squeezed Mix's hand as she watched Oliver lay his head against the headrest and close his eyes against the peacefulness he felt.

"O. Baby, wake up. We're stopping for something to eat," Valentina roused her sleeping son. Oliver opened his eyes and stretched his long legs.

"Where are we?"

"Somewhere Mix pulled up on one of his fancy apps," she replied.

The tin roof and glass front brought a wide smile across

Oliver's face. He wrapped his locks into a bun and slipped a gray hoodie over his head.

"Good choice, Mix! Ria's Bluebird has these crazy ass eggnog pancakes!"

"Excuse me, Son?" Valentina chided.

"My bad, Ma. You know how good food excites me," Oliver kissed his mother on the cheek and bounced past her to the door.

The dark wood panels left a lot to be desired by way of ambiance, but the stellar menu made up for the decor in spades. The spot was packed. The threesome was seated against the windows that overlooked the famed Oakland cemetery. Mix went on and on about the reviews from his app.

"Hon, remember O is quite an up and comer on the ATL food scene. He could probably tell us more about this place than any old app!"

Valentina's pride for her son's accomplishments was evident. Oliver blushed a little and told them that the place was a great restaurant for vegetarians. Mix and Valentina were fit and health conscious. Mix adhered to a strict vegetarian diet, while Valentina's diet allowed for fish and eggs. They maintained their physiques by practicing yoga and swimming. Mix was an avid runner, but Valentina kept to indoor activities.

Valentina steered the conversation to Lacey, just as the colorful waitress left them to their meals.

"So, O. You think you're in love with this Lacey person, huh?"

Mix lifted his head from a mountain of skillet potatoes, sautéed mushrooms, zucchini, and kale. "Valentina, we agreed to a nice Sunday together." He politely reminded his wife.

"Everything is nice. It's a beautiful day. We're enjoying a pleasant meal and making small talk. What's not nice, Mix?"

Mix, sensing her determination, returned to his potatoes, leaving Oliver on his own. Oliver prepared himself for battle.

"Ma, I'm a grown man. I know what I feel about Lacey," he said as he forked at his pancakes.

"I know that you're grown, but I don't know how much you know about love."

Oliver nearly choked. He struggled to clear his throat amidst laughter.

"I'm thirty-one years old. She's not my first," he laughed again. "Not by a long shot."

Mix laughed too—garnering an austere look from Valentina, which he shrugged off.

"Oliver Darwin Barnett, Don't be crass."

"I'm not trying to be disrespectful, but you started this conversation." Oliver stuffed more pancakes into his mouth and sipped from his coffee. He looked directly into his mother's eyes. "I see there's more. What is it, Mother?"

"Have you told her that we're coming to Savannah with you?"

"Yep! I have."

"And?"

"And what, Woman?" Oliver taunted his mother.

"How does she feel about that?"

"She's thrilled! Can't wait to spend some time alone with you."

Valentina laughed and threw her napkin at Oliver.

"Ma look, I love her. Please give her another chance. Lacey is an acquired taste, I'm not going to lie," Oliver chuckled and ran a hand over his locks, "but I know if you two can just put the guns away, you'll really like each other. You're-"

"If you fix your mouth to say, we're a lot alike, I may just slit your throat," Valentina said, pointing a knife at him.

"Valentina!" Mix snapped, sending Oliver into another fit of laughter.

"Cami and Ali may come down too. That would help, wouldn't it?" Oliver added between chuckles.

Valentina drew in a long exaggerated breath.

"I guess so. I'd like to spend some time getting to know Camisha?"

"Just Camisha?" Oliver prodded.

"And, Lacey. Okay?" Valentina mumbled between a curled top lip.

Oliver leaned across the table a kissed his mother again. "Thank you, Mother."

CHAPTER ELEVEN

Savannah Smiles

November ushered in some the loveliest Autumn weather Georgia had experienced in years. The days were bright and sunny and the nights were clear and brisk. Valentina and Mix had moved back to Ohio, which greatly pleased Lacey. She had practically moved to Atlanta and was spending more quality time with Oliver. Valentina's nightly phone calls were tolerable for Lacey, since there was no threat of her stopping by at the crack of dawn. Lacey hated when Valentina stopped by unannounced, forcing her to share Oliver's limited space and tiny table for two. Oliver and his mother would sit at the table leaving Lacey inelegantly relegated to the full size bed, pretending to work. Lacey shuddered at the recall and made a mental note to buy a proper room divider for Oliver's place, or better yet, get him into a more fitting place.

"Sweetheart, do we absolutely have to ride to Savannah with her?" Lacey grumbled, as she folded another of Oliver's crisp, white chef's jackets. "I don't mind driving. I really don't."

"Lacey!" Oliver was exasperated. "Mix and Mom both have long legs. Would you really be cool with them riding in your backseat for hours? Come on, Lacey Baby. Play nice."

Lacey shrugged behind Oliver's back.

"So what time will, Cruella be here?"

"Is that your best attempt at playing nice?" Oliver shook his head. "Go ahead. Get it all out before she gets here."

"I'm done. I love you." Lacey crawled across the bed and kissed him. He smiled and pushed up her glasses.

"I know you do. Now, let me finish packing, woman!"

The drive to Savannah was pleasant, much to Oliver's delight. Lacey was talkative and engaging with Mix. They talked about their travels and places they wanted to see. Mix shared colorful anecdotes about growing up in seaside Bergan, Norway and tried his best to teach Oliver and Lacey to pronounce the word *fjord*. Up until Lacey asked if Bergan was near any fjords, Oliver or Valentina had never heard the word. Mix lit up when Lacey offered him the opportunity to speak about his homeland and Oliver swelled with pride, because his woman knew something about Norway. Valentina drove the group along, mostly in silence or quietly humming to herself. From time to time Mix would take her free hand is his, and she'd offer him a polite smile.

"Ma, have you gone to Norway with Mix?"

"Yes. We went after honeymooning in Iceland."

"Wow. Iceland. Did you ever see yourself going to Iceland? Was it cold? Did you see a fjord?" Oliver jokingly asked.

"Fee-yord," Lacey chuckled, correcting Oliver's pronunciation of the word.

"Are you fluent in Norwegian, Lindsey?" Valentine snapped, casting a nasty glance in Lacey's direction through the rearview mirror.

Lacey looked to Oliver, and remained silent.

"Most young people in Norway are English speakers anyway, Dear. So Lacey doesn't need to be fluent," Mix decidedly offered in Lacey's defense.

Oliver reached for Lacey's hand, but she pulled away and turned her body towards the window. Oliver sensed her anger, and defended her too.

"Ma. That wasn't necessary. Please don't make me regret inviting you."

Inviting! The hairs on Lacey's neck stood on end at hearing that he'd invited his mother to join them, but she'd agreed to play nice, and decided to address it with Oliver privately.

Before he knew it, they were turning on to E. Gaston Rd, a quaint Spanish oak lined street where the Olde Savannah Inn was located. Lacey nearly jumped out of the car—leaving everyone else behind. Once checked in and settled into their room, lacey lit into Oliver.

"You invited that witch after you invited me? I thought this was going to be a romantic getaway for us, Oliver!" Lacey stomped her feet, strengthening Oliver's spoiled brat characterization of her.

"Lacey, I thought it would give you two a chance to get to know each other on neutral ground." His eyes pleaded with her for understanding. "Ali and Cami will be staying here, too."

He saw a softening in her posture and kept moving towards complete diffusion. He pointed out the private terrace, just through the brick archway. "If that's not pure romance, I don't know what is, Lace," Oliver whispered just over her shoulder.

Lacey was taken in by the peaceful oasis with its calming scents of jasmine and honeysuckle, and the towering Victorian queen-size porch bed.

"It is beautiful out here," she quietly relinquished.

"And we can have breakfast served right out here on the terrace."

"I know what you're trying to do Oliver Barnett."

"Do you now?"

Oliver slipped a shoulder out of her top and lightly kissed it. Lacey closed her eyes and leaned her head, allowing Oliver to place soft kisses along the length of her graceful neck. He turned her to face him, took off her glasses, and lifted her cashmere sweater over her head. Lacey slid her silk camisole over her curvy hips and stepped out of her lace panties. Oliver looked over her nude form, as though it was his first time seeing her naked. He swept her up in his arms. He laid her on to the bed, and loved her to sleep in the midday sunlight.

Oliver slipped out of bed and covered Lacey's golden brown body with the Italian bed covers. He dressed, and kissed her on the forehead before calling room service for an early supper and bottle of chilled white wine. Oliver was very excited about the opportunity to teach cooking classes. The fact that they were titled, Master Classes, made him feel very accomplished. In dealing with his family drama, Cami's wedding, and his refereeing the spats between Lacey and his mother, Oliver was left with very little time to plan his menu and curriculum for the upcoming week. He planted himself on the cushioned Adirondack lounger across from the porch bed where Lacey laid peacefully sleeping, and started scratching out menu ideas and witty tips. A knock on the door broke his dogged concentration and awakened Lacey.

"Room Service," a male voice announced from the hall.

"Okay. Just a second!" Oliver yelled. "You wanna get dressed, Beautiful?"

"Where are my glasses?" Lacey felt around the bed. Her voice filled with slumber.

Oliver handed her the glasses, and pulled the French doors closed behind him. He opened the door to find Ali and

Cami wielding a room service cart full of silver trays.

"What the hell?" Oliver wondered aloud with a grand smile spread across his face.

"Surprise!" Cami yelled and hugged her friend around the neck. .

"I'll say," Oliver quipped. "What are y'all doing here?"

Ali pushed the cart in ushering Oliver aside.

"What the hell do you mean? You knew we were coming," Ali answered.

Oliver moved further aside to allow them in to the room. "I was expecting you guys at the week's end."

"Where's Lace?" Ali asked, looking around the room.

As if she were cued, Lacey breezed into the room looking every part a pageant queen. The afternoon of sex shone on her face. Her eyes were blazing behind the tortoise shell eyeglasses, when they fell on her big brother's face. She was thrilled to have her own army of one there to stand with her against Valentina, if the need arose. She practically jumped into Ali's arms.

"Lenny! I'm so glad you could make it."

The brother and sister exchanged a knowing look. Oliver and Cami exchanged their own looks.

Oliver was sure Lacey and Ali had orchestrated this change of plans. The couples enjoyed an early supper of grilled pork tenderloin, island fried rice, and rum cake with caramelized pineapples for dessert.

"So where are you two staying?" Lacey casually asked.

"Upstairs, in the Renaissance suite."

Oliver nearly spit the beer he was drinking across the room. Lacey coolly pat him on the back and asked if he was okay.

"When did you get reservations here?" Oliver asked after he'd composed himself.

Cami shot an approving look at her husband, and they all noticed it.

"Ali booked this room weeks ago! What's going on, Ali?" Cami demanded. "Lacey?"

Lacey spilled, turning to Oliver and taking his hand in hers.

"Babe, don't be mad, but, when you told me that Tina was coming with us, I asked Lenny to come too."

Oliver sat stunned. He calmly took his hand back.

"Oliver, don't be mad. She hates me! And you didn't even talk to me about inviting her," Lacey whined.

Cami shook her head and stood to leave.

"Ollie, I knew nothing about this, but I'm sure everything will work out. I'm looking forward to getting to know Valentina and Mix." She gestured for Oliver to get up to hug her, and he complied. "I'll deal with my half of the gruesome twosome," she assured Oliver with a giggle.

He laughed, too and thanked her. "I'll call you later and we'll go over your menu ideas. I know you're all over the place. Aren't you?"

He laughed and nodded.

"You know me so well. Thanks, Cami Cam. I don't know what I'd do without you."

"And you'll never have to know, because I've got you, Ollie Dollie."

"Yeah. Yeah. Come on let's go and let the penalty phase begin," Ali bellyached. "You owe me Lace, because now I'm in trouble."

Cami hugged Lacey and wished her a good evening, before playfully pushing Ali out of the room.

Oliver quietly pushed the food service cart out into the hallway. After Ali and Cami were out of sight, he took a deep breath before reentering the room. She was ready for whatever angle she took, and prepared to defend her actions.

"You want a bath? They have a lot of those oils in there."

She was set back on her heels. She hadn't anticipated this angle, and didn't know how to respond. "Um, sure. Are you going to join me," she asked cautiously.

"Of course. If you'll have me."

Lacey unpacked as she listened to Oliver run the bath. She was completely dumbfounded by his reaction. Even more, she was unsettled by his calmness. She'd packed an array of lingerie and sleepwear to address any and every mood her man expressed, and given this curveball, she thought it best to launch a full out, La Perla assault. She hadn't expected to have to wear the luxurious, silk chiffon and Chantilly lace baby doll with the matching butterfly thong this early in the week, but her gut told her it was necessary.

The soft hued creams, pinks, and lavenders continued into the French inspired powder room. For some odd reason, perhaps it was her guilt, the powder room with its pedestal sink and old-fashioned cast iron, claw tub that sat nestled amongst a bank of stain glass windows seemed to taunt her. It was as if the beautiful room, heavy with scent the lavender oils Oliver had added to the hot bath and the light of the setting sun, was all too good for her—all too glorious and all too extravagant for her. The guilt she carried weighted her usual easy gait. Oliver was sitting shirtless on the edge of the tub lighting candles when she walked in. He flashed an easy smile, but his eyes and shoulders bore defeat. He held out a hand, and helped her ease down into the hot, scented suds.

"Aren't you getting in," she asked.

"Yes," he answered dryly.

"Babe, I'm sorry."

"Lace, I don't want to talk about it. I have too much to prepare for this week and I've spent too much time refereeing between you and Tina. I give up. You win."

His words sincerely hurt Lacey. He hadn't spoken to her harshly, but he sounded defeated--by her.

"Please, Oliver. Don't say those words to me," she said as she pleaded with him to join her in the tub.

"What words, Lace?" His tone was heavy with lethargy, and slightly agitated.

"That you give up. You said you wouldn't give up on me. I begged you not to give up on me. Remember?"

Oliver sighed loudly, and put his head into his hands. Lacey watched silently and held on to his muscular thighs with both her hands.

"It shouldn't be this hard. I need to just focus on work, and let you and Tina figure out how to fit into my life." He shrugged and twisted at his locks. "I don't know. I just don't think I should have to choose between you two. She's my mom, Lace. Right or wrong, she's my mom and she's here now. And you're the first woman I've ever loved." He looked Lacey in the eyes, searching for the right thing to do. Lacey felt awful for putting that look into his usually carefree eyes, and the strife in his usually light hearted manner.

"You're right, Oliver. You shouldn't have to choose. You

don't have to choose! She's your mom, and I should know better. I do know better." Lacey laid her head on his leg. "Babe, I'm so sorry. And I'm going to fix this. I swear. Now, please get in the tub. Please."

Oliver leaned over her kissed her on the mouth. "I knew a few candles and a hot bath would bring you to your senses," Oliver teased and slid into the tub behind her. He wrapped his arms around her waist, and told her he loved her very much, to which she replied,

"Thank you, Sweetheart."

Sunday morning greeted Lacey in the sun-drenched bedroom, with the comforting smell of rich dark coffee and freshly baked chocolate croissants. She stretched her long legs the length of the bed and reached over for her lover. Not feeling him beside her, she sat up to find him outside on the terrace on one lounger, and Cami on the other. She reached for her silk knee length robe and tied it around her waist.

"That sounds good, Ollie. Butternut squash is in season! So how does it work? Will you give them a list or do you do the shopping?"

"Is food all you people talk about?" Lacey interrupted, joining them on the terrace. She planted a kiss on Oliver forehead and another on Cami's.

"Hey, Sleeping Beauty."

"Hi yourself, Sis. So, am I no longer the Ice Princess? Am I the sleeping one now?" Lacey teased Cami. "Where's that husband of yours?"

"He's out for a run with Mix and Tina."

With Mix and Tina? Without the cover of her glasses, Lacey's indignation registered clearly across her face. She quickly righted herself, noticing Oliver intensely watching for her reaction.

"They both run, huh? That explains Tina's fabulous body."

Oliver smiled and slid over on the lounger, making room for Lacey. She smiled, but politely declined in order to go wash up.

"Save me a croissant and a cup of coffee," Lacey ordered, pointing at the tray of pastries as she left for the bathroom.

"Well, that went well." Cami noted.

"It did, didn't it?" Oliver smiled smugly.

Lacey wrapped a silk scarf around her soft brown hair, and started the shower.

Lenny you freaking traitor! she thought to herself. She'd enlisted him as her ally and he wasn't in to day one before he was cozying up to Oliver's witch of mother. She knew what she'd told Oliver, and she intended to earnestly try to get along with the Obsidian Witch, but she was not going to share her man and her brother with Valentina Rose Barnett-Johannessen. She got into the steaming shower, stomping her feet like a peevish toddler.

Monday morning was the first day of work for Oliver, leaving Lacey and Valentina to one another's whims, and he'd enlisted Cami to referee. Cami arranged a spa day for the three of them and a round of golf for Mix and Ali at the nearby Savannah Harbor Golf Resort & Spa. She'd promised Oliver and Ali that she'd do her best to bridge the gap, between Lacey and Valentina, and she intended to give her best effort.

The waif-like young woman with the pixie haircut, who had greeted the threesome and gotten them into their suite for the day, returned carrying a mother of pearl tea set and leather bound itineraries outlining their day.

"Again, my name is Heather, Ladies," she smiled warmly. "I have here I have for you, Oriental Beauty Oolong tea and your commissioned services for the day."

She handed each of them an itinerary and began to read it aloud.

"At nine a.m. we have Oriental Essence Massages here in your suite. This massage concentrates on the stress areas of the body," she said, using her hands to demonstrate. "Our signature oil blend of warming ginger, mandarin and frankincense all come together to realign the mind and emotions."

Lacey cleared her throat, closed her eyes, and dramatically massaged at her temples. Both Cami and Valentina picked up on the dig.

"We could all use a realignment of our emotions, Heather." Valentina said.

"Indeed," Cami added.

The concierge smiled, and continued reading the itinerary.

"At 10:30 a.m., we have the Advanced Skin Renewal Facials. This treatment consists of a deep brush cleansing that gently exfoliates and brightens." She simulated circular motions on her own face. "Then a relaxing facial massage using rose quartz crystals follows. To complete the facial, a lifting and smoothing mask along with our signature serum will brighten, firm and even skin tone, leaving your complexion smooth, supple and looking radiantly healthy!" she exclaimed. "Manicures and pedicures will follow and complete your journeys."

Cami smiled politely at the eager young woman, then

nodded to Lacey and Valentina.

"Finally, at 12:30, we'll meet with Mr. Robinson and Dr. Johannessen for lunch at the Aqua Star. The restaurant features spectacular views of the Savannah River! And our Executive Chef Steve Black combines the freshest seafood with tropical elements for a refreshing combination sure to delight you all.

"My son Oliver is a chef, too," Valentina interrupted Heather again. "He's a featured chef for the Food and Wine Festival here this week," she beamed. "It's why we're here. He's teaching Master classes all week."

Lacey sighed loudly.

"What is your problem, Lacey?" Valentina snapped.

Lacey coolly adjusted the tie on her fluffy, white robe before answering.

"Nothing at all, Tina. Nothing at all."

"Well what's with all of the posturing? And clearing your throat?"

"You know what, Tina? No. Nevermind. Go on, Heather," Lacey ordered.

"No. I don't know, Lacey. Enlighten me," Valentina edged on, standing with her hand on her hips.

Lacey shrugged and smiled mischievously.

"You want to go there? Let's do it!"

"Let's," Tina encouraged.

Heather was visibly shaken. Cami moved in to intercede. "Ladies, let's let Heather finish reading the itinerary. It sounds likes it going to be a great day to realign emotions, and get to know each other better. Right?"

Heather nodded verbosely.

"Just a minute, Sweetie. Ms. Lacey has something to

say." Valentina said, holding up a finger to Heather's face.

"Yes! Yes, I do," Lacey scoffed. "I find it laughable that you have the audacity to feign a sense of pride in any of Oliver's accomplishments. You show up here years after he's raised himself. You and your Scandinavian white knight touting his successes, as if you had anything to do with them. You should be ashamed of yourself!"

Cami whipped around facing Valentina and Lacey. "Look! Let me break down the way this day," she shook her head and chose other words, "this *week* is going to go. You two will not bicker, nor will you take shots at each other all dang on week. You will not! I won't have it. And I mean it with every fiber of my being," she promised through clenched teeth. "I will not let your petty squabbling mess up his week. My very best friend; your son," she said pointing to Valentina. "And your boyfriend!" she turned to Lacey. "Oliver has been offered the opportunity of a lifetime, to make money doing something he loves to do in front of some very influential people. People who could change his entire life! Do you understand how important this is for him?"

Lacey nodded shamefully and Valentina sat beside Lacey on the palatial silk settee.

"I'm sorry, Heather. Please, go on." Cami assured the nervous young woman.

"That's it," Heather nervously answered with a polite smile, before disappearing through the tall chrome finished French doors.

Emboldened by their retreating postures, Cami turned her attention back to the stewing women.

"You two listen to me closely," she said, wagging a

finger at them both. “Oliver could’ve come on his own and completely focused on the task at hand, but no. He wanted to invite two of the most important people in his life to join him, to get to know each other—not to distract him with a bunch of petty jockeying!”

Cami pointed at Lacey.

“He loves you. You scare the crap out of him, but he loves you anyway.”

She turned her attention and finger to Valentina next.

“He loves you, too. You’re his mother. He’s been waiting for you all of his life, and now you show up and take shots at the woman in his life. This is going to stop! Today!” Cami folded her arms across her chest. “Got it? Whatever beef y’all have with each other, grill it and eat it. The only beef I want Oliver focusing on is the beef he’s teaching these rich people to braise and serve with butternut squash bisque and Baked Alaska with chocolate sauce. Got it?”

She pointed at both of the ladies one more time, to drive home her fervent command.

“Now let’s get up and enjoy these bougie treatments Ali has arranged for us.”

Lacey burst into laughter.

“I knew that itinerary sounded like my brother, and nothing like you at all!”

Lacey stood and hugged Cami. Valentina joined the ladies in the giggly hug.

“I’m sorry, Camisha. You’re absolutely right and I hear you.” Valentina looked at Lacey and extended her hand. “Lacey, let’s start over. I’d like to get to know you, and I hope you’d like to get to know me, too.”

"I would. The man I love wants nothing more than to have us get along. And I don't want to get in the way of him building a relationship with his mother—or in the way of him making this money!"

"I know that's right!" Valentina agreed with a high five. "But as a point of clarification about Mix saving me—no one saved me. I trusted in God and worked the process to save myself. Mix came along long after I had kicked the drugs. I need you to know that," her voice softened as she turned her wedding band around her long slender finger. "No one saved me, Lacey. I saved my damn self," Valentina concluded with absolute finality.

Lacey adjusted her glasses and bowed her head respectfully in Valentina's direction. Cami smiled at the reconciliation and the thought of how much she sounded like her mother, Camilla.

CHAPTER TWELVE

Sheltered

Oliver laughed heartily listening to the recount of Cami's, "Come to Jesus" meeting with Lacey and his mother. He was thankful for whatever had transpired at the spa, and for Cami's budding confidence. The days that followed were as smooth as silk. Valentina and Lacey weren't exactly besties, but they didn't bicker or take gut shots at each other—at least not when he was around.

Camisha Robinson was by far Oliver's closest confidant. He couldn't imagine being any closer to her, even if they were blood relatives. When he first saw her at the Genesis House, the shelter where he was placed as a thirteen-year-old runaway, he thought she was the pretty, but dangerously frail and skittish. She was a shy and nervous little girl. She jumped out of her skin every time her mother barked at her.

"Damn girl! Get in here!" "Camisha hurry the hell up!" "Camisha where's my damn purse?"--her mother seemed to always be yelling at her.

Oliver recalled the day they met. He and Cami were among a group of about five kids who lived in the Genesis House and attended the middle school. They were on a big yellow school bus going on their eighth grade field trip to the Fernbank Museum. No one wanted to be seen with the kids from the shelter, so they always found themselves together on the school bus --she gave him the window seat. Everyone knew who the kids from the shelter were, because they didn't wear the bright, white

Cortez Nikes or Eastland Silverado ankle boots with the strap-and-buckle detail. They wore whatever shoes they grabbed from the donations box that weren't too worn or dirty, most times the size didn't even matter. They didn't match their Ralph Lauren polo shirts to their Baby-G watches or their Tommy Hilfiger overalls to their Tommy Hilfiger boxer shorts. Oliver didn't have a fresh high top fade, like the Fresh Prince of Bel-Aire, and Cami didn't wear colorful scrunchies and butterfly clips in her wild unruly kinky coils. Her rail thin frame and wild hair reminded him of the Richard Pryor joke he told from Sunset Boulevard about the time he was running down the street while on fire and he was the match – but she'd given him the coveted window seat with a whispered agreement, "I'll get it on the way back." That simple gesture meant the world to Oliver and solidified their friendship.

Not many people had reached out to him since he'd arrived in Atlanta. The mothers in the shelter all treated him like a criminal. He was there alone, with no mother or grandmother, which could mean nothing good, given their past experiences with men. The women at the shelter always double-checked their doors when he was in the dayroom. They called out to their daughters or younger sons whenever they saw them keeping company with Oliver. He didn't trust them either. He imagined the ghastly ways they'd screwed up their own lives and the lives of their children. Maybe it had been drugs, or some shady characters, that ended them there in the shelter with him. He held himself in high regard, because he was there as a resourceful survivor, not as a failure of an adult like they were.

Shelter life was interesting. The place was very well kept, but cold and sterile. Each family had their own room, appointed with bunk beds, a locking chest of drawers, a tiny round table with one chair and twenty-inch color television. There was a shared area, which the residents affectionately called the "Day-room" with two large round tables, and a large TV bolted to a stand. There were board games, a boombox and a video game console for the kids, and a work room outfitted with three desk-top computers and a bank of telephones for the adults.

Maxine Allen and her husband Rodney founded and ran the Genesis House. They'd bought the old Victorian home and renovated it themselves, for the sole purpose of providing a safe place for women and children who needed a new beginning. Maxine was a strapping woman, with wide hips, big hands and an easy gap toothed smile. She wore her wiry, honey blonde colored hair in a very low, cropped style like a man. She took one look at Oliver the night Officer Brames delivered him to their doorstep, and wrapped his scrawny body in her warm embrace. "We'll find space for him, Brames. He'll be just fine – yes he will," she declared as she rocked Oliver as though she'd been looking for him all along. The recollection still made Oliver smile nineteen years later.

Oliver would always remember the very day that bound he, Cami and Camilla Robinson family. The kids stepped onto the creaky old white, pink and green porch of Genesis to find Cami and Camilla's few personal belongings neatly piled in the corner. They could hear Camilla's cusses sailing through the air like thrown daggers.

"Fuck all of y'all tired bitches in here! None of y'all ain't got shit and I'ain got to be up in here kissing Max's dike ass!"

"Camila, that's enough. Please just get your things and leave."

Maxine pleaded with Camilla and reached for Camilla's

arm. Which sent Camilla into a rage-filled lunge at Maxine. Every wild punch she threw was thwarted. Oliver remembered being impressed by Maxine's deftness. Maxine grabbed Camilla by an arm and held her against the wall until Camilla settled.

"Camilla please, just go. I don't want to call the law on you and your baby's here. Please don't make things worse than they have to be. You knew the rules and you broke them."

"You just think somebody want's Rodney's old whorish ass!" Camilla jerked again, trying to free herself, but Maxine was a strong woman. Cami stood just outside of the open screen door watching the whole outrageous scene. Her eyes were wide, but emotionless and she stood completely silent.

"Bitch, let me go!" Camilla yelled again and tried to pull her arm free.

"I'm going to let you go on the count of three. And I want you to leave here peacefully."

Camilla scanned the room taking in all of the whispers and shaking heads of the women and children who'd gathered to witness the spectacle. Their watchful gazes crept up her legs and up to her back, making her skin crawl. Her eyes fell on Oliver, and then on Cami. She grew even angrier, exploding all over her dumbstruck daughter.

"You ungrateful little bitch! You just gon' stand there and watch her do this to me? I'm yo' momma!"

Camilla jumped up and down, cursing her daughter until Maxine threw her to the floor. The sight of her mother being thrown to the ground jarred Cami into motion. She ran over to the women and begged Maxine to let her mother go. Oliver stood helplessly wide-eyed, clasping on to his tattered, second hand Nike back pack. He wanted to come to the aid of his friend, but he knew better than to risk the roof over his own head.

"Ms. Maxine please! We're leaving! Just let her go. Please!" Cami cried. Something in Cami's voice touched Maxine and Camilla both, because they both stopped struggling. Maxine walked away and locked herself in the office. Camilla ran her hands over her hair and clothes, gathered the items that had fallen from her purse and walked out the front door with her nose in the air. She told Oliver to keep an eye on their things until she returned for it.

He dutifully nodded and patted Cami on the back as she followed her mother down the steps and out onto the street. Just as the sun was setting, Camilla returned to gather their things. She rolled up in a black GMC pickup truck with two burly black men who wore dressed like cops or security guards of some type. She stopped as she passed a still and speechless Oliver, handing him a crisp twenty-dollar bill.

"Camisha will give you our new address and phone number. You can come visit us whenever you want. But, you can't stay – and I know you smart enough to know that. Right, boy?"

Oliver nodded that he understood, and hugged Camilla. He was sure he'd never see them again, but the next day in school, Cami handed him a folded piece of paper with 2954-B Browns Mill Rd. scribbled in Camilla's handwriting. And the rest was history – they were his family.

*****

"How'd I do today?" Oliver asked with his head laid across Lacey's lap. She moved a fallen lock of his hair away from his forehead and leaned over to kiss him.

"You know that you were good."

"Just good?"

"Outstanding, Love. What was that you made with the ice cream and egg whites?" she feigned interest.

"Baked Alaska," Oliver answered dryly. It didn't go unnoticed.

She put down the Coastal living magazine she was reading, lifted his head from her lap, and laid beside him on the bed. His boyish face and square jawline was perfectly symmetrical—studded only by his soft brown eyes. She kissed him softly at first, then more deeply as he stiffened against her. Just as he let out a small groan, a knock at the door cut through the heady atmosphere.

"You have got to be kidding me," Lacey mumbled, as the knocks grew more aggressive. Oliver laughed and kissed her more passionately. The knocks ceased and they could hear the voices agree that they must've gone out already. Oliver adeptly removed Lacey's drawstring panties. His eager mouth obediently followed his eyes and hands to Lacey's caramel tone mound. He covered her with his mouth, and licked her from her hottest spot to her growing clitoris, sending Lacey's voice into a high-pitched shrill. "Shhh. Shhh. Shhh," he hushed her again with a devilish grin. She couldn't speak. Instead she bit down on her bottom lip and nodded compliantly. After her second toe curling orgasm, she listlessly agreed to a hot bath, later, she would join the others for whatever they had planned for the evening.

"How do you think things are going between you and Tina?" Oliver asked as he lowered his colt like, muscular body into the mountain of steamy bubbles.

"I think things are going well. Have you asked her?"

Noticing the bite in her answer, he took the fluffy washcloth and began washing her back in soothing circular motions. He summonsed his cool and went on.

"I haven't really had any one on one time with her this week."

"What do you think she'll say?" Lacey fired.

"Babe, I don't know. Chill out."

"I'm sure your spy, Cami has filled you in on our every breath."

"My spy?" The back rub stopped, and Lacey grimaced a little. "You called your brother to stay here with you all week—completely disregarding what I asked you to do."

"What did you ask me to do?" she said as she turned her head to face him.

"I asked you to try to get to know my mother. And what did you do? Huh, Lace?"

"What did I do, Oliver? You tell me!"

"You went behind my back and called Ali to run interference! I'm not stupid, despite what you may think," he added. His addition stung.

"Whoa! Now that's not fair. I don't think you're stupid." His comment shocked her and she was visibly shaken. "Where did that come from?"

Oliver regretted the snide remark, and wished he hadn't said it.

"Answer me, Oliver. How did you come up with that?" She pressed.

"Forget about it." He moved to stand up, but Lacey grabbed him by the hand.

"No. I won't forget about it. Talk to me. Do I make feel like I think you're stupid?"

"Lacey, I know you don't think I," he paused, searching for the right word. I know that you don't take what I do seriously."

She didn't deny his assertion. "I don't have to. You do."

He winced. Her frankness still caught him off guard some times. He wasn't used to a woman being so matter of fact.

"But, Babe I want you to. I want you to respect what I do. How can you be with a man who you don't respect?"

"I do respect you, Oliver." Her face showed genuine confusion. She turned to face him, with her long legs crossed Indian style, in the Jacuzzi tub. "Where is this coming from? Who you are and what you do aren't one in the same."

"But, what I do gives me an identity, like what you do gives you an identity."

Lacey pondered his point before shaking her head in opposition.

"That's not true. I run numbers, but I'm not some stuffy bean counter. Am I? And you cook. But, you are so much more than a cook, so much more than a musician." Lacey took Oliver by the hands and straddled his lap. "You are a strong, resilient, caring man and I'm sorry, but cooking and playing African drums didn't make you those things." Her sparkling hazel eyes darted across his face seeking any signs of a deeper understanding for how much more she thought of him. "You've got to know that I love you, Oliver Barnett. I respect you. Hell, I exalt you. You are the most fascinating man I've ever known. I don't get the cooking thing or know if you want to do it for the rest of your life, but it doesn't matter. What matters is that you get it and that you get that I love you dearly."

The fervor in her declaration made Oliver's chest swell.

And her wet breasts made his cock stiffen again. He took her face in both hands and kissed her.

"You still don't take what I do seriously. That didn't get lost in your sweet, nor your wet thighs, Ms. Robinson."

She laughed and hugged him tighter.

"I've never loved a man, the way that I love you."

"You stole that from the Queen of Soul."

"Did I?" Lacey grinned. "Maybe I did," she acquiesced with a little nod and another passionate kiss.

Oliver grasped her round ass, positioned her hourglass figure just so, and entered her again.

"Last one, then we've got to find everyone else for dinner. Okay?"

Lacey closed her eyes tight against the ecstasy at the meeting of her thighs and lustfully agreed with a silent nod.

Oliver and Lacey floated into the Aqua Star laughing, hand in hand. They looked every part the happy, young hip couple. Oliver's long dreadlocks were neatly twisted into a bulky bun, placing his strong jawline center stage. He was a hipster, and it showed in his dressy attire--a burgundy brocade tuxedo jacket with a navy blue dress shirt and a paisley printed bow tie. He looked happy and Cami smile broadly. Lacey's feminine essence luminesced in her eyes, across her face. Her golden shoulders peeked out from the chic rose-colored waterfall duster coat. The sleeveless jacket flowed fluidly over her body, framing her killer silhouette. They were definitely starting to rub off on each other. Oliver was in a suit, albeit not a conservative one, but a suit nonetheless. And Lacey was actually wearing a hint of color.

"She's glowing in that color," Cami leaned over and whispered to Ali.

"She's glowing from getting screwed," Ali shuddered at the thought. Cami playfully shoved him.

"Hi, All!" Lacey sang. Mix and Ali stood to welcome her.

"Sorry, we're late." Oliver apologized, helping Lacey out of her coat before pulling the chair out for her. Lacey wowed in a figure-flattering dress with long sleeves and shoulder cutouts.

"You look nice, Lacey." Valentina offered, making Oliver beam brighter.

"She should. It took her forever to get ready." He teased and sat beside his girlfriend.

"Not to mention the time it took to pin up your son's hair!" Lacey retorted.

Everyone laughed. Ali signaled for the server who returned in a flash to take their drink orders.

The restaurant was lovely. Heather had not exaggerated in her praise of the views of the Savannah River that the Aqua Star offered. The city lights danced off the river as a lazy tugboat drifted by their window table.

"This is a beautiful restaurant," Mix said.

"It is. And the menu looks really good. I think I'm having the she-crab soup. O, do you know the chef here? What did Heather say his name was?" Valentina asked the women.

"Steve Black. I believe."

"Yeah, it was Steve Black," Lacey said, endorsing Cami.

The server returned with their drinks, and the chef in tow. Oliver stood, extending his hand to Chef Black.

"Good evening, Chef."

The men shook hands and embraced. Oliver introduced everyone before excusing himself. He disappeared behind the kitchen doors with Chef Black before returning nearly fifteen minutes later, wearing a bright smile on his face.

"He's invited us back for Sunday's Jazz Brunch. We'll be dining at the Chef's table. He wants to join me for my Friday class." Oliver was blushing like a schoolgirl with a crush.

"Babe, that's wonderful!" Lacey said, congratulating him with a kiss.

"Congrats, Bro!" Ali and Mix stood to shake Oliver's hand.

"Ollie, I am so proud of you! You've come a long way, Kid."

"We've come a long way." Oliver and Cami hugged each other tight.

Valentina shifted uncomfortably in her chair, but mustered a small congratulation to her son.

Noticing her discomfort, Mix patted her thigh and took her hand in his. Tears pooled in her eyes. She took her napkin and dabbed at them.

"Ma, don't cry. Come on now." Oliver walked over to his mother and knelt beside her.

She waved him off, but was overcome with sobs.

"Ma! What's going on with you? What's the matter?" Valentina fought hard to compose herself, but the tears and sobs proved to be formidable opponents.

"I'm sorry," she . "I don't know what's wrong with me," she tearfully explained. "I'm so sorry, O. I really am." Oliver held on to his mother, attempting to console her. He helped her to her feet, and attentively escorted her out of the restaurant. They walked outside to the dock, just outside of the window where their party sat. Valentina wasted no time explaining her outburst to her son.

"O, I am so sorry for not being there for you when you were a child. I was so screwed up. I'm afraid that I won't ever be able to make that up to you. I am so proud of the life you've made for yourself, but every time I hear you and Camisha talk about, *making it*, it crushes me, because a child shouldn't have to make it! And that's all my fault. Your brother is one of the smartest and most charismatic men I know and he's sitting in prison, because of choices I made. And Benjamin, he's just so angry. He's trying to cut himself off from his whole family. I did that! I did! I chose drugs, and sorry as men over my children—over my own flesh and blood." Her six-foot frame seemed diminished and frail, wracked by the sobs. Oliver stood close to his weeping mother, but could not bring himself to touch her. Feelings of resentment had found their way back into his heart, surprising him. Her admission of guilt had stirred them up, making them feel fresh and new. Intellectually he knew she was sick with addiction and he knew she was trying her best to make amends to he and his brothers, but none of that mattered in that moment. He could not console her. They stood in silence until Valentina regained control of her renegade emotions. She turned to Oliver and apologized again. His ego freed his arms and leg allowing him to draw her nearer. He held his mother closely, until her sobs subsided.

"I love you, Ma. You have to forgive yourself. I'm working on forgiving you, and so is Izzy. So it's the least you can do. We are family and no family is perfect. You got me?"

She squeezed him tighter and kissed him on the cheek. "I got you."

"Can we please go back inside? We haven't even ordered."

"O, One more thing." She stopped her son.

"Yeah?"

"You and Lacey make a lovely couple. And it looks like she makes you happy."

Oliver smiled again.

"She does. She makes me feel a lot of things," he chuckled. "But happy is definitely one of them." He gave his mother's hand a squeeze before they rejoined the group.

CHAPTER THIRTEEN

The DaCosta Files

Oliver was surprised to see Ali walk through the glass double doors of the shop – surprised and confused. He hadn't seen Ali at the shop since they'd last met with Cami's biological father, Mr. DaCosta, just days before his and Cami's wedding. They had worked as a team to orchestrate her father's return to her life.

"What's up, Brother?" Ali greeted Oliver with their customary bro hug and dap.

"Chilling. What are you doing here in the middle of the day?" Oliver asked, his voice filled with apprehension.

Ali chuckled a little and rubbed at his meticulously trimmed beard. He was an imposing figure with the build of a heavyweight boxer, just as his name implied. He was wearing his signature aviator sunglasses that covered his already dark, brooding eyes and he had taken to wearing a full beard.

"Am I no longer welcome here, O Man?" he asked with a chuckle. "Mr. DaCosta called. He asked me to meet him here.

Although Oliver and Ali had essentially worked out their roles in Cami's life, and the fact that Oliver was dating Ali's sister, there was still an air of tension between them whenever the ladies weren't around. Oliver laughed, thawing the ice and dapped up his new brother-in-law again.

"Not at all, Man. I just haven't seen you around here in a long time, and I didn't see Cami with you. That's all. Mi casa es su casa, Brother! Can I get you anything?"

Oliver walked around the stainless steel counter and poured himself a cup of green tea. Ali declined.

"I wonder what's up, because Mr. D called me, too."

Ali's interest was piqued. He hadn't heard from James DaCosta since he and Cami had returned from their honeymoon. He knew that Cami had talked to her father and to Mrs. DaCosta, but neither of them had been by the house since the wedding reception/bon voyage party.

"Did he mention what he wanted to see us about? Undoubtedly it must be something about Cami, but why all the secrecy? Why couldn't he just talk to me over the phone? Or come by the house?" Ali wondered aloud.

"And why does he want to talk to me? You're her husband now," Oliver added.

The two sat befuddled until a cool breeze snapped them from their private thoughts as James DaCosta walked through the café doors.

"What's up fellas?" he said, extending his hand to each of them. "Thanks for meeting me. The traffic is a bear out there."

James DaCosta was by any measure, an elegant man--thoughtful and humble. He'd always followed the rules. He finished college with a good education, he married well, and worked hard to establish a good life for himself and his young wife. He'd made mistakes just as any other man, but the one that had stayed with him, hanging over his pristine reputation like an anvil, had also produced what he thought of as his greatest accomplishment – his daughter, Camisha. In spite of his pride for Camisha, no one outside of his wife and Camilla could ever have known about her.

James had met Camilla Robbins at a friend's bachelor

party where she and two other young women were there working as dancers. Camilla was a stunning young woman. She had captivating, greenish brown eyes, long wavy hair and curves that went on for days. She was brash and quick-witted. After a few hours of conversation, and one too many drinks he took her up on a fateful offer for a "little extra". Six months later, following a few more dates with Camilla, his wife showed up at the Precinct asking him why a sixteen year old girl was claiming to be carrying his baby. James was a twenty six year old rookie with the Atlanta Police Department and his wife was Evangeline Herron of the Atlanta Herrons, one of the most powerful families in the city. Evangeline's family was not pleased about their first born marrying a beat cop, and didn't hold James in high esteem—if word got out about him impregnating a teenager, it would have surely ruined his life.

"I wanted to meet with you guys face to face, and truthfully, I wanted your take on something rather sensitive I've been looking into," James said to the anxiously awaiting men.

"Let's sit over here."

Oliver directed Ali and James to a corner table near the rear of the shop.

"What's all this about, Mr. DaCosta?" Ali asked, cutting to the chase.

"Please, call me James. We're family now."

Ali was uncomfortable with James's familiarity and instinctively recoiled. Oliver noticed.

"Is this about Cami?" Ali was running out of patience. Oliver admired his fiercely protective stance regarding his new wife. James recognized the angst in Ali's voice and got to the point of the meeting.

"Yes. Well, it's more about her mother."

The mention of Camilla put Oliver on edge as well.

"What about Camilla?" Oliver demanded.

"The whole accident has really been nagging at me. The idea of the guy who hit her staying by her side at the scene, but never showing up to the hospital to check on her, it just didn't set well with me. There is no record of him calling or visiting. And Camisha said that her boyfriend said that they'd fought before she left. Right?"

Both Oliver and Ali nodded in silence. James went on.

"And he didn't show up at her funeral or at the house afterwards, did he?"

James was sounding every part the detective. And his line of questioning was raising the antennae of both Oliver and Ali. They looked at each other for confirmation. Neither of them could recall seeing Carl at the gravesite or at the house. They shook their heads in wonder.

"What's all of this mean, Mr. D?" Oliver asked.

James quietly shook his head.

"I don't know. Maybe nothing, but my gut tells me it's all related. My wife thinks I should leave it alone and let Camisha move on with her life."

He sat pensively, resting his chin on his fists.

"I don't know. I mean I'm just finding my way back into her life, and I don't want to mess things up between us. But, I have to ask myself if I'd want to know what happened."

They all sat silently taking in all of the questions James had raised.

"And that's what brings us here. You two know Camisha best. What do you think I should do? Do you agree with Evangeline? Should I just leave well enough alone?"

"Yes," Ali answered without hesitation.

"No!" Oliver countered. "You didn't even know Camilla. How can you make decisions about her death?"

"I know my wife. And she's my only concern," Ali snapped.

"You know your wife," Oliver scoffed at Ali's rebuttal. "You've known her all of a year and you think you can decide what she gets to know and not know? Well, I know your wife, too and she'd want to know if her Momma was killed? Camilla was all we had. She was all Cami had all of her fucking life, Man?" Oliver pushed back in the chair he was sitting in so forcefully it hit the wall with a loud thud, drawing curious looks from the customers in the shop.

"No disrespect, Mr. D, but Camilla was the only parent there at night when she was sick. The only parent there to stand up for her on those days when kids chased her home. Camilla was jacked up, but she kept us fed, clothed and safe. We deserve to know what happened to her."

Ali and James sat silently listening to Oliver's impassioned case for further investigation into Camilla's accident.

"None taken. And you're absolutely right, Oliver," James replied.

Ali stood and put on his chrome aviator sunglasses marking the end of the meeting.

"All I ask is that you handle your investigation with discretion. And if anything comes of it, let me know before you speak to Cami."

"Absolutely." James stood and shook Ali's hand. "And Lennox, your parents have every reason to be proud of you.

Take care of my daughter. I'll be in touch."

Ali patted Oliver on the back as he passed and asked to speak to him privately. Oliver walked out behind him.

"O, I'm sorry if I came across callously back there. I forget how much Camilla meant to you, too. I just know how hard it was for Cami to lose her mother and before James came into the picture she felt very alone and afraid. She's doing well now and I don't want anybody putting upsetting ideas into her mind. I appreciate your affections for her, but I have to insist that you don't mention any of this to Cami until I say so."

Oliver was floored; his indignation shone in his eyes. He ran his hand over his dreadlocks, tightening the black band that held them in a neat ponytail. But, Ali was unaffected and held Oliver's glance until he spoke again.

"The last thing I want is to upset Cami. You don't have to worry about me mentioning anything about this to her. She'll hear it from you first."

"Thanks, Brother," Ali said as he dapped up Oliver again and got into his black Audi S5 and was gone as quickly as he had appeared. When Oliver reentered the shop, James was waiting for him at the counter.

"He's just being protective of his wife. Surely you can appreciate that," he explained to Oliver.

"No doubt. But, he'll regret not telling her," Oliver replied knowingly and returned to his station behind the counter. "Can I get you anything, Mr. D?

"No, thanks. But, whatever you can tell me about this Carl character would be helpful."

CHAPTER FOURTEEN

Moving

The white picket fence that marked the boundary of the Robinson family's property was somewhat of an historic landmark in Flatrock Branch, Alabama. Usually a welcome sight for Lacey, it was quickly becoming a trigger for longing and musings about the road not taken.

"Momma! Daddy! I'm home," Lacey yelled as she walked through the front door of her parents' home, and dropped her keys into the antique brass bowl that sat atop the entry table.

"We're in here, Lacey Baby." Her father boomed from the kitchen. Lacey smiled at the sound of her father's voice. She was without a doubt a daddy's girl and getting a loving bear hug from her daddy always righted her wrongs. She walked in to find him sitting at the small white kitchen table with her uncle Ulysses hunched over a pile of paperwork.

"What's going on in here?" She asked as she scavenged through her mother's well stocked refrigerator. Tess's refrigerator rivaled any fresh market in the world. She grabbed a plastic container, popped it open and took a sniff of its creamy contents and decided it was her mother's famous chicken salad. "Winning!" She exclaimed with a fist pump. She grabbed a fork from the cabinet and carried her prize to the kitchen table where her father was squinting over a document. Thomas Robinson glanced over the top of his rimless glasses at his daughter.

"Are you going to eat from the Tupperware?"

Sensing his disapproval, she skulked back to the kitchen cabinet and grabbed a small plate.

"Better, Captain?" She retorted.

"Much. Now help us look over these contracts for Ulysses and Katy B's new restaurant."

"New restaurant? I didn't know anything about a new restaurant. Congratulations, Uncle Ulysses!"

Ulysses was a soft spoken and unassuming man. He was small in stature and meek in demeanor, the complete opposite of his wife, Katy B who was pleasantly plump, boisterous and bubbly. Katy B had never met a stranger, whom she wouldn't hug and feed. Ulysses offered a gentle smile and tilted his head towards Lacey in thanks.

"There's a lot you don't know about around here, because you're never here anymore," Tess Robinson interjected as she walked into the room with her arms filled with brown paper bags. MJ and Katy B bounced in behind her with loaded arms, also.

"Hey, Cousin! Welcome home!" Mary-Anthony cheered. She excitedly wrapped Lacey in her arms. Her mother, Katy B bumped her out of the way with a buxom hip and hugged Lacey next.

"Lacey Baby, don't listen to your ornery momma. Love looks good on you, Girl! Real good."

"Yes, it does!" MJ chimed in.

"Does it, Tommy?" Tess asked, teasing her daughter.

"Indeed, Wife. My baby girl looks very happy."

Tommy answered without looking up from the papers. Uncle Ulysses stood up to help unpack the bags.

"You stay right there, Tommy. We don't need your help."

"I didn't think you did, Wife. I trust that you have it all in hand."

Tess threw a kitchen towel at her husband, setting off a storm of laughter throughout the kitchen. Lacey walked around the kitchen island and hugged her mother.

"Hey, Mommy. Sounds like you miss me."

Tess blushed and swatted at her daughter's backside.

"I do. I miss you very much."

She pulled her daughter close for another hug and kissed her on the cheek. "And you are glowing, Love. I couldn't be happier for you. When can we start to spend some time with your beau? We'd like to get to know him. Right, Tommy?"

"Right, Wife."

"Please help those men make heads and tails of those contracts," Tess whispered to Lacey, with another peck on the cheek. "I love you, Lace."

Lacey spent another hour or so with her family before gathering up her Uncle's paperwork and heading down the hill to her home.

Lacey poured herself a big glass of Chardonnay, lit a few candles, and cranked up the volume on her wireless speakers before lowering herself into a hot steamy bath. She closed her eyes and let the bluesy grooves of Alabama Shakes transport her. Brittany Howard's soulful voice asked all the questions she wanted to ask. It was as if the bandleader was reading her thoughts.

My lines, your lines / Don't cross them lines / What you like, what I like / Why can't we both be right?

The swag and sway of the music blended with the effects of the Chardonnay, creating a hazy atmosphere in Lacey's austere and still home, bringing her to unexpected tears. The warm, salty tears easily rolled down her cheeks and into the cooling bathwater. She didn't fight against the emotion, she leaned into it. She knew exactly what was going on. The doubts were creeping back in. They always seemed to patiently await her return. They must have waited in the kitchen cabinets, in the linen closet, underneath her bed sheets. They crouched in hiding waiting to break her—waiting to steal her joy.

You and that boy don't stand a chance. He's never going to settle down. He'll tire of you soon and being moving right along. Don't get your hopes up, Ms. Tuskegee University. He doesn't even fit into your life. He's a nobody.

Savannah had been wonderful—much better than she had anticipated. She and Valentina had made some headway and she'd gotten to spend time with her brother and Cami. Most of all, she got to spend time with Oliver, in a romantic B+B. He'd treated her like a queen. A soft smile tugged at the corners of Lacey's mouth at the memory. Just as she sank into the scented bubbles of her warm bath, the phone rang with Oliver's ring tone, spreading the smile brightly across her face.

"Hi, Sweetie," she purred into the phone.

"Hi yourself. What are you up to? Your music's loud."

She loved that she could feel him smiling from hundreds of miles away.

"I'm soaking. I'm in the tub."

"Aww, come on. You spent the entire week with a tub," Oliver laughed.

"When's your lease up for that dump anyway?"

Oliver laughed again. "In four months, Your Highness."

"Have you been looking for something else?"

"Should I be?"

"Oliver don't be difficult. Seriously. Have you?"

"Answer me. Should I be looking? And what should I be looking for? Two bedrooms? A bathtub? Walk-In Closets?" He was teasing her. The line went silent.

"Hello?" Oliver asked.

"I'm here."

"What's wrong?" Lacey could hear the worry in his tone.

"What do you want from me? From this?"

The line fell silent again. She could hear Oliver breathing. She pictured him lying flat on his back across his bed, with one arm behind his head, staring at the ceiling searching for the right thing to say.

"I want you. Us."

"You sure about that, Oliver? You've never had an, Us. And quite frankly never have I. How do we know how this is supposed to work? I live hundreds of miles away and I can't keep this up indefinitely."

"Indefinitely." Oliver pensively repeated the word. "Is that something you're down with?"

"What?"

"Indefinitely."

The silent pause was back. Lacey sank deeper into the tub and stared at her own breadboard ceiling.

"I think so. I don't know. I don't know what you want, Oliver."

"Yes you do. I just told you. I want you."

"You're just saying that, now."

"You're asking me, now."

"Am I supposed to uproot my life for, now?"

"Lace, I don't know what we're talking about. But it feels heavy. It feels like you have something you want to say, but you are not saying it. So please, just say it."

"I want to move to Atlanta," she blurted out.

"Then move to Atlanta."

"I want to be there with you."

"And I want you here with me. I don't understand what's hard about any of this. Your brother has a completely empty condo here. So what's the problem?"

Your brother has a completely empty condo here. The words sunk in her gut like a cement block. A painful knot lodged itself in her throat, as she fought back tears. She felt a familiar icy sensation shoot up her spine, making her sit up straight in her bathtub.

"Goodnight Oliver." Lacey hung up the phone and rose from the lukewarm water. She clicked her speakers off and dried off to the tune of Marsha Ambrosia's, Say Yes – Oliver's ringtone.

*****

"What the fuck just happened?" Oliver exclaimed aloud, as he realized Lacey was no longer on the line. He called her several more times, but she wouldn't answer. As the night went on, her phone went directly to voicemail. He was stunned and confused. He couldn't figure out where things had gone left. He replayed the conversation over and over in his mind. He'd said that he wanted her. He'd said that he wanted her to be in Atlanta with him. He'd been completely open to the idea of indefinitely. He was stomped and picked up the phone to dial Cami, but she didn't answer. Desperate for a female interpreter, he dialed his mother, who picked up immediately.

"Hey, O! How was it going back to your day job?" She asked cheerfully.

"Interesting. But, we'll have to talk about that later. I need an interpreter right now."

Valentina frowned. "An interpreter? For what language?"

Oliver laughed at his mom. Her response was needed comic relief. He went about explaining his version of the conversation between he and Lacey and her strange behavior. Valentina sat quietly listening to her son's account. When he was done she chuckled and asked if he was crazy.

"Son, there's this exercise used in counseling called mirroring."

"I know what mirroring is, Ma. What's it have to do with this though?"

"Bear with me. I'm going to mirror what you just told me, OK."

Oliver regretted calling his mom and sighed annoyingly.

"OK. Go."

"Lacey wants to move to Atlanta to be with you. You want her there in Atlanta with you, but in her brother's completely empty condo, on the other side of town, not in your space – with you."

Oliver sat processing the feedback his mother had given him, and felt like a jerk. "Ma, that's not what I meant. I just know that my spot's not good enough for her. There's not even a tub in here. Or a decent place to sit for a cup of tea," Valentina added. "So are you going to move into her brother's condo with her?"

"Hell no!" Oliver snapped.

"Well Son, it sounds like you have some things to figure out. I don't know what you want to do with your life, but time waits for no one, O."

She was right, and he knew it. Oliver sat up and loosed his long dreadlocks, sending them cascading down his back. He picked up his phone and texted Lacey.

I only meant that my place isn't good enough 4 u. I know that. I have 4 months here, but I want u here in the ATL ASAP. I said it all wrong. I luv u. Pls talk 2 me.

Oliver didn't sleep at all that night. He'd stayed up wracking his brain, searching Craigslist for the perfect place for he and Lacey. He knew she'd come around. And when she did, he'd have all the right answers.

The buzz of his cell phone woke him. He was filled with hope and he wasn't disappointed, it was Lacey.

"Babe, I'm so sorry. Did you get my text?"

"You're an idiot, Oliver Barnett."

"I know."

"So. What do you think? Can you tolerate showers for at least four more months?"

"Are you asking me to move in with you?"

"I am."

"Are you sure, Oliver? I don't want to cramp your style and I surely don't want to be hurt."

"I've never been surer of anything in my life. We can look for our next place together."

"Our place?" Lacey smiled.

"Yes. But, Buckhead ain't on the menu, so don't even think about it."

Lacey could've floated to the moon. She was happy, but

then she imagined telling her parents that she was moving to Atlanta to live with her bohemian boyfriend. The thought made her cringe.

The sight of her mother and father milling around the house the next morning, made her very nervous. They looked so carefree in their flannel robes and house slippers—completely oblivious to the choice their only daughter had made to abandon them and move to Atlanta to live in sin with a runaway, who was in several ways, still running away. She took a deep breath, and climbed the steps to their front porch. She paused just outside of the door.

"Lacey Jackson Robinson, get your narrow behind in here and stop that hemming and hawing around out there!" her mother ordered.

She dragged on into the house.

"What are you up to?" her daddy asked with a kiss to her forehead.

"May I have a cup of coffee first?" Lacey procrastinated.

Tess poured her daughter a cup of hot coffee and added cream and sugar, just the way Lacey liked it. She put two fried eggs and a slice of toast on a saucer and slid it to Lacey. Thomas and Tess watched their daughter over their morning papers and awaited her announcement. Lacey took her time slicing thin triangles of her fried eggs and taking small bites of her buttered toast, while watching her parents watch her. She knew she couldn't stall for much longer, so she started small.

"So Oliver and I have been seeing each other for some time now," she sad as she took a sip from her coffee mug. "And things have gotten rather serious."

"Do you love him?" Thomas asked pointedly. His candor

shocked Lacey.

"Yes, Daddy. I do."

"Does he love you?" he asked.

"Yes. I feel pretty sure about that."

"So does your brother," he added.

"Excuse me?" Lacey asked, befuddled.

"Lenny told me that after the trip to Savannah, he knew that the young man loved you."

Her father's words meant a lot to her, and Lenny's acceptance meant even more. Tears welled up in her eyes.

"Really, Daddy? That means the world to me. I always want to make you proud."

Tess sat quietly—too quietly for Lacey's comfort.

"Mommy. You're unusually quiet," Lacey goaded her mother.

Tess shook her head. "I'm just letting you get to what you came to tell us this morning."

Lacey wasn't sure what to make of her mother's posture.

"I – I think I want to move to Atlanta. I mean, I am moving to Atlanta."

Mr. and Mrs. Robinson sat in complete silence for what seemed like eternity to Lacey.

Mr. Robinson nodded his head and the corners of his mouth turned down. Mrs. Robinson stood up from the table scraping the chair against the wood floor and took an exaggerated breath in. She walked around clearing the table and placing dishes in the sink.

"I can't say I didn't see this coming." Tess said.

"Neither can I," Thomas said, shaking his head.

"Lacey do you have a plan? Have you thought this

through?" Tess asked.

"Have you ever known her to not have a plan? A well thought out plan of action?" Thomas answered his wife.

"I guess not. But, love's unchartered territory for her."

Lacey felt like a child, sitting there while her parents spoke of her as if she weren't in the room and thirty-two years old.

"Daddy I'll still run the business and I'll still be able to make store visits. Maybe we can look into expanding to Atlanta, or at least to the Western Suburbs of the city."

Thomas nodded again. Tess ran water into the farmhouse sink and started washing up the breakfast dishes. From time to time she'd mumble something under her breath and shake her head full of shiny, silver tendrils. Lacey was a little disappointed by her mother's reaction, because it had been her who told Lacey to follow her heart.

"Lacey, I have no doubt that you will continue to do a fine job running the stores. This is the twenty first century and you are a sharp businesswoman. You've never let me down and I don't expect that you'll start doing so just because you're living a few hours away." Thomas reassured his daughter from his favorite chair.

"Where will you live, Lacey?" Tess asked.

Lacey recalled Oliver's words, and lied to her parents.

"At Lenny's. He has that condo out there sitting completely empty."

Tess's shoulders relaxed, and she faced her daughter with a bright smile.

"I'm sure he won't mind that at all. Have you already discussed with him? He'll like having you there with him," she rambled on, happy again.

"Lacey, I know that you're smart and resourceful. You're a good girl and you'll be fine. You'll do the right things."

Her father's words wore heavily on her and in her spirit she knew, that he knew that she had lied.

CHAPTER FIFTEEN

All Kinds of Proposals

Oliver sat at the new pine trestle table Lacey had bought him, staring at the yellow Post-It note with Benji's phone number scribbled on it. When he agreed to call his middle brother, as his oldest brother had asked, it was with complete sincerity. But every time he went to dial the numbers, he couldn't find the nerve. The thought of Benjamin erupting on him or even hanging up on him bothered him greatly. He didn't know what he'd say to his brother. He hadn't spoken to him in over a decade—not one word. His cell phone rang, giving him a reprieve. The robotic voice on the phone announced a collect call from Isaac Barnett, *A Prisoner in a United States Federal Prison System.* Oliver accepted the call. It was as if his big brother knew the he needed a little pep talk.

"What's good, Izzy?" Oliver greeted his brother.

"Not much, Short Stuff. I'm still in prison."

The brothers laughed and small talked about the upcoming holiday season and how many visits they could arrange, taking into account Oliver's budding career as a chef and the holiday catering gigs he'd already booked.

"If all goes well, and I keep my nose clean, I'll be able to see you in action next year, Master Chef Barnett," Isaac teased.

"That would be great. Better than great. I can't wait to see what you make of yourself. This world ain't ready for you, Brother. You're going to kill it. We're going to kill it. The Barnett Boys."

"Yes, Sir!" Isaac exclaimed.

Oliver could hear the smile and hope in his big brother's voice. It made him hopeful, too.

"Speaking of the Barnett Boys," Oliver led in. "I was just sitting here looking at Benji's number."

"You haven't called him yet, O?"

"No. I just lock up every time I try to."

"Lock up? What the hell does that mean? Just punch in the damn numbers. Say, 'Hey, Ben. I miss you and so does momma and Ike. We want to see you.' What's so damned hard about that?"

"What if he hangs up?"

"What? You sound like a ten-year-old! You call his ass back. And keep calling him back until he don't hang up. That's that, O. We don't give up on each other. We all we got. You do understand that, don't you? No new family will replace us—your blood. We survived, because of each other. Benji stole dinner for us, damn near every night! Benji ran the numbers for P. Cole, so we could have milk and cereal for breakfast. Do you remember all of that?"

Oliver didn't remember any of it. He was so young. He was just a little kid. He never questioned from where his meals came? Again, Isaac read his mind, relieving him from finding the right words.

"I know you were young. Kids don't think about where their food comes from or who had to do what to get it. But, Benji pulled his weight to see that we had. Trust me. He loves you. Call him."

"I will. I love you, Bro. And I've never tried to replace y'all."

"That was cold. I know. My bad. I shouldn't have said that. You were trying to survive too and you did, Little Bro – you did. I'm proud of you, O."

The robotic voice interrupted to inform the brothers that the call would disconnect in one minute.

"Thanks, Izzy. I'm still just trying to survive. I'm calling as soon as we're done."

"Well, we're done. Love you, Short Stuff."

The next call Oliver made was to his brother Benjamin, who did not hang up.

Oliver was the happiest he'd ever been. Everything was going better than he could have ever imagined. Lacey had decided to move to Atlanta after the holidays, and her plans were moving along seamlessly, although she'd decided to move into Ali's condo after all. She'd explained that she couldn't bear the thought of disappointing her parents. Oliver secretly breathed a huge sigh of relief. He loved Lacey and wanted her nearer, but he did not know if he was completely ready to share his space or be responsible for someone else's well-being - especially someone as complicated as Lacey. Oliver had never lived with anyone, as an adult or even been in a serious relationship. Lacey would be considered a lofty starting place for anybody, and especially so for a free bird like Oliver. He and Cami were always fired up for Thanksgiving and this Christmas promised to be extra special, because Benjamin had agreed to spend Christmas in Atlanta with his family. Life was good and Oliver was on cloud nine.

Lacey woke up to Oliver's deep chestnut brown eyes staring at her. She smiled and snuggled closer to him.

"Good morning, Handsome." she purred.

"So, I get that Ali's spot is a cover up, but for who?" Oliver asked without returning her smile.

His sternness took her aback a little. She sat up in the bed and looked down at him. She slid closer to him and placed his head in her lap.

"For whom?" she said, correcting him. "I don't understand what you're asking. What do you mean, "A cover"?" She sad as she twisted at his locks.

"Yes you do," Oliver chuckled and rolled over facing the window.

"Babe, please don't start a fight."

"A direct question shouldn't start a fight, Lace."

"No it shouldn't. However, starting a conversation with me and then turning away will. Now, what do you mean by a cover?"

He sat up and faced her again.

"Lacey, you're smarter than the average bear. You know exactly what I mean."

The greenish golden flecks in her hazel eyes seemed to dance in the morning light that peeked through the dusty, plastic blinds—chipping away at his resolve.

"What I don't understand is, who the cover is for; your parents or your brother."

Lacey felt like a cheater who'd been caught in the backseat of a Chevy by a chasing camera crew. And it angered her more than it shamed her.

"Moving into my brother's was your idea! You were the one who suggested that I move to Atlanta and live in my brother's 'completely empty condo,' remember?" she snapped. "And now I'm being nailed for doing just that?"

Oliver hadn't meant for her to live in Ali's place. He'd

sensed her reluctance to move in with him and offered her a less immoral and restrictive alternative—one he thought would work for the both of them, or so he thought in that split second. However, the reality of Lacey being at his place every night, living out of a designer duffle bag, took him right back to the times when she was hiding him and their relationship from her family. He felt like Pony Boy from the Outsiders—a low class greaser from the wrong side of the tracks who the Soci Prom Queen slummed around with when her rich, Soci friends weren't around. But, she was right. He had made the suggestion.

"I didn't know what I was talking about. I was wrong for suggesting that."

His forthrightness always pleased her.

"Are you no longer thinking that arrangement will work for you, Mr. Barnett?" she said, snuggling up close to him again and wrapped her arms around him. Oliver wrapped his long, lean arms around her waist and settled into her womanly curves.

"I don't want to start all of that sneaking around again, Lacey. You know how I feel about it. You know that about me."

"Well, what do you suggest now, Mr. Barnett?"

"I suggest we start looking for somewhere nice – that we can both afford. And don't even think about Buckhead!" Oliver warned again.

"Is that all you're proposing?" Lacey teased.

"It's a suggestion, not a proposal," Oliver fired back.

The quickness of his response covered the room like a wet blanket. They both fell silent for what seemed like a very uneasy hour. Lacey loosed Oliver's waist. He grabbed ahold of her more tightly. No words were necessary. His grip around her waist and his shallow breathing against the back of her neck said it all, not yet, Lacey. But I do love you.

*****

The shop was abuzz with activity and sounds of clanging metal baking sheets and hissing espresso makers. Business was good and Oliver had taken to the role of manager like a fish to water. Cami was there for her bi-weekly check-in. Cami had been promoted to District Manager and her first act as DM was promoting Oliver to Store Manager. His numbers easily supported her decision to promote her best friend. Both, the staff and the customers loved him.

As soon as the business part of Cami's visit was done, Oliver gestured for her to follow him. He led her to the long, dark conference room table at the back of the store.

"What's up, Ollie Dollie? You seem out of sorts."

"I am!"

Oliver laid his head against the walnut wood tabletop and stretched his lanky arms out reaching for Cami. She took his hands in hers.

"Talk. What's wrong? You're scaring me."

"Everything was going so good, Cam. So good!"

"OK. What happened?"

Oliver recalled the whole *move in with me* conversation with Lacey and the fateful use of the word, *proposal* to an attentive Camisha.

"Why'd you use that word, Oliver?" Cami asked.

"I don't think I did. I think she used it!" Oliver almost whined.

Cami touched the top of her friend's bowed head and giggled.

"Do you want to?"

"Want to what?" Oliver snapped up.

"Propose?"

"Hell no!"

Cami's shock and what looked like disappointment registered clearly across her soft features.

Oliver spoke quickly to remove the disappointment from her eyes.

"I don't mean it like that—I mean, I love that girl. I do. But, marriage is not on the horizon for me. I'm not even able to imagine ever being married. I'm just not that guy. You know that, Cam."

Cami shifted uncomfortably in the aluminum chairs she'd picked out for the shop and carefully considered her next words.

"Then what are you doing with her Oliver? You know that Lacey's the marrying type. Her family has their own wedding chapel! She's getting married! So what are you going to do with her, Oliver? She's thirty, not twenty!"

He banged his head against the table and gathered his locks into a high topknot.

"I'm just trying to live. Hell, I don't know. I hadn't even thought about marriage before that one word hit me in the dammed face!"

Cami shook her head at her friend's gross level of immaturity.

"Why did you ask her to move in if you knew there was no future for the two of you?" Cami pressed.

"No future? There is a future for us!" Oliver snapped, "Just not as husband and wife."

Oliver kept his forehead pressed against the cool tabletop.

He lamented the thought, because he knew it wouldn't last the way he wished it would.

"Ollie, I love you, but you know that's not going to last for a woman like Lacey. You're going to break her heart. Ollie, you're better than this."

"Am I?" He peeked up at his best friend.

Cami slapped the tabletop, drawing looks from the other employees and customers, alike.

"Dang it, Oliver! I told you not to get mixed up with her! I begged you! But no, you just had to have her and for what? A roommate? She's not that kind of girl, Oliver! You knew that!" Cami was infuriated. "You knew that," she repeated.

"Why are you so goddamned mad, Cam? Calm down," he whispered, looking around at the onlookers. "I'm not playing her. I'm just not marrying her."

Cami stood and pulled her cross body bag over her shoulder. Oliver stood, too. The childhood friends hugged, just as they always did upon their goodbyes.

"I think you're more concerned about how this affects you and Ali more than how it affects Lacey. Lacey and I are good. We're happy. We're great! So please, just chill out and please don't make a big deal out of this. Please, Cam?"

"Let her go, Ollie," Cami whispered into Oliver's ear.

"I can't. I love her," Oliver replied in kind.

Cami was seething on the drive to the North side. Part of her knew that Oliver was right. Her concerns were largely for her own relationship being negatively impacted by his inability to settle down.

"This is bad," Cami remarked to herself as she merged on to I-75 North.

Ali tossed his gym bag into a corner and lifted his sweaty tee shirt over his head. Cami still thought her husband was the sexiest man alive, with his perfectly caramel complexion, round shoulders and ripped abs. He tossed his shirt into the wicker hamper and walked over to the bed where his wife was working, and kissed her on the forehead.

"Why aren't you wearing your glasses, Woman?"

"I don't need them for computer work," she answered without looking up from her work.

He laughed and walked into the bathroom and started the shower.

"How'd your visit with Oliver go today?" he asked from behind the closed bathroom door.

Cami found the question odd, taking in to account she visited Oliver's shop at least once a week, and he'd never shown any interest in those visits. She smelled a rat and answered suspiciously.

"It was fine. Why do you ask?"

Sensing her alarm, he thought it best to redirect.

"Just making conversation, Love. Have you spoken to your dad?"

Hearing the words, "your dad" disarmed her. She was still getting used to having a dad, so hearing the words, and they still sounded foreign to her.

"Yes. He wants to have dinner soon," she answered.

"Oh yeah," Ali answered evenly and climbed into the steamy shower.

The tone in her voice gave up nothing, and he was pleased to have dodged that bullet. He lathered himself with a woodsy scented shower gel and formulated a plan to find out how much

Cami knew about the awkward "proposal" conversation that had so rattled his baby sister. He knew that his wife was bright and fiercely devoted to her best friend, so his approach had to be delicate, or he'd be initiating an unwanted fight in his happy home.

Cami had remained steadfast in her decision to stay out of Oliver and Lacey's relationship since its fateful start, and on the few occasions when Ali breached that agreement, she completely iced him out. And no one could pull off the cold shoulder like Camisha Ann Robinson. She was an introvert by nature; so not speaking for days on end was no challenge for her. It was highly preferred. Ali knew that if he tried to involve her in Oliver and Lacey's on again off again relationship, there would be hell to pay. He was acutely aware of what a minefield he was navigating by mentioning the conversation, but his baby sister was in knots over the exchange. He was compelled to ask, but he also wanted to mitigate as many negatives as he could. He toweled off and decided that a bottle of Malbec and good sex would best set the mood for the interrogation.

"Yes, an orgasm and some pillow talk should do the trick," Ali shared with his reflection in the fogged up bathroom mirror. He wrapped a towel around his waist and initiated his campaign to get his wife to spill.

Ali dried off, and left for the kitchen, leaving his wife banging away on her keyboard. He quickly returned with an uncorked bottle and two red wine glasses. He sat them on the bedside table, and clicked on some mood music. Frank Ocean's cover of Aaliyah's hit, "At Your Best (You Are Loved)" poured out of the premium sound system covering the room with Ali's intentions.

"What are you up to?" Cami crooned as she closed her

laptop with a sexy smile spread across her face.

"I'm trying to get a little quality time with my beautiful wife. Is that alright?"

"It's better than alright." Cami lay back against the diamond tufted boucle headboard and beckoned to her husband.

Ali obediently crawled across the bed into Cami's open legs. She wrapped her arms around his neck and kissed him. She pulled at the towel that was loosely wrapped around his waist, but he stopped her.

"Slow down, Love. I'm trying to set a mood—keep the home fires burning."

"Oh, they're burning, but I'll play along," Cami blushed. Ali filled a glass for Cami and handed it to her.

"Who's the second glass for? Are you drinking wine?" Cami questioned with a furrowed brow.

At times like this one, Ali hated that she was so sharp and intuitive. He had to think quickly.

"I don't know why I grabbed two, but I'm not taking anything back to the kitchen right now," he explained between wet kisses to her taut tummy. He removed her shorts and panties and continued kissing her down the insides of her thighs. The rising temperature between her legs successfully redirected her attention. She moaned from the intense pleasure of her husband's touch and forgot all about her sneaking suspicions.

Ali leaned over his sleeping wife and lightly kissed her mouth. She was sound asleep. He turned the music down a bit and crept off to the bathroom with his cell phone. He hoisted himself on the double vanity and dialed his sister.

"Hey, Lace."

"Hi. I have to call you back. Are you okay?" Lacey answered.

"Yes, I'm fine. Why can't you talk to me now. What are you doing? I talked to Cam."

"About what we talked about?" Lacey anxiously asked.

"Yes. So do you still need to call me back?" Ali playfully cajoled his baby sister.

"Hold on. Give me a second."

Lacey hurried off to the courtyard just at the bottom of Oliver's rusty wrought iron staircase, to stall him as he grilled salmon steaks for dinner, and returned to her brother who was waiting on the phone.

"OK, what did she say?"

"She said that Oliver loves you. He thinks you want to be engaged, because you asked about a proposal or something."

"What! Why does he think that?" Lacey interrupted. "It was just a word! There are all kinds of proposals, not just proposals for marriage?"

Lacey paced like a caged animal and nervously adjusted her eyeglasses.

"What am I supposed to do, Lenny?" she pleaded.

"Calm down, Lacey. He thinks it's what you want? She didn't say, but it sounds like he's freaking out about it, too."

"Really? You think so?" She whined with a hint of hope in her voice.

"Hell, I don't know. But I'm confused as hell. If you don't want him to propose, what do you want?" Ali asked.

"Not that! We're still getting to know each other, Lenny. We're in a good place."

"Is being engaged a bad place?" he pressed.

"It is at this point! He lives in a hovel. He has no idea

what he wants to do with his life. He only knows what he doesn't want to do–and that's be a grown up." Lacey explained.

Ali was exasperated. He sighed dramatically, slumped his broad shoulders, and ran his hands over his thick wavy hair.

"Then what are you doing, Lacey? Why are you even considering living with him?"

Lacey didn't answer right away and her brother waited patiently.

"I'm going to live with him, Lenny."

Ali said nothing.

"I couldn't disappoint mommy, so I didn't tell her."

"Or me. Or daddy. Does anybody know what you're doing?" he asked.

"Not really," Lacey shamefully admitted. "I practically live with him now! So what's the difference?"

"Goddamn it, Lacey! You know the difference! If you didn't know, you wouldn't have lied to your family. This is exactly the type of shit that makes me not trust him!"

"Don't be angry with him! He doesn't know that you all don't know," she said, lying once again.

"What? So you're just a common liar now? You're just lying to everybody in your life--since you've hooked up with him?" Ali rued the thought.

"Lenny, come on. I know you love me, but I didn't start hiding things upon meeting Oliver, and you know it."

Her last words were an implication hurled directly at her brother, who had been hiding her secret from their parents for years. Ali didn't want to rehash that particular time in their past. He drew the call to a close. "I've got to go. If Cami hears me getting in your business, she'll erect the Wall of China on me. Be careful, Lace. And please don't string him along. I don't even want to think about what it would do to my wife if you hurt her best friend."

"What? Of course not! I love Oliver. I'm just not interested in getting married any time soon."

"But, you're moving in with him," Ali interjected. "Lacey, I'm starting to feel like I don't know anything about you."

"Don't say that, Lenny. You know exactly who I am. You just want me to be someone else. You want me to be your seventeen year old, awkward virgin little sister. But I'm all grown up. Lenny, I was in high school when I got pregnant," Lacey said, in a solemn whisper.

"I love you, Lacey, and nothing can change that."

"I love you, too."

"Hey, Lace!" Ali said.

"Yes?"

"Call Cami and invite us over for dinner."

The siblings laughed and Lacey agreed to make the call in an appropriate, unassuming amount of time.

Ending the difficult exchange with her brother on a light note eased Lacey's angst. She rejoined her man's side at the high end, Napoleon Mirage gas grill she'd bought him, to celebrate his successful week at the Savannah Food and Wine Festival. She saddled up to him, wrapped her arms around him, and pressed her face against his back. They stood that way for a while, not saying a word.

"Ali called. I think he invited himself over for dinner."

"Yeah?"

She nodded against his back, and he continued minding the salmon stuffed portabella mushrooms. "I told him about our living arrangement."

"I'm guessing by your mood, he blessed it."

Lacey turned Oliver to face her, flashed her mega-watt smile, and batted her glittering eyes at him. She made a little pout and kissed him on the lips.

"Don't be cross. He knows how much I love you. He has no choice but to accept it. I'm an adult." She kissed him again and he was more affable. He bit his bottom lip showing his one dimple, and held her back to look at her fully.

"Are we OK, Babe?" He asked tenderly.

Lacey knew exactly what he was asking, thanks to her brother's reconnaissance. She tip toed to meet him at his eye level.

"We're perfect—just the way we are. I couldn't be happier, Oliver."

His deep brown eyes darted across her face for any signs of uncertainty, and he found none. In that moment, she was even more beautiful than the day he met her.

"I think you could be happier in a bigger place with a bathtub, maybe in Virginia Highlands or in Midtown," he teased.

"Yeah, I think you're right. I'll call an agent tomorrow."

"An agent, for a rental? Jesus, you're so high maintenance."

"Whatever, Man." She playfully waved him off. "I'm not leaving my next home to you and Craigslist!"

CHAPTER SIXTEEN

Boom!

The crisp Thanksgiving morning started early for Oliver and Ali. The sun was brilliant and lit the rust and wine colored leaves magnificently. It showered a golden hue over the otherwise cold and soggy morning. Thanksgiving brought with it the usual frenetic energy. There were food and wine pairings to execute, linens and place settings to arrange, and of course a feast to prepare for the Cami and Camilla's orphans. The Feast for the Orphans was a tradition started the first Thanksgiving Cami spent in her own house. So many of their friends in Atlanta were transplants from other places. Many of them couldn't afford to, or didn't go home for Thanksgiving for varying reasons. Therefore, Cami, Camilla and Oliver would cook a big meal and have them over on Thanksgiving. Every year, the trio would try a new dish that they called the 'twist'. The only request was for everyone to bring to bring a new gift to be donated to the women and children's shelter where they'd all became a family. Camilla loved Thanksgiving and she was a great help around the holidays, Oliver missed her sorely.

"Man, I'm really missing Camilla today." Oliver admitted to Ali. "I can only imagine how Cami's feeling."

Ali drew in a deep, soulful breath, and nodded for Oliver to lift his end of the stack of folding tables.

"Yeah. She's a trooper, but I know she's hurting. Last year around this time, she was still on auto-pilot, and we were still blending our lives together."

Oliver chuckled as he walked backwards through the kitchen door.

"Blending, huh? I seem to recall it as her throwing your bachelor crap into the basement."

They laughed in unison.

"Yeah, she was not feeling the sixty inch and surround sound. Was she?" Ali joked.

"Nope! But the new man cave is much appreciated, my brother."

"Mi casa es su casa," Ali playfully replied.

Lacey and the Robinson women were all busying around the kitchen, chopping and washing, mixing and dicing. Cami was in her comfort zone and she looked to be lit up from her core. She was truly at her best around the holiday season. The stories about Camilla were front and center, filling the house with warmth and joviality. Mr. Robinson and Ulysses sat out on the patio stoking the outdoor fireplace, watching the young men carry out the heavy lifting.

"Son, have you heard from your father-in-law? Will he and his missus be joining us for dinner?"

Ali had heard from James, and instinctively shot a look in Oliver's direction. "Yes, Sir. They'll be here," he answered as he and Oliver passed his father and uncle for table linens.

When he was sure he and Oliver were out of earshot, he asked if Oliver had heard anything more from James DaCosta.

"Have you talked to him about Carl since the last time?"

"No!" Oliver snapped. "And I don't want to either."

Ali frowned at Oliver. "What the fuck are you talking about?" he whispered through his clenched teeth. "You were the one who pushed to know!"

Oliver shook his head wildly, and wagged his finger at Ali. "I told you that I wanted to tell Cami. You said not to, and I'm not down with that; so count me out. If Cami's not going to know, I'm not going to know. So, don't tell me any more about it," Oliver demanded. "I'm not about to start keeping secrets from her. She wouldn't do that shit to me, and I'm not doing it to her." Oliver shook his head vehemently.

He moved to walk away with his arms full of white linen tablecloths. Ali shoved him in the chest, preventing him from passing.

"Ali, don't put your hands on me, Bro. You wanted to play your husband card; so you deal with this shit. Cami does not like being handled. And since you wouldn't listen to me – I'm out. I am out!"

Oliver moved to walk away again. And again, Ali stopped him from passing with a hand to his chest.

"Are you kidding me right now, Oliver? You're in this shit, too!" He leaned into Oliver's face and whispered, "You can't un-know what you know. And you didn't tell her either."

The kitchen window opened, startling the men.

"Is everything OK out there?" Cami asked through the kitchen window, just over the gardenia bushes.

The men composed themselves and nodded in her direction. She stood at the window watching them for a few more seconds before disappearing from their sight and reappearing in the back yard where they were standing arguing in lowered voices.

"Today! You two are going to start fighting today? Grow up! Think about me today," Cami cried.

Like sad little boys, admonished for wrestling in their

Easter clothes, Oliver and Ali sorrowfully bowed their heads. The tears streaming down Cami's round cheeks gripped at their hearts. She'd been trying her best to keep her emotions in check. She'd been missing her mother's presence in the kitchen so bad; it literally caused her physical pain. She smiled and diced with a huge lump in her throat for the entire morning and to see the two of them bickering was all she could bear.

"If you two can't behave like adults today, I don't want either of you here."

She pointed her finger between the two of them and angrily wiped at her tear stained face.

"I mean it! I will not tolerate any fighting or negativity in this house today. I won't! Do you understand me?"

The men nodded silently and apologized. Ali reached out to hug her. She swatted at his outstretched arms and pointed at him again.

"Shame on you! Get it together," she scolded Ali, before turning to face Oliver again. "And especially on you, Oliver. You know what this day means to me and to my mother."

She shook her head and left the men standing dumbfounded and conscience-stricken. They stood there processing the hurt they'd heaped on Cami, on a day they both knew would be hard for her.

"I'm sorry, O. You're right. I am her husband, and I made the call. I have no right to hold you responsible for my wife's well-being," Ali apologized.

"Yeah, but she's my sister, which make her my responsibility, too. We'll figure this out," Oliver sighed and shoulder bumped Ali. "I gotta say though, I like how ballsy she's getting," Oliver added.

Ali smiled sheepishly. He jammed one hand in his pocket, ran the other hand over his head, and slowly nodded in agreement.

"I'll tell her everything tonight." Ali settled.

"Thank you, Man. 'Cause I can't even look her in the face. She deserves to know. She can handle it. She's tougher than you know, Bro."

Dinner was another success! There was great food and great company, lively music and animated storytelling. Cami was every part the gracious hostess with her charming and doting husband at her side. The party moved effortlessly outdoors to Ali and Cami's al fresco patio and garden. The setting sun put on a spectacular light show, just before the strung globe lights powered up. Mr. Robinson and Oliver drew the men around the outdoor fireplace with live music, cigars and cognac, while the women settled around the large teak table with cups of coffee and second helpings of Camilla's famous almond lavender pound cake. The women's chatter was melodic amongst the rhythm of the garden's stone water feature --harmonizing with the hollow twangs from Oliver's guitar.

"How's married life treating you, Camisha?" Evangelina DaCosta asked her stepdaughter with a warm smile.

All of the women smiled with anticipation for Cami's answer. Tess, Katy B and MJ hadn't spent much time with Cami over the past year, and wanted to know how life had been treating her, too.

She shyly lowered her warm brown eyes, and with a girlish smile, she sipped from her mug.

"It's been good. I'm a lucky girl to have found someone like Ali." She tilted her head, and glanced over at her husband, who was lovingly watching her. “He’s a good man.”

The listening women responded in a chorus of, “Awwws,” painting Cami’s face with an amorous glow. The conversation turned to Lacey and Oliver. Cami was very happy to no longer be the center of attention. The Robinson women were fully engaged with interrogating Lacey about her love life, when Evangeline leaned close, and placed her hand on top of Cami’s.

“Honey, how are you doing? I’m sure this time of year is tough for you,” she said lovingly.

“Yes, it is. This was her favorite holiday,” Cami explained. “But, having my in-laws here, and you,” Cami placed her free hand atop of Evangeline’s, “helps a lot.” She said with a genuine smile. Evangeline was a lovely woman. She was elegant and accomplished, but warm and relatable at the same time. She’d forgiven the unforgivable and had embraced her stepdaughter.

“Thank you for saying that, dear. You are truly a special young woman, Camisha. We’re blessed to finally have you in our lives.” Evangeline and Cami sat hand in hand with tears welling up in their eyes.

“I know all of this nasty business with Carl can’t be easy for you,” Evangeline said.

Confusion spread across Cami’s face.

“I’m not sure what you mean. What business with Carl?” Cami asked.

Evangeline loosed her hands and looked around for her husband. Cami did too.

“James!” Evangeline called to her husband. “Can we talk to you for a second?”

Evangeline stood, took Cami by the hand and excused

herself. She directed her husband to follow her and Cami into the house. Ali followed the party through the kitchen door. His stomach was turning flips. He hadn't expected to have this conversation until he and Cami were alone. Oliver joined the on looking women at the table.

"Babe, what's going on," Lacey asked.

"Let's just wait and see." Oliver calmly answered. "Anyone need refills? Is everybody good?" he asked, trying to distract the curious guests.

Ali directed everyone into the family room where he sat his wide-eyed wife in her favorite spot near the fireplace, and handed her a glass of Malbec. Cami's eyes darted across everyone's faces. It was clear that they all knew something that she didn't and it was making her very uneasy.

"Ali, what's going on?" she asked directly. Ali sat on the arm of the leather club chair with his wife.

"How much do you know?" he asked cautiously.

"She obviously doesn't know anything about her father's investigation." Evangeline answered sternly.

"I can explain," James said, breaking the air of suspense. "I had so many questions about Camilla's accident, and the person who hit her," he started.

"So did I." Cami said, eliciting several surprised looks. "Like why did the person never come to see her at the hospital? I mean he stayed by her side at the scene, so he must've cared somewhat."

"Exactly!" Carl exclaimed and moved closer to Cami on the sectional sofa.

"So you opened an investigation?" She asked anxiously.

"Yes."

"But what would you know about any of this, Ali?" Cami looked up into Ali's piercing sable brown eyes for answers.

He took the glass from her and held both her hands in his.

"Mr. DaCosta called me and Oliver when we returned from Savannah. We met him at the shop, and he told us about his suspicions."

Cami calmly took her hands away from Ali, and looked at her husband and then at her father. "Oliver knew about this, too?" she whispered.

Ali could see her emotions toiling and threatening to boil over, at the mention of Oliver's involvement.

"Cam, Baby. Don't be mad at Oliver. He wanted to tell you right away. Be mad at me, I ordered him not to," Ali assured her.

"No one orders Oliver to do anything," she repudiated. "Please, excuse me."

She stood and walked down the hallway to their bedroom and closed the door. Ali and the DaCostas sat motionless in the family room.

"James, I asked you to leave this alone," Evangeline scoffed. "And then the nerve of you to exclude Camisha, as if she's a child." She shook her head disappointedly.

"I'll talk to her. Everything will be fine." Ali said nervously. "I hope." He said to himself.

Ali went out to explain the scene and asked Oliver to get his family settled in the basement while he went to talk to Cami. He saw the DaCostas to their car and his aunt and uncle along with his cousin, MJ off, as well.

Once everyone was settled in their respective places, Oliver and Lacey helped Ali tidy up around the patio and clean the kitchen. He wanted to stall for as long as possible before having to face his fuming wife. He wanted to have all of the right things to say, all of the right answers and all of the best things to do to make this all right for his marriage.

Ali wished his sister and Oliver a goodnight and found Cami laying in the chaise lounge in the sitting area of their bedroom, staring at the ceiling fan. He went to sit beside her, but was warned not to. He sat on the bench at the foot of their bed, at least twenty feet away from his wife, and quietly watched her until she spoke.

"You decided, that I couldn't handle knowing about the investigation into my mother's death. You - who only knew her for a few months decided. And you, ordered my best friend, her godson to keep it from me," Cami calmly recounted the details of the betrayal. "Oliver and I have never kept things from one another. Never." She kept her back flat on the chaise and her eyes glued to the ceiling fan. Her tone and words were deliberate and measured, filling Ali with anguish.

"Cami, Babe. Let me explain."

"Don't. You've done enough. And your explanations, at this point, are useless. I'm sure you've thought of all the right things to say—just the right way to market this BS to me. Right, Lennox? It's what you do. You tell people how to feel, what to buy, how to be. Right, Lennox? You're a pro."

He'd never seen Cami that way and he wanted to bring back the sweetness and gentility to her to tone, but he didn't know where to begin.

"Babe, please. Don't say that. I only wanted to protect you." he pleaded.

Ali walked towards the sitting area.

"Lennox, do not come near me right now."

Every time she called him Lennox, it cut him with the precision of a surgical grade scalpel. He stood frozen in between the bed where he'd started the day making love to the most beautiful and loving woman he'd ever known and the sitting area where this hardened, unfamiliar version of his wife lay calling him out of his chosen name. His heart broke into pieces.

"I want you to leave."

"Leave? And go where, Cami?"

"I don't care. But I can't look at you tonight. This is her holiday and you ruined it. I want you out!"

Ali silently packed a bag and left the bedroom with no further arguments. He wanted to go downstairs to talk to his parents, but couldn't find the energy. He left the house and booked himself into the Airport Hilton.

The buzzing of his phone woke him at three in the morning. His head was pounding and his mouth felt liked it was stuffed with cotton balls. He scratched himself and answered. It was Oliver.

"Dude, what the fuck happened? Where are you? Lacey said your mom called and said you'd left in the middle of the night."

Oliver hadn't let him get a word in edgewise, since he'd answered the phone.

"Oliver, slow down." Ali struggled to a sitting position. "She knows about the investigation. And you were right. I should have told her, as soon as I knew."

"How was she when you left?" Oliver asked his voice filled with concern. "Should I go over there?"

"Not until the morning. She may be mad at you too. But, she's mostly mad at me." Ali sat at the edge of the bed rubbing the top of his bowed head. "Oliver, I've never seen her like that. She was so angry and cold. She reminded me of Camilla," he remarked.

Oliver sat silently recalling the last night Camilla and Cami were at the shelter. It was the first time he had witnessed Cami shut down—not out of fear, but out of anger and frustration.

"I've seen her that way before. I should have just told her," Oliver said.

"No. It's all on me," Ali argued. "You wanted to tell her, but I knew better. I practically ordered you to keep quiet."

"No one orders me to do anything, Ali. I wanted the easy way out, and I kept my mouth shut. That's all on me. I knew better. Cami and I have never kept secrets from each other. She would've never done that to me."

"You sound just like her," Ali chuckled. "O, tell me that we'll be alright. You know her better than anyone does. Tell me that I didn't lose my wife tonight."

Oliver shook his head and lit a joint. He took a long drag from the joint and blew the smoke into a circle above his head.

"Naw, Man. That girl loves you something fierce. You're in deep, but you're not losing your wife," he said, taking another pull. "Ali man, you've got to starting believing in her strength. I know she looks delicate. I mean, she *is* soft spoken, but she's a survivor. She takes whatever life throws at her and just keeps pushing. She's a tough one," Oliver concluded.

"Thanks, O. I hope you're right."

"I am. Get some sleep." Oliver put the joint out on the

windowsill. "We'll hook up with your family for some breakfast, and in a few hours, we'll explain all of this to. By the time we get back to your house, Cami will be better. She'll never be rude to your family, but your ass will be back in the vise when they leave. Get some rest, man."

CHAPTER SEVENTEEN

My Brother's Keeper

The weeks following Thanksgiving were among the worst of adult Ali's life. For the life of him, he couldn't understand why his wife remained livid with him, but had completely forgiven Oliver. He was back in the bed with her, but she was as cold as ice. She still cooked him breakfast every morning, and dinner every night, but exchanged very few words with him. He'd come home to find she and Oliver laughing and bantering over Christmas dinner menus or she and Lacey excitedly digging through decorations. She'd had lunch with her father and stepmother at least twice that he knew of, but she was treating him like the sole assailant, as if he'd acted alone in the betrayal. He'd try talking to her directly about how she was making him feel. He'd enlisted Oliver and his mother to plead for his forgiveness. He sent flowers and gourmet food baskets. He'd even bought her jewelry – nothing worked.

"Cam, how long do you expect to carry on like this?" Oliver questioned his best friend.

"I don't know. I don't have an exact timeline," she answered coolly.

"You're killing that man. And for what?"

"To teach him not to keep things from me."

Cami said, perusing the Italian wines that lined the DeKalb Farmers market's wine section.

"You see Oliver, my husband thinks I'm soft. He thinks I'm a fragile flower or something. If I give in too easily on this,

I'll be living under Ali's whims and decisions for my life for the rest of my life. I love him, but he has to start believing in me. He has to start accepting me for the strong woman I am. I've navigated a pretty ugly world without him, " Cami explained as she accepted and rejected bottle after bottle of DOCG labeled wines.

"I hear you, Cam. But to Ali's defense, he doesn't know what you've navigated. Have you even told him everything? About Genesis house? About the bullying? About the evictions and shit?" Oliver pressed.

Cami didn't answer right away. She directed the buggy to the Butchers section of the bustling market, and leaned over the refrigerated glass cases of lamb and goat.

"I'll tell him, in time—in my own time, though," she finally answered.

Not accepting her response, Oliver continued pleading a case for Ali.

"Why aren't you still mad at me?" He asked very carefully.

The question stopped Cami in her tracks. She stood there in front of the case of expertly butchered carcasses staring at nothing in particular, before standing to face her nervous friend.

"You have no desire to control people or situations. You've never tried to handle me or manipulate my thoughts or decisions. You were handled by him. I'm sure you knew that you were being handled, but in your style of least resistance—you let him. You wanted the situation handled by anyone other than you. It's how you operate. If you don't make a decision or a commitment, you don't have to deal with the fall out. You can just pick up and go."

Cami's words hit Oliver and they hurt. Right there in the middle of the smells and sounds and hurrying crowds of people and competing languages and dialects of the International Farmers Market Oliver scurried through his memories of he and Cami's life together, trying to recall just one memory of her hurting him so deeply. He took a small step away from her. His eyes scanned hers for some sign of remorse. Upon finding nothing but steadfastness, Oliver took an elastic band he was wearing around his wrist, pulled his locks into a messy bun high on top of his head, and stepped around Camisha to the meat case. But then turned so quickly Cami had to take a step back in order to not be hit by him.

"I'm sorry, Cam. What the hell does that mean? 'I don't want to make decisions.' Is that how you see me? As some kind of lazy slacker who let's other people handle me and make decisions for me? Really, Cam?"

"Oliver, think about it. What decision have you really made for your life, since you came here to Atlanta? What have you really ever had to work for?" Cami asked pointedly.

"Wow!" Oliver staggered. "Who works for me, Cam?"

"I do!" she yelled, pointing to her chest. "Name one job you've ever had that I didn't give to you. One! Checkers? Me! Circle K? Me! Valet parking at Saint Cecilia's? Me! Even your job right now, managing the shop—me! And what about your breakout at the Viceroy? It's always been me! Camisha and Oliver—we're a package deal, because I believe in you, Oliver. I need you to be all right. I need you to be good. You've always been there for me – no matter what. You protected me as a kid. You were my only friend, all of my life. I owed it to you to take care of you, b it hampered you from having to do it for yourself."

She turned back to the meat case. "I'm sorry. It's the truth. You're in a perpetual state of arrested development."

She stood closely to her best friend, and took his pinkie finger with her own and smiled at him.

"You know how much I love you. I'd do anything for you, Ollie, but you know I'm right."

When he didn't pull away, Cami pointed out a tied rack of lamb.

"We should totally do a rack for the entree! I can't wait to meet your brother."

Oliver understood that it was the end of the conversation and acquiesced, just as Cami estimated he would.

"A rack it is, Boss Lady."

*****

The city donned in its most festive apparel. Glittering with holiday decorations and twinkling lights by the tons. Oliver teetered between excitement and anger from one moment to the next. He was thoroughly excited about being under one roof with all the people he loved, and about sharing what he loved and what had saved his life with his mother and big brother. However, Cami's words at the Farmer's Market rattled around in his mind like an unsettled spirit. Had she always seen him as some kind of needy loafer who just let life happen to him? Or as a runner who scurried away when things got tough? And what really nagged at him was, that Lacey had accused him of something very similar, when she asserted that he didn't "even have goals" or when she'd chant, "Cami. Cami. Cami" To him, further asserting his dependence on his best friend.

"Did you and Cami finish the wine pairings for this Grand Christmas Feast?"

Lacey asked over her glasses, as she clicked through her mountains of emails. Oliver walked over to the bed where she still chose to work instead of the fancy table she insisted he needed at his place, and kissed her puckered lips.

"Yeah, I think we're all set."

He was exhausted and needed a few minutes to himself. He locked himself in the bathroom, and turned the shower on to full blast. Oliver sat on the commode and clicked through his voicemail. One from Stephen Black caught his attention and he played it.

"Hello, Chef Barnett this is Chef Stephen Black of the Aqua Star, here in Savannah. I'd like to discuss an exciting opportunity with you. Give me a call. I look forward to hearing from you soon."

The message sat Oliver on edge with exhilaration. He couldn't believe that Chef Stephen Black had actually reached out to him. His chest filled with pride. He rushed out to tell Lacey, who had drifted off to sleep. He lifted his phone to call Cami, but remembered that they were still in an awkward place since their visit to the Farmers Market. He decided it was probably best to wait until he actually knew what the exciting opportunity was, before he shared it with anyone. He smiled broadly and jumped in the shower.

The Atlanta Airport was widely regarded as the world's busiest airport and it was flaunting the haughty distinction the day before Christmas. The traffic into the airport stretched for miles and crept along at a snail's pace. Lacey and Valentina had insisted on riding with Oliver to pick up Benjamin who was due to land in about a half an hour. Oliver couldn't tell who was more nervous, his mom or his girlfriend. Lacey had fussed over what to wear for hours the night before. She settled on dark teal silk blouse and skinny jeans with a chic tobacco brown leather biker jacket and matching riding boots. She wore, what she called her "good luck" tortoise shell and cream ombré cat-eye glasses.

His mother had arrived in Atlanta two days prior to Benji's expected arrival to inspect Oliver and Lacey's new apartment, but she claimed she only want to help furnish the guest room for Benji's stay. She and Mix bought a Christmas tree and decorations for the new place. They bought a top of the line mattress, and a chest of drawers for the guest room. Lacey brought one her favorite Ikat club chairs into the room, along with a small bedside table, lamp and water pitcher set with a matching drinking glass. Oliver was ticked by all of the hullabaloo the women were making over a three-day stay for a man who would probably never pour a drink of water from a glass pitcher situated at his bed side. He jeered, but he too was excited to see his big brother after so many years. He wanted to make his home as comfortable and inviting as possible.

"I am so nervous, O. I'm feeling sick to my stomach," Valentina confessed as Oliver's SUV inched along the jam-packed airport parking lots. 'Things didn't go well the last time we saw each other."

Olive recalled Mix's frantic visit following their return from visiting Benjamin in North Dakota.

"We'll work through it, Ma. He agreed to come, didn't he?" Oliver said.

"But you know how prickly he can be. How'd he sound when you talked to him?"

"He sounded like nice Benji. He said he was happy to

hear my voice and last night he sounded, dare I say, excited. He said he's spent the last few Christmases alone and was looking forward to having a family Christmas. He's really excited about seeing Izzy, too. It's going to be good, Ma. I promise."

"A family Christmas, huh?" Valentina quietly reflected.

Oliver noticed the remark, but made no interjection. They had never had a good family Christmas, not that he could remember, and he was looking forward to having his first with his own family, in his own place.

Lacey had secured, with the help of her real estate agent, an authentic sixteen hundred square foot two story loft in the Old Fourth Ward district of the city. The space was all Lacey with its exposed brick interior, wall of windows, hardwood floors, twenty-foot ceilings and enormous skylights. But the location and kitchen were handpicked for Oliver. It was directly across the street from the Ponce City Market, and boasted luxurious Wolf kitchen appliances. The couple had their own a private entrance, a fantastic roof-top terrace and large side courtyard complete with grilling area, for Oliver's beloved gas grill and his bike. It was still close to the dance studio where he played for the kids and in the heart of his most treasured neighborhood. Lacey had insisted on a vintage plank top dining table that seated twelve, with Louis ghost chairs. She justified the extravagant purchase because her man was a chef and they'd surely host dinners at their own home, and not always have to depend on Lennox's and Cami's house. And she was hell bent to be all moved in by Christmas, in order to host at their own beautiful home. It would be the first time her family would meet Oliver's family, and she wanted nothing more than to host such a momentous occasion in her own space—not her parent's space or her big brother's space, but in hers - hers and Oliver's.

Benjamin and Oliver yelled to each other from mere feet away at the congested Airport Arrivals landing. They couldn't possibly know who to look for after eighteen years. As a thirteen-year-old Oliver was much shorter and didn't have long dreadlocks, and Benjamin was a chubby sixteen-year-old loner with acne-marred skin. When Oliver spotted a man matching the clothing Benji described, he waved his cell phone wildly and yelled to his brother.

"Benji! Benji! Over here!"

The brothers rushed to each other and excitedly embraced. Benjamin held his younger brother at arm's length to look him up and down, and then drew him in again for another enthusiastic embrace. Oliver's brown eyes spilled over with easy, warm tears. His heart was filled.

"My God, O! You're a full-grown man. And you're long, just like Ike and Momma! You look good, baby brother." He rustled Oliver locks and put him in a playful headlock move. "And what's with all of this hair, Man?"

Oliver felt like a little brother again and was overwhelmed by how much he'd missed Benjamin. He grabbed the duffle bag his brother had sat down, and led him to his Jeep Cherokee where Lacey and Valentina were standing curbside. As if Valentina had fabricated the entire acrimonious reception in North Dakota, Benjamin wrapped his mother in a full embrace, just as lovingly as he had greeted Oliver.

"I'm sorry, Momma. I just want to start over," he whispered into his weeping mother's neck.

Oliver and Lacey were both touched by the scene and, quietly loaded Benjamin's belongings into the truck.

"Benji, this is Oliver's lady friend, Lacey Robinson." Valentina proudly introduced Lacey, while wiping at her eyes and leaving traces of tissue all over her smiling face.

Benjamin politely extended a hand to Lacey, who politely accepted it with a shy smile. She nervously pushed her glasses up her nose and told Benjamin how much she'd heard about him and couldn't wait to get to know him. He smiled in kind and held the passenger side door open for Lacey. The ride back to the East side was filled with laughter and happy tears for the Barnetts. Valentina couldn't have been happier than she was in the backseat of the late model Jeep Cherokee with two of her sons joyfully calling her, Mom.

The Barnett brothers stayed up late into the night talking about Atlanta and North Dakota. Oliver cooked for his brother and served him like a king. They talked about Isaac and the few good times from their childhood days in Ohio. Oliver talked to him about shelter life, and meeting Cami and Camilla. Benjamin told his baby brother about his three children and naming them after scientists and inventors, just as they had been. The brothers chatted as if not one day had been lost between them. Benjamin was very different as adult. The person sitting across from him on the velvet, tufted couch was nothing like the person Oliver remembered back in Ohio. The old Benji was bitter and antagonistic. This Benjamin was more like Izzy, charming and quick witted. He was no longer chubby, and long gone were the acne marks of his youth. He'd grown a few more inches, just not as many has his little brother had. He wore his hair cut evenly and close to his head with a completely clean-shaven face. He and Oliver had matching almond shaped, cognac brown eyes framed by the same thick shiny brows. Benjamin wasn't as strikingly handsome as Isaac, nor did he possess the enigmatic charisma that Oliver that wielded. But, he was undoubtedly another good-looking Barnett brother.

"So Izzy's here in Atlanta, huh?"

Something in the room shifted with Benji's abrupt question about Isaac, raising the hairs on Oliver's neck.

"Yeah. He's been here for about three years now."

"How is he?"

A small nervous chuckle escaped from Oliver, making him all the more uneasy. An eerie recollection of the Benji he remembered crept up. Benji's slanted eyes grew dark and more narrowed even more.

"He's the same old, Izzy—charming whatever he wants out of whomever he wants it from. His body is the only thing about him that's locked up," Oliver answered without batting an eye.

Benjamin stood up and walked over to Oliver's battered old piano. He banged on a few keys with his back turned to his little brother.

"Did he tell you about the day he got busted?" Benjamin asked.

"No."

"You sure?" Benjamin plucked at a few more piano keys setting an ominous soundtrack to the direction in which the conversation was heading.

"I'm positive. Why?"

"Why what?"

"Why are you asking?" Oliver demanded.

He turned to look at his brother, who kept his back turned. Benjamin picked up the bronze picture frame that held a picture of Oliver with his arms wrapped around Lacey's shoulders, kissing her on the cheek at Ali and Cami's wedding reception.

"She looks like money," Benjamin answered instead.

Oliver was not deterred. Benjamin returned the picture to its resting place on the floating shelves, just over the piano.

"Why are you so worried about what Izzy told me about the day he was busted, Benji? Did you two have some kind of beef about it? 'Cause he's never mentioned it to me, one way or another. He's been worried sick about you. Momma even hired an investigator to find you. Everyone's been looking for you. There ain't no beef for you here, Brother."

"No beef, huh?"

Benjamin walked over to the floor to ceiling wall of windows that looked out onto the bustling Ponce City Market. Something in his posture softened, but he kept his back to Oliver.

"I saw it all go down, and I did nothing."

"What the hell do you think you could've done for him, if he was being arrested?" Oliver retorted.

"I should've went back to the house and started flushing shit. I don't know. I just watched from the playground with everyone else. I didn't even go over to try to help him or ask what was going on. I just stood in the crowd like I didn't even know him. I'll never forget the smirk on his face when he saw me watching," Benjamin ruefully recalled the chaotic scene.

"He didn't say anything to me when they walked him past all of us to the police car. He just shook his head at me and mouthed the word, 'punk' to me," Benji shook his head trying to loosen the unsettling memory. "And I haven't seen or heard from him since that day."

"You were a kid, a smart one. If you'd done anything else, there would have been two Barnett boys in prison right now. And no part of me believes that Izzy would have wanted that for you. No part," Oliver pensively shook his head. "Benji, we were all just scared little kids left to fend for ourselves." Oliver defended his middle brother's inaction.

"Yeah. But I've been grown for a long time now, and he sent out the cavalry to find me – from behind bars!" Benjamin chuckled at his brother's reach.

Oliver walked over to his brother and put a hand on his shoulder.

"I was afraid to call you. Everyday I'd sit at that table," Oliver gestured to the round trestle table in the breakfast nook. "And hold your phone number in my hand."

Benjamin turned to his little brother.

"Afraid of what?"

"What you'd say to me for disappearing and letting so many years get between all of us. Benji, you've always been kind of an ass, Bro."

Benjamin and Oliver laughed and broke out into the ducking and swaying of a brotherly slap boxing match.

"Seriously, B- I didn't know what to expect, but then Izz called. He told me that you took care of us—that you made sure we had breakfast every morning, and that you worked your ass off to provide for all of us. So, I needed to man up and call you. And he was right – as usual."

Benjamin was touched by Izzy's endorsement. He reached out and hugged his baby brother in the middle of the floor to ceiling wall of windows. Lacey called out from above the men.

"Do you guys need anything down there?"

"No, Ma'am! Sorry, if we woke you," Benjamin called up to her.

She walked half way down the iron staircase wearing a silk robe over sweats and UGG boots.

"No! I'm in the office working. I'm so happy to have you here, Benjamin."

"Call me, Ben. Come down and kick it with us."

"I couldn't. I'm sure you two have a lot of catching up to do," Lacey politely refused.

Oliver playfully waved his girlfriend off.

"Aww man, Benji she builds empires for a living and that work never ends," he teased.

"I was wondering how my baby brother was affording all of this, as a baker."

Oliver knew that his brother was only joking, but his words tossed more dirt on him. Lacey had first pushed him into the hole with the 'Goals' talk and then his mom, tossed a handful on with her, 'Time Waits for No One' comment and Cami had shoveled on enough to practically bury him with their Farmers Market conversation. He mustered a smile when the pair looked at him.

"I do more than bake, Benjamin," he tried to say as evenly as possible.

"He sure does," Lacey sang. "He's quite the up and comer on the culinary scene in the city. People pay a lot of money for Oliver to teach them to cook fancy food. You'll see tomorrow!" she boasted proudly.

Benjamin smiled broadly at Oliver.

“We’d better all turn in—or Santa won’t come. And since you’re balling now, Little Bro, I know he comes to this neighborhood!”

CHAPTER EIGHTEEN

Bad Timing

Isaac woke his brothers Christmas day bright and early. His voice was childlike and filled with excitement at hearing his two younger brothers together for the holiday. They carried on like anxious little boys talking over one another, laughing and slapping at each other. Isaac wanted to know everything about the visit with Benjamin. Was he taller? Was he nice to their mother? Had he met Mix? What'd he think of Lacey? He wanted a play by play of what they'd be doing for the day. What was on the menu? What did Oliver's apartment look like? When would they be coming to visit him? Who got what as gifts? His heart was filled, but breaking at the same time. Isaac wanted nothing more than to be with his family for Christmas breakfast, and opening gifts with his mom. He laid in his cell and imagined them all around a larger than life Christmas tree, opening presents and drinking hot chocolate. He imagined them all sitting around a big dining table filled with silver serving trays and gravy boats. Given Lacey's class and grace, he was sure there would be crystal wine and water glasses lining an elaborate table setting dressed with sparkling lights and boughs of holly. He smiled about how far his family had come and could hardly wait to have them all there with him on Christmas day, even if it was in a Federal Penitentiary. Then the unsettling images of his little brother's girlfriend crept back into his mind. He often found his thoughts drifting to her. For Christmas, he envisioned Lacey descending a lighted staircase wearing something pink and silky.

In his private thoughts of her, she was always wearing pink. He bolted up and shamefully shook the image from his head.

The Barnetts ascended on Ali and Cami's home. The couple welcomed them warmly. A very eager, Cami was bursting with happiness for Oliver's good fortune. He'd for so long been an army of one, buzzing around her kitchen with she and her mother, grinding coffee beans and beating eggs. He'd never felt like a plus one, but an integral part of her family. Something tugged at her core that felt a little like loss at seeing him with his own blood relatives, but her feelings of joy far outweighed any other feelings. The strain that the tough words between she and Oliver had caused, did not escape her, and she wanted to apologize to her friend, but she knew that her words weren't meant to hurt him. She felt that apologizing might convey that she felt guilty about what she said or that she was motivated by anger about his betrayal. All of which was true, but she'd meant every word of what she'd said to her friend. She had always taken care of Oliver, and with a glad heart. Furthermore, there was no doubt in her mind that she would do it all over again, if he ever needed.

Oliver bounced out of Lacey's car and wrapped his best friend in a big hug. He hurriedly waved Benjamin over to the carport, where he and Cami stood holding hands. She was shaking like a leaf and ran her free hand over the apron she was wearing and then over her long wavy bob.

"Camisha Robinson, meet my big brother, Benjamin." Oliver said proudly.

Benjamin extended both hands to Cami, who used them to pull him into a warm hug.

"Being Oliver's brother makes you my brother," Cami

gushed.

Benji liked her instantly and felt a strong brotherly affection towards her. A broad smile spread across his face. He felt happiness radiate through his limbs as each one of the Robinsons poured out of the kitchen door to greet him with big smiles and bright, welcoming eyes. Lacey had joined her brother and mother with linked arms and looked on at the love fest. Oliver and Lacey introduced Benjamin to Ali and his parents.

"Let the man into the house. It's cold out here," Mr. Robinson said and held the kitchen door open for everyone to enter.

Breakfast was all done and the dining room table was set. A fire was burning and the house smelled of fresh ground coffee and Camilla's famous orange glazed cinnamon rolls. Valentina stood beside Cami at the stove and wrapped an arm around her waist.

"Everything smells so good, Camisha. How are you?" she said, smiling at Cami.

"I can't complain, Ms. Tina," Cami sighed. "I really miss her during the holidays. She was at her best at this time of year."

"I hate that I never got to meet her in person. I wish I could have wrapped her in my arms, and given her big hug for giving my baby a home and a family," she said, as she gave Cami another squeeze around the waist. "O was lucky to have you two."

"We were lucky to have him. She loved Oliver like he was her own."

The two stood there quietly taking in the festive scene. Cami returned to the coffee pot and began filling mugs.

"You must be feeling pretty full, having your boys together for Christmas." Cami noted.

The mention brought tears to Valentina's eyes. Full, was exactly what she was feeling. She couldn't have been any happier. She pursed her lips as she struggled to contain her emotion.

"I'm very happy. Very happy." She answered. "Lacey said that the boys were up all night laughing and talking."

"Yeah, I heard," Cami said, laughing.

"Oliver called this morning. I can't recall ever seeing him so happy."

"Really?" Valentina asked with a surprised look.

"Absolutely. Oliver's usually so laid back. He's always pleasant, but kind of guarded–you know? He's always joking around and being light about stuff, but, today he's open. I see it all over him." Cami watched Oliver with the other men around the giant fireplace. "Lacey's had a lot to do with him opening up too."

"I bet. She's a tough cookie, that one," Valentina laughed.

"You can say that again," Ms. Tess interjected as she sashayed into the kitchen. "It's been a long time, Valentina."

The women hugged. Ms. Tess breezed by Cami and kissed her on the cheek.

"Hand me a knife so I can start serving up these Camilla rolls." Ms. Tess said.

Cami obediently grabbed a knife from the drawer before handing it to her mother-in-law.

"How have you and Tommy been holding up with Lacey's move to the city?" Valentina asked.

Her question paused the room, and its occupants seemed to float into the air in extremely slow motion. Ms. Tess shifted uncomfortably and forced a small smile as Mr. Robinson, Ali and Lacey looked on from the family room.

"We're doing just fine. Lacey's an adult, so I knew we'd be losing her sooner or later. I just didn't expect it to be this way. I thought she'd leave us with a husband," Ms. Tess shrugged and slid a few plates across the granite kitchen bar.

"Lacey's smart and resourceful, Tess," Mr. Robinson chimed in, defending his daughter.

"And standing right here in the room," Lacey snapped.

Cami moved to lighten the mood. She grabbed Ali's phone from the bar and clicked on the sound system. The Supremes', "A Few of my Favorite Things" spilled into the room. Valentina began to sing along, "Raindrops on roses and whiskers on kittens. Bright copper kettles and warm woolen mittens." She lightly bumped Tess's, who reluctantly joined in, followed by Lacey and Mr. Robinson. Oliver winked at his best friend, and picked up his guitar from the stone hearth.

The weather was beautiful and the sun shone brightly for Benji's Christmas day in Atlanta. It was a much-needed break from the freezing cold of North Dakota. The roads were unusually clear in the city, and Oliver was grateful for it all. Not even Jesus's birthday could squelch Atlanta's bumper-to-bumper traffic, but God was showing great favor to the Barnett family. Valentina drove along I-20 like a native, no longer needing Oliver's direction.

"I'm guessing the Robinsons are not down with yours and Lacey's living arrangements," Benjamin asked. "And when'd you learn to play the guitar?" He laughed.

"Not so much," he said lightly. "It's just a little something I picked up as a kid—the piano and the drums, too!"

"Add that to list of things the Robinsons aren't *down*

with." Valentina scoffed under her breath. "They think they're so damned high and mighty."

"Now. Now, Love." Mix quietly patted his fiery wife's hand as she shifted into third gear. Benjamin and Oliver laughed at the scene that played out in the front seat. The tall cinder block walls of the prison came into view, dashing their light-hearted moods. The ominous cloud that often covered Benji's countenance set in. Oliver quietly watched his big brother's slanted eyes darken, retreating into himself. The party of four moved through the visitor's search and sign in process in absolute silence. Benjamin second guessed his decision to come at least twice, demonstrated by all out stops and turning around to look back towards the exit. The banging of the heavy metal doors startled him. When they entered the mermaids and scuba divers painted walls of the Visitor's area, Oliver slid into one the little metal chairs like a seasoned veteran.

"He'll be coming through that door over there,"

Oliver said, pointing out to his nervous brother. In mere seconds, Isaac Barnett shuffled through the matte gray painted metal door, stopping to let the guard unlock the wrist and ankle shackles in which he was transported. His bright smile was on full display and his eyes danced like a child's on Christmas morning. He visibly fought back tears. Valentina could not contain her excitement. She jumped up and ran over to her firstborn son, who carefully ran his hands over her long silver locks and kissed her on each cheek. They walked across the room hand in hand, with Valentina's head resting on her son's arm. Mix met him with a hug, while Oliver and Benji stood and waited to greet their big brother, who excitedly grabbed them both up in a big bear hug. He held on to Benjamin longer and whispered something into his ear.

"Merry Christmas, Fam!" Izzy boomed as he plopped down into the tiny seat, banging his knees on the table. "God-damn it! You'd think I'd know by now that my knees won't fit under these little ass tables," he laughed and stretched his long legs alongside the table, crossing them at his ankles.

"Y'all smell good—like cinnamon rolls and oranges or something."

They all laughed.

"You should look into the culinary arts when you get out. 'Cause you nailed that, Izzy!" Oliver chuckled. "Cami cooked breakfast for all of us—Orange glazed cinnamon rolls."

"Nice," Izzy dramatically nodded his head. "No Lacey today?"

"Nah. You know her parents are here, so she's playing hostess to them," Oliver explained.

Isaac grimaced.

"Oh, well. So, Benji, you got to meet Cami, huh?"

"Yeah. She's just like a little sister. Right?"

"Wouldn't know. I've never met her." Izzy looked over at Oliver.

"You haven't met her, yet? How is that even possible," Benjamin asked.

"Funny, ain't it? He's brought his old lady here, but never his Cami."

Izzy answered in an accusatory tone. Valentina found it odd, too.

"That is strange, O. Why haven't you brought Cami to meet your brother?" She asked.

Oliver was very uncomfortable with the inquisition. He

balked at all of them, and quickly changed the subject.

"Did you get the card Lacey and I sent?"

"Yes! Thanks for that, Bro. It's definitely the fanciest card on my block. I'm getting a lot of hell about all of that glitter, though," Isaac slapped at Oliver. "But seriously, O thanks for the money."

"Lacey picked it. And you're welcome," Oliver said, averting his eyes.

"So Ben Ben. What the hell are you doing in North Dakota, Brother?"

Benjamin smiled sheepishly.

"It's where the money's at. I have mouths to feed and hair weaves to keep tight," he joked. "Them baby mommas of mine don't play about their money."

"Damn, Bro! How many are there?" Isaac asked.

"There are only three. Tonya has the two oldest and Candace has my baby girl."

"He named them after scientists and inventors, Ma! Just like you did," Oliver proudly connected.

Visibly moved, Valentina smiled shyly at her husband, who returned her smile.

"Yeah, I did. Alexander and Garrett are nine and seven, and Stephanie Rosemarie turned five in October," Benjamin rattled off.

"Rosemarie?" Valentina blushed.

"Yes, Ma'am. Rosemarie. She's named for my mother," Benji razzed her.

Mix nodded approvingly, and rubbed his wife's lower back. She composed herself and pat Benjamin's hand.

"How often do you see them?" Valentina asked cautiously.

"I get back every two or three months. The company pays for it. It's pretty extreme out there in the Dakotas," he answered unabashedly.

"What do you think of our rich, white pops?" Isaac joked.

Mix smiled, and shook a finger at Isaac.

"You are a joker, Isaac," he chuckled.

"Mix is good people. Ma's done well for herself." Benjamin reached out for her hand again and she obliged. "I'm proud of her. And, I'm glad y'all found me. I'm especially glad y'all didn't just write me off; God knows I deserve it."

"Stop that shit right now, Little Bro. We all did the best we knew how, and none it matters now, because we made it, and we're all back together." Isaac held out hands to his little brothers atop the cold stainless steel table and they linked hands with Mix and Valentina.

"This visit was way too short." Valentina whined as she squeezed her firstborn son.

"Pray for me tonight at dinner. OK, Momma?"

"OK," she cried. "I love you, Isaac."

Isaac hugged everybody one by one and tearfully wished them a merry Christmas. He ordered Benji to keep in touch and to send pictures of his niece and nephews. Benji promised he would and walked away from the group.

"Love you, Bro. And I'll be back to see you after the New Year," Oliver said.

"With Lacey. Okay?"

Oliver nodded with a bright smile.

"As if I could keep her away," he quipped.

"But, will you bring Cami?" Isaac asked pointedly.

"I'll try," was all Oliver offered, as he hugged his brother.

Oliver genuinely didn't know why he hadn't brought Cami to meet Isaac. Of course he'd considered it, but he never did. She didn't even know that he had a brother living in Atlanta before a few months ago, and they'd never talked about why. Most of the ride back to his house he wondered why he hadn't told Cami about Isaac and from where the apprehension stemmed.

Lacey was at the loft when Oliver returned. Valentina dropped him off and took Benji back to the hotel with she and Mix. She wanted to spend some time catching up with him, she explained on the ride from the prison. Lacey was very agitated. She was banging around pots and pans in the kitchen and didn't hear Oliver's key in the front door. He walked up behind her and wrapped his arms around her waist, startling her. She dropped the skillet she was hanging on the copper pot rack.

"Jesus, Oliver! You scared the life out of me," she slapped at him, then kissed him longingly on the lips. "God, I missed you," she whispered against his mouth with her arms laced around his neck. "I should have gone with you guys. My mom makes me crazy," she whimpered.

Oliver leaned back to look at her. "You look good in this kitchen, Lacey Baby," he said, smiling.

He picked her up into his arms, and sat her on the cold limestone kitchen island. He cozied up between her thighs and kissed her deeply. Lacey wove her long fingers into Oliver's thick locks, and wrapped her legs around his waist. She pulled him firmly against her throbbing center using only her long legs.

"Is that for me?" Lacey purred against Oliver's full lips.

"All for you. Merry Christmas, Baby."

"Well, let's get this thing unwrapped," she said, as she grinded against his stiffness.

Lacey unbuttoned his jeans and slipped his underwear down to his thighs with the deft artistry of a master violinist.

"Look at you wearing jeans. Did you get all dressed up for your big brothers?" Lacey teased.

"Can we please not talk about my brothers right now?" Oliver pleaded between moans of pleasure. He passionately kissed Lacey's creamy, brown décolletage. In one agile move, he raised her thighs, slid the shorts she was wearing to the side, and entered her.

The afternoon sun was high in the sky. The glow of Oliver and Lacey's nude bodies intensified as they lay panting on their plush, teal velvet sofa. Lacey intertwined her curvaceous legs with Oliver's, and kissed his chest sweetly. The couple lay quietly watching the sky and listening to the syncopation of their breathing, the rhythmic beating of their hearts. Oliver sighed deeply and sat upright.

"Lace, this may not be the best time to do this, but I want to give you some time to think about what I'm about to tell you," Oliver said carefully.

Lacey reached for the glasses that she'd strewn across the floor during the throes of lovemaking. She sat up and faced him. He recognized the icy scowl, and the glint of fire in her cat like hazel eyes. He quickly moved to mollify the threat of her rage. He quickly pulled her between his spread legs and wrapped his arms around her. He felt her muscles relax a little and he kissed her on the forehead.

"Chef Stephen Black – the one from Savannah. Remember him?" He didn't wait for her to answer. "He wants to sponsor me for a Culinary Tour of France. Master chefs do that for young chefs new to the game, like me." He waited for her to say something. But, she only shifted against him and pushed her glasses up her nose. Oliver loved the way her hair smelled. It reminded him of freshly baked vanilla pound cake and how he imagined Hawaii would smell.

"A Culinary tour of France. How would that work?" Lacey asked in a measured tone.

"I would go to France in May and work in different kitchens all over the country. I'd take classes during the day and work in the kitchens at night." The excitement he felt built with his every word. "I'd start in Provence and end in Normandy."

"How long would you be gone? Two or three weeks?" Lacey asked.

"Three months."

Lacey felt the all the blood drain from her face. She couldn't peel her eyes away from the lighted marquee letters that hung over the Ponce City Market. She could feel Oliver's breath on her neck and she felt the light kisses he put on her shoulders, but she couldn't take her eyes off the sign. She felt like her mind should be racing, but it was completely blank. All she could do was count the light bulbs that made up PONCE.

"Lace, I want you to come with me," he declared, freeing her from the paralysis. She sat up and faced him again. She searched his face for any signs of deception or pity, but there was only sincerity. She shook her head to lose the cobwebs that had quickly set up. He took her face in both hands and kissed her.

"I don't want you to say anything right now. Just think about it. May is a long time from now. Okay?"

She nodded and let him kiss her again before lying back against his sculpted chest. Lacey didn't know how to feel about Oliver's news, but she knew that she wanted to talk to MJ about all of it.

Oliver's proposition consumed Lacey that evening over the grand Christmas dinner surrounded by their family and friends. It would only be for three months and she could take a leave of absence – she was sure her father would support it. But, her father wasn't getting around as well as he used to and she couldn't ignore the difficulty he endured with going over those bank papers for Uncle Ulysses and Aunt Katy B's new restaurant. They hadn't spoke about it, but she'd noticed. How could she leave him for three months? She didn't think Lennox would cover the work in her absence. He'd been commuting back and forth between Atlanta and the West Coast with his own work. Valentina spoke, breaking Lacey's dogged distraction.

"You seem a million miles away. Are you okay?"

Lacey nodded, but didn't speak. She handed a stack of dessert plates to Valentina and forced a trite little smile. Taking the hint, Valentina kissed her on the cheek and carried the plates to the black wood and mirrored buffet cabinet. As she passed her son, she ordered him to check on Lacey. But, Oliver was acutely aware of Lacey's distress. He couldn't take his eyes off of his lady, as she cruised around the loft like a robot. She gave an obligatory smile here and there, but she was definitely out of sorts. He deeply regretted having mentioned Chef Black's offer before their families were due to arrive. "Bad timing, man. Bad timing." Oliver whispered to himself.

CHAPTER NINETEEN

Jump at De Sun

Lacey curled up against the tall wrapped headboard and pulled the silk comforter over her legs. She'd lay still, pretending to be asleep until she was sure Oliver had left to take Benjamin to the airport for his late morning flight. She felt awful about not seeing Benjamin off, but she really wasn't ready to talk to Oliver again before she had a chance to call her cousin. She'd successfully avoided having any one on one conversation with him throughout Christmas dinner and she'd showered and climbed into bed, while he and Benjamin stayed up into the wee hours of the night. MJ always made sense of things for Lacey and she always seemed to have more family insider information than either she or Lennox. MJ and her mother were very close, and Aunt Katy B respected MJ's opinions. Their relationship was very different than Lacey's and her mother's.

"So he wants you to summer in France with him?" MJ asked.

"Yes."

"And what's the problem with that?"

"He'll be moving all over the country every two or three weeks. All over the damned country, MJ! That'd be like us moving from here to Texas, and then from Texas to Chicago and then from Chicago to Seattle – all in three months! In twelve weeks! He'd be in classes all day and then working at night. What would I do with myself in another country all alone? I wouldn't get to settle in and meet people, before we'd be on to the next Region!"

Lacey voice broke and she bit the inside of her cheek to maintain her composure.

"That's crazy, MJ. And I have a business to run. Remember that?" Lacey whined.

"Lacey, you have a lot to think about, but you do know that you cannot ask that man to stay. Don't you?"

"I know." Lacey whispered.

"Look. It's only three months and you can take a week or two to visit him while he's there."

"MJ. Do you think he asked me to check the box? He knew I wouldn't leave my daddy in a lurch. Right? Surely he knows that."

"Are you mad at him?" MJ asked.

"I think I am." Lacey pondered her cousin's question. "He just convinced me to move all the way out here and then to move in with him and now he's just going to up and leave me? And with no discussion?"

"What the hell are you talking about? He did discuss it with you, Lacey Baby."

"No!" Lacey cut her cousin off. "He's already made up his mind to go. He invited me to come with him. But, no, he did not discuss it with me." Lacey yelled.

The women sat holding the line before one of them spoke again.

"Lacey, you're being a brat about this. This could be an opportunity of a lifetime for Oliver. You complain about his lack of ambition and then when he asserts himself, you complain about that, too. A talented and caring man loves you and wants to take you to France with him for his big shot and you're bitching about it? You are unreal!" MJ took a breath to calm herself.

"Lacey, whether you go or not, you have to support him - enthusiastically! Do you understand me?"

Lacey knew her cousin was right, but the whole thing hurt so badly. She didn't want to lose him to France or lose him due to her childish insecurities, and especially not now. She felt physically ill over the mere thought of Oliver being half way around the world, experiencing new things and meeting new people without her - and growing more and more away from her. She took her glasses off, pulled the covers over her head and cried herself back to sleep.

*****

"It would've been cool to have you around a little longer." Oliver admitted as he steered his truck into the busy airport. "I know Izz would love to have seen you for longer. For him to be the convict, he's by far the most emotional one of us."

Benji and Oliver laughed about their big brother. He was indeed the most loving of the Barnett brothers.

"I'll be back soon. I promise." Benji assured his little brother. "I think I'll try to get the kids from their crazy ass mommas and make it a Spring Break trip or something."

"Momma would love that. But, you know she's going to spoil those kids when she gets back to Ohio. She may give me a break now that she knows how to get her hands on her grandchildren."

Benji chuckled at the thought. He was very thankful that his family was whole again and wanted a relationship with his children. He loved the idea of his children having grandparents who loved them and fussed over them.

"You know she's going to make up for our childhoods through them. God be with their mothers and other grandmothers." Oliver laughed heartily. "Man, you have no idea how smothering she can be since she's sober and making up for lost time. Thank you for having kids for her to smother."

"Speaking of having kids," Benji laughed. "Are you and Lacey trying to keep her condition a secret?"

Oliver nearly drove his truck into a barricade.

"What the fuck are you talking about, Man?" Oliver exclaimed.

He tried to look at Benji's face and keep his eyes on the traffic ahead of him. Benji was equally as stunned by his younger brother's reaction.

"O, are you serious? I know I'm the baby maker of the family, but damn! I saw it as soon as I got in this truck two days ago. She's glowing like the fucking North star and her tits look like they're going to explode. And those mood swings yesterday...Man you're about to be a daddy."

All of the images that Benji mentioned flashed through Oliver's mind and all of them glared at him prolifically.

"She was upset yesterday. I'd just told her that I was going to take a gig in France for a few months."

Oliver pulled up to the Departures curb and banged his head against the steering wheel. His throat threatened to close and he could hardly take a deep breath. Benjamin pat him on the back.

"Damn, O. I hate to leave you like this, but I thought you knew. And now you're leaving the country?" Benjamin sat with his brother and tried to comfort him.

"What the fuck!" Oliver hit the dashboard. "I can't leave her now. Why now? Nothing ever goes right for me! Just when I take a step forward, I take two steps backwards." He exploded.

Benjamin smacked Oliver across the head with his open hand and grabbed him by the collar. "You? Nothing works out for you? Man up, O! Do you think a classy broad like Lacey wants to be pregnant and not married? Hell! Her folks can barely stand to look at you about their little princess and you think this is something she wanted to happen? Like this? Hell no! Did she ask you not to take the job in France?"

Oliver shook his head no.

"Exactly! Look, I don't really know Lacey. And I can't even say that I know her type. But, from what I can tell, she's put herself out there to be with you – so don't get all in your feelings about what goes wrong for you. You live in a beautiful home with a beautiful woman who is way out of your league. You have friends who love you and you do something that you love to do. You told me that Lacey doesn't sweat you about money and shit like that. And you don't even have a regular job. Do you? I'm sorry, O. But to me little brother, it looks like you're the one winning. I'd bet Lacey's freaking out, which is why she hasn't told you, yet."

Benjamin leaned over to meet his brother's far away gaze.

"Just go home and talk to her. You tell her that you know and that you've got her back. Now get yourself together, because I've got to catch this plane to get back to work. I don't have a sugar Momma who takes care of me." Benjamin teased.

Oliver shot his bother an icy glare.

"Don't even joke about that. I take care of my damned self! I pull my weight." Oliver yelled.

"Chill out! I was just fucking with you. I love you, Little Bro. I'll call you in a few days to check on you."

He hugged Oliver again and was gone as quickly as he had appeared days earlier.

It was a miracle that Oliver made it back to the city without smashing the truck into a highway divider. His mind whirled like a Dervish. *What kind of game was she playing? Was she playing a game? Should he mention or let her mention when she was ready? Should he turn down Chef Black's mentorship?* Oliver knew that this was a situation he had to keep to himself and handle himself. He drove the truck into their private two car garage and turned the engine off, but he sat in the truck running through his options. He settled on asking her right away. He called Lacey from the garage.

"Hey, Lace. Is there something you want to tell me?" he asked with painstaking care.

Lacey was groggy from her despair induced slumber. She wiped her eyes and felt around for her glasses, before answering Oliver.

"Babe, I'm very proud of you and I don't ever want to stand in the way of you following your dreams. I'm not going to lie, I know I can't go to France for three months, and I'm going to miss you something awful – but I'd never ask you to choose." The corners of Lacey's pouty mouth turned down. "So, I'll support you in any way you need me to. Congratulations." She said half-heartedly.

Lacey's answer to his question confused him even more.

"What are you talking about France for, Lacey? I want to know if you're pregnant?"

"Pregnant! Lacey popped up. "What are you talking about? Why would you ask me that, Oliver?" she yelled at the phone. But something in his question jarred her. She had been feeling queasy, anxious and really tired. But all of the rushing around for the Holiday season, in addition to getting moved into the new place easily explained those symptoms. But there was also the breast tenderness and bloating, which was normal around that time of the month – which had not come, yet! She sat up and swung her legs to the hard wood floor.

"Oliver! Wait. What? Why are you asking me that?" She cried pleadingly.

He heard the terror and tears in her voice and knew that he'd just dropped a bomb on her, too.

"Babe, calm down. Benji said some shit that got me thinking. I'll get a pregnancy test. Okay?"

Lacey couldn't speak and only shook her head. Warm, salty tears dripped from her chin into her lap. It was though hearing the words signaled her womb and it wrenched. She vomited on her bare feet.

"Lacey, calm down, Love. I'm on my way up! Stay with me. Okay?"

Lacey stayed glued to the spot on the edge of their queen size bed, holding the phone to her ear and watched the pink lumps of vomit ooze from her feet onto the white fur rug. Oliver was at the bedroom door in seconds. He ran to her side, climbed onto the bed and held her until her trembling settled. She looked at Oliver and then back down at the mess on the rug.

"Let me clean up this mess." She said calmly. She stood to her feet and staggered.

Oliver held her up and asked her to get back in bed. She obeyed him and climbed back under the covers. He reappeared with a basin of warm water, soap and a washcloth. He removed her glasses and cleaned her up. He cleaned up the floor and removed the bedcovers.

"Babe, listen we don't know anything right now. I'll go buy a pregnancy test and something for you to eat. Something you can keep down. OK, Lace?"

He sat beside her and looked into her usually glittering eyes, to find them completely flat and brimming with tears. She had slipped into some kind of trance, which completely freaked him out. Lacey was always operating. She was always two steps ahead. She was saucy and cunning and always ON. Seeing Lacey in such a vulnerable state made him feel guilty about thinking maliciously of her intent.

"Lacey, please snap out of this, Babe." He pleaded with her. "Whatever happens, we're in this together, which means it'll all be good. I love you. And we're going to be fine. I promise you." He looked for his words to register in her eyes. She gently nodded and tried to force a smile. With that, Oliver stood to leave. She grabbed him by the hand.

"Please don't tell Cami." She begged of him.

She noticed Oliver's brow furrow and confusion flash across his face. "I just want to keep this between us, until we can decide what's best." She explained desperately. She angrily dropped his hand. "Don't look at me like that. You're with me! This is between you and I, goddamn it!"

And just like that, the old familiar Lacey was back. Oliver silently complied without further discussion and left the room. Over two pregnancy tests and Jump at De Sun's Ten Spice, Cashew and Vegetable soup, the verdict was in—Oliver and Lacey were having a baby.

****Le temps passe****

CHAPTER TWENTY

Baby, Melodrama.

"So, how's Luca adjusting to Marseille?" Lacey asked, as she stretched her legs and stared out the window of her office. Tobias walked in and whispered to her that her parents were there. She nodded and returned to her, and Oliver's daily call.

"He loves being on the water. But, I gotta tell you Lace, between Momma and Madame Mathilde he is going to be hard to deal with when he gets back stateside."

Oliver laughed and nervously twisted at the strands of his short afro. He still loved Lacey so much it physically pained him every time he heard her voice. Three years, and half way around the world hadn't dulled the power she wielded over him.

"Trust me I'm used to it." She laughed too. "Every time he and daddy go fishing he begs my mom to make him a bouillabaisse, like Madame Mathilde makes with the fish she gets from the Port. It gets her so worked up!"

"I bet you like that." Oliver smiled.

"You know I do." Lacey sang. "How are you, Oliver? Are you still fending off people calling you Olivi-Aye? I know how much you hate that name."

"You know! These people really want to change my name. Don't they," he laughed, rubbing his hand across his head. "But, I'm still that little shelter kid from Ohio."

They laughed easily for a while and then the mood turned solemn.

"You're not going to marry that dude. Are you, Lace?"

Oliver asked.

"Funny. I would have never guessed that Tobias would be the thing that got you and Lennox to agree on something," she said.

"How are his face and ribs healing after that beat down my brother Ali put on him?"

"Really Oliver? That was almost two years ago. Grow up!" She blushed.

"Alright. Alright." Oliver laughed a little longer, before settling down. "But seriously, Lace, you can't marry him. Anybody but that lame ass dude. He doesn't deserve you. He didn't in High School, and he doesn't now. I can't even understand what you're doing with him! And having him around our son," he said, shaking his head. "Lace, the whole deal is ludicrous. You've got to know that!"

Lacey sighed deeply and spun around in her leather office chair. She smiled flirtatiously. Oliver's jealous tirade pleased her to some degree. When Tobias called her and asked her for an opportunity to apologize for how he had handled her pregnancy in high school, she agreed, partly because she was lonely and in a dark place. Oliver had just served her with a court order for joint custody of Luca, which clearly sent his message--he was done with the cat and mouse games. And moreover, he was moving to France without her.

Tobias had made a good life for himself and was exactly the kind of guy with whom Lacey had always imagined herself. He was living in Atlanta and was on the fast track at his firm as an entertainment attorney. He was romantic and sophisticated. He looked great and had earnestly made every effort to make amends for his past wrongdoings. He was politically engaged and goal oriented. And to top off all of his attributes, her mother loved him. She'd practically handpicked Tobias as her daughter's replacement for Oliver. Oliver had hardly settled in Marseille when Tess reached out to his mother for his phone number.

"Anybody but him, huh? How about you? Are you still on the menu, Mr. Barnett? Or does Gigi have your heart?"

"Ha! There you go. And you know her name ain't Gigi. You also know that my heart belongs to but one. I can't ever see myself asking another woman to marry me."

The line fell silent. Lacey often replayed Oliver's proposal and her prideful refusal. It wasn't romantic or at all the way she'd always imagined her proposal would be. She'd just pee'd on the last pregnancy test when he stumbled over to the tub's edge and buried his head in his hands. She'd always remember the way his locks covered the entire top half of his seated body. He looked up at her, his eyes filled with tears. "Don't worry," he'd said. "I'll marry you. I'll do the right thing," just like the immature child he was back then.

"If memory serves, you didn't ask this woman. You offered me a life vest that you deemed I needed," Lacey snapped. "Let me speak to my son, Oliver!"

Any time the proposal conversation came up, the pleasantries ended. Oliver greatly regretted the way he'd handled that entire situation. He was scared and his knee jerk reaction set all of his progress to melt Lacey's heart back centuries. In an instant, right before his eyes, Oliver witnessed tall, glossy sheets of ice completely encase the love of his life's heart – in that instance, he knew that she was gone.

"I'll have him call you. Mix took him and his little friend,

Augustine sailing today. Momma said she told you about it when she talked to you yesterday."

Tess walked in and found her daughter red faced and teary eyed. She walked over and rubbed her shoulders, startling Lacey. Lacey hurriedly wiped at her eyes and put her glasses back on her face.

"Yeah, she mentioned something about Mix being excited about teaching him to sail," she calmly said and told Oliver she'd look forward to hearing from Luca later on, before ending the call. Tess closed the office door and pulled a chair from the corner of Lacey's office. She sat knee to knee with her daughter and took her by the hands.

"Lacey, be true to yourself." She put her forehead to Lacey's forehead. "If Oliver is the man you love, then love him. Yes. Tobias is the kind of man I've always dreamed of for you. He's accomplished. He's handsome. And he's from a good family."

"Mommy." Lacey interrupted. "He's not perfect."

"No one is. Neither are you, Love." Tess gently chastised her daughter.

"I know Mommy, but Toby hurt me years ago." She hung her head and cried aloud.

The primal sound that shook her daughter's body shocked and terrified Tess. She fell to her knees and hugged her sobbing daughter tightly.

"Lacey Baby. Baby. What are you talking about, Baby? How did he hurt you?"

Lacey couldn't speak. Uncontrollable sobs and hiccups wracked her. She couldn't reconcile which truth discomposed her more – that Oliver was the man she loved and had pushed away or that she was sleeping with the man who had carted her off to an abortion clinic and walked out on her as she slept.

"I got pregnant in high school." She sputtered. "He took me to Birmingham for an abortion and just left me. Mommy he left me sleeping on the living room couch! I hadn't heard from him until you gave him my number."

Lacey's words, was struck her mother silent. She fell to her bottom and searched her brain for images of the last night she'd seen Tobias at her home. She searched her brain for clues that she missed that signaled her daughter's distress.

"Lacey," she cried. "Baby, what? When? How did this happen? Have you kept this to yourself all of these years?" Tess's cries matched Lacey's.

"Mommy please don't cry."

"I pushed you and pushed you. And you were carrying this all by yourself," Tess cried.

"Mommy please don't blame yourself. I didn't have to carry it alone. Lenny knew. I told him."

The day Lennox told her and Tommy that he had to go back to school immediately came to her as freshly as if he'd said it minutes before. She clearly recalled scratches and bruises on his hands. But, she casually attributed the scars to his boxing and asked no questions about them. She got to her feet and pulled her daughter into an intense embrace.

"I'm so sorry, Baby. I am truly sorry for my part in this hurt that you've been carrying." She tilted Lacey's face and looked deep into her usually bright and clear, now blood shot eyes. "I'll fix this. I'll do whatever it takes. Mommy's going to handle it." She promised.

When Lacey had washed up and got down the stairs of the luxury loft she and Oliver once shared, Tobias was nowhere to be found and only her mother and father were there.

******

Oliver couldn't recall more splendid sunrises than the ones that shone through his second floor bedroom. They peaked over the horizon, where the Mediterranean Sea met the sky glowing brightly with golden shades of peaches and blues. Farai's crown of voluminous curls tickled Oliver's bare shoulder rousing him completely awake. He sat up and pushed his back against the cool bare wall quietly, trying not to wake her. He loved watching her sleep. Her dark reddish brown skin reminded him of terra cotta planters. It was during her slumber that her high forehead and chiseled cheekbones best displayed the distinct array of deep cocoa colored freckles that dotted her face. He melted when a sexy smile crept across her wide mouth, lifting the lone freckle that sat just above the right corner of her top lip, the fuller of the two.

"Bonjour ma chérie."

Oliver lay beside her and kissed her gently on the mouth. She smiled widely and rolled over.

"You got in late last night."

Oliver got out of bed and pulled the French doors that led to the terrace closed.

"Oui. It was a magnificent show. I wish you could have made it, mon amour."

"Me too, but we had a late party at the bistro. You want coffee or do you want to get some more sleep?"

"I want more of you."

Farai patted the empty spot on the bed where Oliver had just left.

"Viens ici," she purred.

Oliver shook his head and shrugged.

"I don't know what you said. You're going to have to translate that one for me."

She giggled and stretched, "Sois mon petit ricain. My American boy. I said, 'Come here'."

He raised an eyebrow and gave a cocky nod.

"OK! Now that, I understand."

He jumped back into bed and kissed her again. She raised her hips to meet the stiffness between his legs and pulled the gauzy lounge pants he was wearing down with both, her hands and her feet. Farai's sexual appetite was insatiable. She wanted it no matter what time she showed up on Oliver's doorstep. She wanted it when the sun rose and she wanted it "once more" before he left for the bistro. He enthusiastically obliged her desirous nature.

Marseille was arguably the epicenter of the French Hip Hop scene and Farai Sekibo was one of its biggest stars and recognizable social activists. She performed under the name, Baby Melo—which was short for melodrama. Oliver found her moniker quite ironic. After years of dealing with the likes of Camilla, Cami and Lacey, he knew melodrama and Farai was the antithesis of the word. She was a late blooming tomboy, much like Cami had been, with only one feature distinguishing her from the neighborhood boys - her long and wild mass of curly hair. What once made her miserable, was now her signature - her calling card. Coupled with her pronounced Ethiopian features and distinctive freckles, she commanded a cult like following.

He'd met her shortly after his first few weeks in France.

She'd sauntered into his corner bistro with a lively entourage and wearing big round sunglasses. She looked every part the star. She wore a knee length white fur, sleeveless duster over an olive green military style field jacket and bell-bottom jeans. Her mane of soft corkscrew curls flowed freely around her entire torso like an oversized halo. Oliver couldn't take his eyes off of her every graceful move. The way she bit the corner of her plump lower lip, whenever their eyes met made him thicken in his chef pants. He instantly fell for the smoky quality of her voice and laser quick cadence of her French. Her laughter was easy and melodious. Her heavy lidded, bedroom eyes danced between her dinner guests and the kitchen window, where Oliver stood directing his line cooks. He served her table that night and had her over for breakfast, the following morning.

Oliver sat at the tiny, wrought iron table on the terrace and quietly watched a nude, Farai run globs of coconut oil through her wet hair. He loved her hair. He'd never seen a woman with so much hair. Her hair stretched far below the curve of her back, but just below her round bottom and womanly hips. The thick, kinky ringlets cascaded over her proud shoulders and firm breasts. The morning sunlight danced off of her smooth brown skin. He laughed when she broke yet another wide tooth comb, as she meticulously detangled her mane. She playfully cursed him in French and tossed half of the broken comb in his direction.

"You want some help with that, Babe?" Oliver asked coyly and took a sip from his cup of honeyed green tea.

The South of France's Viuex Port was the heartbeat of Marseille and accounted for the city's rich culture and diversity, which instantly drew Oliver in. Though Marseille was the second largest city in France, just behind Paris, its tranquil squares and souk-like markets were what Oliver loved most about his new home. He'd spent his first summer in France under the mentorship of Chef Black and had thoroughly loved every region he toured, but it was the old Port of Marseille that had captured Oliver's heart. While working in Provence, he'd imagined exploring St. Vincent's Abbey and the Bar de la Marine with Lacey and their soon to be born child. He pictured the two of them visiting the fishmongers along the Vieux Port for the daily catch and picnicking at Prado Beach on Sunday afternoons. In his mind's eye he'd already picked out an authentically French villa situated in a peninsula about three minutes from the sea. There would be a large terrace and a private garden with an unobstructed view of the sea, a large living room with a fireplace, because the winters were cool on the water and a study for Lacey, when she came to her senses - and he fully counted on her coming to her senses.

Despite how busy Oliver stayed during his work-study in France, he returned to Atlanta just weeks before the birth of his first child just as he had promised he would. Oliver and Lacey's seven-pound son, stormed into the world with a head full of straight black hair and his mother's hazel eyes. Oliver named his son Luca. Not for a famous scientist, like he and his brothers were named, but he did keep with the scientific theme. LUCA was the acronym for the Last Universal Common Ancestor, which was the evolutionary theory of a single cell that's believed to be the organism from which all life evolves.

One balmy summer night after closing, Oliver shared the origins of he and his brother's names with a dishwasher named Arnaud. Arnaud was a budding French geneticist who worked at a bistro in Normandy with Oliver by night to fund his studies of genetic coding and its popular tree of life. In the dark the bistro's dining room, the men passionately discussed the theory of L.U.C.A over a bottle of pear cognac. Oliver loved the idea that every living thing he saw was related and wanted his son to feel completely connected and never alone in the world, the way he so often felt as a child and as a young man navigating what felt like a very lonely world.

Despite Lacey's repeated refusals to legitimize their new family, Oliver was sure that when she held their son, she'd abandon her prideful stance and marry him. He was sure she'd do what was best for their family. But, she wouldn't budge on her decision to raise Luca alone. Oliver enlisted all the help he could recruit to reason with her. Ali pleaded with his obstinate sister, her father came to Atlanta to talk to his daughter and MJ had practically stopped speaking to her, out of sheer anger at her cousin's perceived ungratefulness. All of which further enraged Lacey and emboldened her resolve to raise their son alone. Lacey had it in her head that their child would hold Oliver back from experiencing his full potential on the World's culinary stage. She had sincerely convinced herself that she was doing what was best for Oliver, because she loved him. She was deathly afraid that Oliver would one day resent her and their child if she married him and consequently kept him anchored to Atlanta. After another rejected proposal for marriage, another year of bickering with the mother of his child and another year of living in Atlanta while being forced to live apart from Lacey and Luca, he could simply take no more. Oliver heavy heartedly accepted an offer to run his very own kitchen in his beloved Marseille. He took Lacey to court to formalize their joint custody agreement and left the country.

CHAPTER TWENTY-ONE

Daddy Dearest

Madame Mathilde Lepère was truly French. Her family hadn't immigrated from Greece or Italy or even from Corsica. She was born and bred, French. She stood out because of her smile. She was chatty and had a self-effacing sense of humor. She showed up to dinner late and never over dressed for a soiree. Unlike many of the other French women Oliver had encountered, she was warm and approachable. She wasn't overly sophisticated, and didn't hate Oliver's accent. She found it very cute. She was instantly intrigued by the single Black American with the long ropes of hair, who worked very late hours, played the piano and always waved to her as he climbed the steps to his two-story apartment. The French relationship with privacy was complex, and her husband begged of her not to be bothersome. But her curiosity overcame her French sensibilities and her husband's requests. After only two or three weeks of learning her new neighbor's name, she had him over for dinner.

Mathilde wasted no time before pointedly inquiring as to why he always seemed so forlorn. And as equally as pointedly Oliver painstakingly told Mathilde all about Lacey and their disheartening end. He proudly showed her pictures of Luca and told her he'd be spending his summers and every other Christmas in France with him. And since French women thought themselves the best at everything, especially at the art of love, she heaped unsolicited advice on him regarding how to win Lacey back, at every opportunity.

"Oli-ver, you must not give up on your love. Run after her! Call her every day. Send her flowers."

"All the way from France, Mathilde?" Oliver chuckled and took a sip from his tea cup.

"Yes! Especially from France! Women love to be chased. You must seduce her at every opportunity. Not like you Americans do—no! But through conversation, tell her how the scent of the sea over these beautiful roses you have here, keeps you up at night longing to have her here, with you. Tell her how you love to hear her voice when she answers your call. Oui? Do you understand?" She probed.

Oliver belly laughed at his overly dramatic neighbor. But, he took note of her suggestions.

"She doesn't want to be married. Well, at least not to me. And I'm cool with that, Mathilde."

"Pssh!" She dismissed Oliver's claim with an elegant, well-manicured hand. "You Americans are so foolish. Marriage is not a be-all and end-all. It is not the only responsible or loving way of bonding, Oli-ver. French men fall in love ten times a day! And you seem to have fallen in love a lit-tle, with the beautiful young woman with the hair." She dramatically drew big ringlets in the air. "Who keeps very late hours? Oui?"

She didn't wait for his response. She nodded authoritatively ending the day's lesson.

"I must go now. But, I have a lovely duck for dinner tonight." She pressed a kiss on Oliver's cheek. "Bonne soirée mon ami. I will call. And you will come to pack up les restes. Oui?"

Oliver nodded in agreement. He'd learned that it was pointless to refuse her, leftovers or well-intended advice.

Valentina and Mix accompanied Luca to France every

time the little boy crossed the sea to visit with his father. He was growing like a weed and was as sharp as a whip. Although, Luca had never known his parents to live together as a couple, he knew that he didn't like the idea of his mother dating. Luca mentioned his mother's friend Tobias on more than a few occasions during his visit. He spoke of his mother's new arrangement with great importance.

"Dad, you've got to do something! He's over all the time."

"Well, Luca. Your mom's a grown up. And she's allowed to have friends." Oliver said evenly, as he basted dough on the butcher-block countertop.

"Uncle Lenny doesn't like him."

Luca sat propped on a bar stool watching for his dad's reaction.

"I heard Auntie Cami telling him to try to give Mr. Tobias a fair chance. She said that mommy is lonely because you're so far away." He tossed over the countertop.

"Should you have been eavesdropping, Luca?"

"I don't know what that means. Is it French talk?"

Oliver laughed at his crafty little four-year-old. He reminded him so much of Isaac. He missed his brother every time Luca stirred up mischief.

"No, it's English. It means to listen in on conversations not meant for you. But, what else did your Auntie say about mommy and Mr. Tobias?" Oliver prodded.

"Nothing, because they stopped talking when I dropped my book."

"Do you miss your cousin when you come here to visit me?"

"Not really. She's so bossy. And she always calls me a

baby! And I'm the oldest. Right Daddy?"

Both Luca, and Cami's daughter were just over a year apart and they'd named her Lena. Luca and Lena were a matched set in the family and Oliver hated missing out on their lives growing up together. Ali and Cami had been over twice since he'd settled in France. She'd promised to make the trip at least once a year and had kept to the deal.

"What are you handsome Barnett men cooking up for dinner tonight?"

Mix and Valentina showed up in Oliver's little kitchen, through the French doors that opened to the garden. She and Mix insisted on staying at a hotel during their two week stay. She thought it very important that Luca and Oliver spent alone time together. Mix playfully rubbed Luca's sandy brown hair and climbed into a pub chair at Oliver's long, narrow kitchen table. He grabbed an orange from the fruit bowl and asked Luca had he told his father about his first sailing lesson. He had in vivid detail. He'd went on and on about how his Grandpa Mix had let he and Augustine take turns at the tiller, watching the wind and running the sailboat. Oliver was grateful for the change of subject.

"O Baby, you really need some color in this place. Everything is just so white!"

"Ma, it's not my place."

"I know, but you're living here. Which reminds me. Have you thought anymore about buying a place here?"

"No, Ma. Why do I need to own a house over here?"

"Over here, huh?" She ruffled his twisted afro and lifted the lid of pot on the stove top. "Sounds like he's here for a visit. Doesn't Mix?"

Mix chuckled at his meddling wife and popped another orange segment into his mouth. He winked at Luca who was sitting beside him.

"Why do you always have to try to pull Mix into your mess, Woman?"

"Thank you, Oliver." Mix chuckled.

"What mess? I'd just like to have my son plant some roots. Somewhere!"

Oliver pointed to a bowl of ice cubes on the kitchen counter.

"Luca, get ready with the ice."

Luca hopped off the tall chair and ran over to grab the silver bowl of ice cubes; he had filled just before his grandparents had shown up.

"I'm ready, Daddy!"

Oliver opened the hot oven and slid the sheet of baguettes onto the upper rack. Luca slid the bowl of ice onto the bottom rack and shut the oven door. Oliver held his hand up high and Luca jumped to high five it.

"Good job, Lukey Dukey!"

"Daddy, I hate it when you call me Dukey! That's disgusting!"

Mix and Valentina laughed wildly.

"My bad, Little Man! My bad."

CHAPTER TWENTY-TWO

Sunrise

Cami and James had come along way over the years, since her mother's death. He was quite the doting grandfather and Evangeline was absolutely smitten with her granddaughter who was named after her. Cami thought it fitting to name her daughter after all of the matriarchs in her life, Camilla, Ms. Tess and Evangeline. It had been Evangeline who'd been at Cami's side through her entire labor and delivery. Holding her hand, coaching her through treacherous contractions and assuring her that Ali would make it in time. Ali nearly missed the entire birth. He jetted from California to Atlanta in an absolute panic and just made it to cut Camille Evangeline Jackson's umbilical cord.

James and Evangeline hosted a most beautiful third birthday party for Lena at their home. The proud grandparents draped every square foot of their stately Collier Hills home in shades of pinks and yellows. The party was fit for a princess. Dozens of James and Evangeline's family and friends joined Ali, Cami and Lena for a lunch of corn dogs, BBQ chicken, Baked Beans, Macaroni and cheese and peach tea. The Robinsons made the trip from Alabama and a few of Lena's classmates and their parents attended. Amidst a full out pink and yellow circus themed birthday party, complete with pony rides and carnival games, the DaCostas and Robinsons fawned over their only granddaughter. Cami missed Oliver's presence so much, but she was immensely proud of him. Watching him blossom was both pleasing and heartbreaking for her. She hated the idea of him leaving his son and Lacey, but she was also proud of him for taking control of his life and no longer allowing Lacey to manipulate him. Surprisingly, Ali was in full support of Oliver taking the job in France and helped him as much as he could without completely alienating his baby sister.

"Did you have lots of fun, Princess?" Evangeline asked.

Lena pranced and twirled in her hot pink and yellow tutu and tipped her top hat to her grandmother Evangeline.

"Yes, Ma'am! And the ponies were my favorite part! I wish Luca could've been here."

"We'll be seeing him in a couple of weeks and you can tell him all about the party. Okay?" Ali assured his daughter.

"Camisha, can I talk to you and Lennox before you head out?" James squeezed Cami's shoulder and nodded to Ali.

The serious tone in his voice concerned her. She looked to her husband for a clue. He looked as clueless as she was. Ali and Cami followed James around the grand spiral staircase at the center of the house to his study. James's office was just as one would expect a man of his position to have – an elegant and classic man's study. The tall walls were covered by raised dark wood paneling, custom cabinetry and topped by inlaid amber ceiling tiles. He directed the couple to a shiny round table in the corner of the decidedly masculine room. Cami sat at the table admiring all of the special touches around the room. The pale blue leather chairs with their odd shape and high backs, the antique brass and lapis globe that sat in the corner, the abalone and mother of pearl flower pot with the most beautiful Phalaenopsis orchid she'd ever seen and finally her eye fell on a gold picture frame that held a picture of she and Ali standing at the altar, during their wedding. The picture sat prominently displayed alone on one of the built in mahogany bookshelves beside his desk.

"What's going on, Mr. DaCosta? I feel like I've been called to the principal's office."

Cami gently laid a hand on top of Ali's and fiddled with his wedding band. Her father laughed nervously and handed Ali a glass of cognac.

"What can I get for you, Baby?" He warmly asked Cami.

"I'm fine. Please, sit down and tell me what's going on."

He sat down beside his daughter and took her by the hand. He smiled at her.

"So you know that Carl was cleared of any involvement with your mother's accident, but I haven't given up on finding out what happened to her."

"Yes. I know all of that." She hurried him along with a nod.

"Well, we have another lead. We were able to track down the owner of the vehicle. Well, the address to where the vehicle was registered." He corrected himself. "The car was registered to an elderly couple named Anderson in Sandy Springs."

"Okay." Cami nodded.

"I went to their home myself to meet with them. They said that the car involved in the accident belonged to their daughter." James took a sip from his glass and wiped at the water ring it left on the table. "And that's where things got weird."

"How so?" Ali asked.

"I asked to see a picture of her. And Camisha," he turned to his daughter again. "She looks exactly like your mother--the way I remember Camille as a young woman."

His voice trailed off. The accusation sent chills up Cami's spine and she squinted.

"What do you mean, exactly like her?" Cami stuttered.

"Do you have a picture?" Ali interrupted.

"I do. I took a picture with my phone."

Carl pulled his phone from the breast pocket of his blazer and pulled the picture up. He handed the phone to Ali.

"Wow! Cam, look at this." Ali's voice trembled, making Cami afraid to see the picture. He pulled his chair closer to her and handed her the phone. The face that stared back at her made her stomach lurch. The woman in the picture had Camilla's light eyes and wavy hair. She had Camilla's smile and the same troublesome glint in her eye that taunted, "I know something you don't know." Cami dropped the phone and looked to Ali for some kind of reasonable explanation. He shook his head in disbelief and held tightly to his wife's hand.

"Her name is Sunrise Anderson—she's a year or so younger than you. Camisha, do you have any idea who this woman is?"

Cami had never seen her before, other than in her own mother's face. She wracked her brain for any recollection of Sunrise. Any run-ins with her on the train or at the shop – anywhere! But, she came up with nothing. Cami was shaken and needed answers.

"How does she fit into Camilla's accident?" Cami pleaded with her father.

"I don't know, Baby. But, I'll find out. You have my word. I'll get to the bottom of it. Cami had Ali put Lena to bed when they got home, while she called Oliver. She figured he'd just be closing up the kitchen and heading home. He answered on the first ring.

"What's up, Cami Cam?" He whispered into the phone.

"Oh my God, Oliver. I forgot about Luca. Did I wake him?"

"No. But, hold on. Let me go out back."

Oliver quietly closed the patio doors behind him and sat at his little garden table with a beer.

"What's up?"

"My dad tracked down the owner of the car that hit Camilla."

"And." Oliver prodded. "Was it on purpose or an accident? Did he know Camilla?"

"It was a she. And she looks just like Camilla, Oliver. I mean just like her, down to the wickedness in her eyes."

"Wickedness, Cami? Damn!"

"You know exactly what I'm talking about, Ollie. You know that look!" Cami insisted.

Oliver struggled to understand what his best friend was telling him. He walked into the kitchen, listened for Luca and took a joint from a coffee can when he was sure that Luca was still sound asleep. Oliver lit the joint and kicked his feet up on the second chair. He took a long drag from the joint and blew circles of smoke into the salty night air.

"Hello. Oliver are you there?"

"I'm here." He coughed. "Let me get this straight. A lady that looks like Camilla may have hit her. Right?"

"Yes."

"How old is she? Did Mr. D talk to her?"

"No. He talked to her parents. She's about my age and he only saw a picture of her."

"Then how'd you see her?"

"He took a picture of the picture with his phone. Oliver, I'm stomped. Do you think she could be related to me?"

"Hell, I don't know. Did Camilla have any family in Atlanta? Where was her family?"

"I have no idea. That was another of her no fly zones. She never had any family that I knew of." Cami lamented.

"Damn. You okay? How are you holding up? What are you thinking?" Oliver fired questions at her.

"I don't know. I just want all of this to be over. First it was all of the Carl stuff and now this!"

"I'm sure. I wish there was something I could do."

Oliver took another drag from the joint and put it out on a garden paver.

"You know, Ollie. Part of me wishes he had never started this investigation. Does that sound awful?" There was an aching pleading in her voice.

"Not at all. You've been through so much, Cam. You should want some resolution. Hell!"

Ali came into the family room and sat beside Cami. He put her feet onto his lap and began massaging them.

"What's up, Oliver?" Ali said towards the phone.

"Tell him I said, 'What's up'. I guess that's my cue." Oliver chuckled. "I'ma let you go, but Cam everything is going to be fine. And you know I'm here if you need me. Plus, I'll see you in a couple of weeks."

"Oh yeah! About that. Ali is trying to convince Lacey to come with us. You know she and Tobias didn't work out?" Cami dished.

"How could they have? That was ridiculous of her anyway." Ali interjected.

"True, that!" Oliver agreed. "That would be cool. I'm sure Luca would enjoy having us all together. He's sorry he missed Ms. Lena's birthday party, too. But we have a little something planned for her visit."

"OK." Cami smiled. "Will you call her, and extend the invitation? That way she won't feel like she's intruding. You know?"

"Not a problem. I'll call first thing in the morning."

"OK. And then call me." She sang. "Oh and Ollie please, don't be a douche. Tell Farai that Lacey's coming. Got it!"

"Got it! Call you after I speak to Lacey and don't be a douche. I'll tell Farai as soon as she shows up. OK, Boss Lady?"

"Shows up." Cami laughed. "You two. Boy have you met your match! Good night. I love you, Kid."

Oliver laughed too. He knew that he had indeed met his match in Farai.

"Love you too. Goodnight."

Oliver hung up the phone and smiled at the bright crescent moon whose light danced along the bay. He couldn't wait to see his family in a few weeks. Then the minor detail of having Lacey meet Farai plucked at his delight. They would have to meet at some point, which was the inconvenient truth of the difficult decision he and Lacey had made for their lives and the life of their son. But, Oliver had never played out the scenario in his mind. Lacey never came to France and Farai never traveled to America with him. She'd met Luca early on in their relationship and they were fast friends. She'd met his mother and Mix and they too loved her. Cami and Ali had briefly met her, while at the bistro one afternoon on their last visit to Marseille. But, Lacey had not. He'd been very honest with Farai about his connection with Lacey and how he'd once hoped they could be a family. But that was all before he'd met her – astrologically, his perfect love match. A little factoid of which she loved reminding him.

Farai Sekibo was Oliver's match in so many ways, and she didn't take any of it casually or think it was happenstance.

"It's very important for me to know everything I can about a man before I get involved with them." She announced their first time together.

"OK." Oliver played along, as he kissed her neck and shoulders.

"Who's your favorite artist?" She asked breathlessly.

"Musically?"

"Yes." She panted.

"Bob Marley. What about yours?" He countered.

"Prince." She licked and nibbled at his ear, making his erection rock hard.

"Good one." Oliver grinded between her spread legs. "Your favorite song?" He mouthed against her open mouth.

"Darling Nikki." She answered and seductively crooned a few lines. "I met a little girl named Nikki, I guess you could say she was a sex fiend. I met in a hotel lobby masturbating in a magazine." She rubbed at Oliver's stiff cock and licked his bare chest.

Oliver held himself back a little to look into her desirous eyes and smiled. Her singing voice was as equally sultry and bluesy as her speaking voice. His head swam with astonishment at his good fortune and kissed her deeply. He reached into her pants, but she grabbed his eager hands stopping him.

"What's your birth sign, Oli-ver Barnett?" she asked.

Oliver couldn't believe her timing and thought she was being coy. But when she held his hands to the couch and sang into his ear,

"They don't say that love's written in the stars for no reason, mon chéri."

He looked into her eyes to make heads or tails of her intentions and she softly bit his bottom lip.

"So?" She kissed him again. "Your sign."

"Aquarius." Oliver breathlessly answered against the discomfort of his throbbing manhood. Farai pulled him into a passionate kiss with one hand and unbutton his cargo shorts with the other.

"Oh perfect," She purred against his lips. "I've been waiting for you, Oli-ver." She moaned against his eager mouth with a sexy giggle. "Vous êtes parfait mon amour – You are my perfect love."

"And you're a nut." Oliver laughed and helped her get his shorts off and a condom on.

In that moment, he knew for sure that their courtship would be an adventure.

Farai was nothing like Lacey. She was very forthcoming and direct. She knew exactly what she wanted and made know game of letting the people around her know it. She was both, free spirited and socially conscious at the same time. She was a very busy woman, but always kept her "Oliver time" sacred and unmoved. She was just easy. Which was exactly what Oliver required after all of the battling and maneuvering he'd experienced with Lacey. Farai's key in the door startled Oliver and the shadow of his form in the garden startled her. He stood and met her in the kitchen.

"Bonjour." Oliver greeted her with a soft kiss.

"I get French at this hour? OK." She shrugged and smiled. "Bonjour."

"Oui. J'adore to sourire." He unwrapped the scarf she was wearing around her neck and kissed her exposed collarbone and shoulders.

"My smile, eh? Com'on now, Oliver. What's all of this about?" She turned her head to allow more wet kisses to her neck and décolletage.

"Let me take you in the garden." Oliver teased with undeniable cockiness.

"Say it in French." Farai ordered with a haughty tilt of her head.

"Umm, au jardin?" Oliver stumbled over the phrase.

"Meh! Close enough."

Farai stepped out of the red and white maxi skirt she was wearing and leapt into Oliver's arms.

He carried her through the patio doors and sat on the little garden table. Farai pulled at his chef pants, straddled his thighs and guided his erect cock into her wet slit. Oliver removed the silk tank top she was wearing and kissed her breasts hungrily. Her brown skin sparkled in the moonlight and the scent she wore intermingled with the saltiness of the sea. She let her hair down out of its high chignon sending it cascading over hers and Oliver's bodies, heightening all of his senses. They held one another as closely as two bodies could be without conjoining and she rode him to a vigorous climax.

The spent couple laid on the chaise lounge in the garden, wrapped in each other's arms quietly watching late night boaters and early morning fisherman head out to sea. He kissed her high forehead and flushed cheeks from time to time and she kissed his chest and toned abs in return.

"So are we going to talk about what's going on, Oliver?"

Oliver adjusted himself and then he adjusted her in his arms.

"Do you want to smoke?" He answered instead.

"No. I want to know what's bothering you."

He took a deep breath and yearned for a smoke.

"Lacey is coming to pick up Luca this time."

"Oh."

Oliver didn't know what her, "Oh" meant so he sat quietly to learn more.

The early morning birds had begun chirping and delicate dew drops had begun releasing the perfume of the juniper bushes and lavender that dotted Oliver's small garden.

"Did she say why?" Farai softly asked in the dim twilight.

"She's coming with Cami and Ali. Did I ever tell you that she and Cami's husband are brother and sister?"

"No. I don't think I knew that." Farai sat up and pulled her top on. "I think I will take that smoke now. Do you want something to drink?" She asked from the kitchen.

Oliver called in to her for a bottle of water.

"Flat or Fizzy?"

"Flat. S'il vous plait."

Farai rolled her eyes as she stepped into the skirt she'd left pooled on the kitchen floor.

"Maintenant il parle francais!"

Oliver didn't understand her words, but he was very clear about her tone. He knew that he would have to talk fast and address all of her concerns completely and earnestly. When she returned she was balancing a round tray filled with a bottle of water, a glass, rolling papers and their mystical coffee can. He took the tray from her hands and gently pulled her into his lap.

"Farai, I want to be with you."

Oliver moved her hair to one shoulder and kissed her on the back. He meant it with every fiber of his being.

"You chose me and you didn't have to. Babe, you have to believe me. I don't take that lightly."

He kissed her again and felt her relax under his touch.

"Lacey will always be a part of my life and yours, as long as I am. I was wrong to think I could keep the two of you completely separate. And now I fear that I've made her seem unreal to you."

"And am I unreal to her, Oliver?" Farai asked.

"No. And that's what's unfair. She's coming here knowing that I have you. And knowing who you are to me. She can just look you up on the internet to see you working and talking and moving about your world. She can read interviews to know more about the way you think. The things you care about. But for you, she's the great unknown. She's but a faceless, voiceless character in the story of my life—my past. For you she only has a name and a relationship to my son. And that's why I waited up for you. I found out tonight and wanted to tell you first thing."

Oliver's words were thoughtful and beautiful, but Farai was a passionate and feeling woman who was falling in love with him. She needed more. She slid off of his lap to sit beside him on the lounger. She looked him deeply in his eyes. He didn't look away.

"Do I have to stay away while she is here?"

Farai's question floored Oliver and his face gave it away. His reaction gave her great comfort.

"Of course not!"

He wrapped his arms around her curvy waist and pulled her closer. He rested his chin in the crook of her neck. He loved the way she smelled.

"FiFi, you are the woman I want. I want you to show up just the way you normally do. You have the key for a reason. Use it just as you normally do. Like a tomcat slinking into my bed at all times of the night." He playfully nuzzled at her neck.

Farai blushed and kissed her lover gently.

"Are you sure?"

"I am more than sure. I hope you can make some time to spend with all of us. It's very important to me for you to get to know Cami. She's a very important part of my life. And so is Lacey. She's Luca's mom."

Farai's full lips spread widely across her freckled face in a brilliant smile.

"OK. I'll clear my week." She took his face in her hands and kissed him again. "But, I already have a show booked for that Saturday night. Maybe you could bring them? I'll make everything very special for them."

Next, it was Oliver who smiled broadly at her generous offer and nodded humbly.

"I'd like that very much, mon cher. You are the best, Farai Sekibo!"

He laughed loudly and tickled her.

"Hush now! Shh! You'll wake Luca." She giggled and kissed him quiet.

CHAPTER TWENTY-THREE

Pen Pals

Isaac looked forward to Lacey's weekly Summer time visits more than anything he could recall in his life. She showed up every Sunday with updates on his nephew and his youngest brother's escapades and adventures in France. He could hardly wrap his mind around one of them living in France, running his own restaurant and dating a "semi-famous" as Lacey reported, rapper. He didn't even know France had rappers. His brother was living a charmed life, and he was very proud of Oliver. But, Oliver's new life was tearing Lacey apart and consequently, wrenched at Isaac. On some deeply private level, Lacey's longing for Oliver made him jealous. She put up a good front, with a stiff upper lip, but Isaac had grown to know her very well, through their one on one visits, phone calls and written correspondence.

Since his nephew's birth, Isaac and Lacey talked at least twice a week, once over the phone and then on Sundays. But it was the letters they shared that truly connected them. The letters shed the most light on who Lacey Robinson really was. Lacey excitedly checked her mail every Monday for letters from Isaac, and he eagerly awaited mail call for her letters to him. She unabashedly shared so much of herself with Isaac Barnett, as he was an attentive and comforting listener. He acted as her counselor and as her friend. She had told him things about her that she had only shared with MJ, and some things she hadn't.

Lacey had grown exponentially through her friendship with Isaac Barnett. He knew all about her fears and her dreams.

It was through her letters to Isaac that she realized how much she'd looked forward to someday walking down the same aisle that her mother and aunt had walked down in their weddings. And how crushed she was to face the painful fact, that she had probably ruined any chance at her own walk down that hallowed aisle, when she pushed Oliver away. He knew about her insecurities and her shortcomings. She'd told him how deeply she resented her brother for leaving her to care for the family business, while he went on to build a life for himself. She recalled how envious she was of his and Cami's budding romance. Lennox was living on his own terms and had met someone who her mother loved and was settling down. All while she was left behind tethered to their family's responsibilities, with no prospects and no hope of ever leaving Flatrock Branch, Alabama. Lacey remorsefully wrote to Isaac about how she had intentionally tried to sabotage her brother's relationship. She thought, in some twisted way that if he remained single, some day it would only be the two of them growing old together and she'd somehow be indemnified for his abandonment. She thought she would always feel regretful for how poorly she treated Cami, but had never admitted it to anyone--not even to Oliver. She didn't think he'd ever forgive her for intentionally hurting his best friend. However, Isaac absolved her of the guilt with three written words, *no one's perfect*. There was nothing off limits in the letters, not even the abortion. She'd opened up to Isaac about just how scared she was as a teenager, when she closed her eyes against the suctioning sounds of the machine that ended any chance at life her first baby had. She was completely vulnerable through her letters to him, and he was completely receptive. He never made her feel judged or unworthy.

Isaac appreciated the letters and visits. He too had grown very fond of the mother of his nephew. Despite his best efforts, Isaac's affection for Lacey teetered between familial and romantic. He found Lacey to be open and thoughtful, not cold and superficial, as she seemed at first. He found her to be very funny and easy to talk to. She was a great mother and fiercely loyal. He saw through her tough exterior and understood why she felt the need to hide behind it. In spite of all of their differences, Isaac and Lacey thoroughly enjoyed being together and deeply relied on one another.

"So are you ready to meet Baby Melo in person?" Isaac poked fun at Lacey.

"I guess so." Lacey frowned.

Isaac tenderly touched her hand. Lacey smiled appreciatively, softening her features.

"How do you think she'll be? Are you going to stay at Oliver's?" he fired questions at her.

"She seems nice," Lacey shrugged. "And Luca loves her! And I don't know. I may stay there. I'll just play it by ear. Oliver thinks it'll be good for Luca if I stayed with them."

Lacey pushed her glasses up her nose and looked down at the scratched metal tabletop.

"Are you nervous or anything? I mean she kind of comes and goes as she pleases, when she's in town. Right?"

She twisted her full mouth and nodded.

"I know. He's gone over the whole situation with me. She'll be around that week, and according to Oliver, she's really looking forward to getting to know all of us." Lacey mocked the enthusiasm in Oliver's voice.

"Damn. That sounds serious." Isaac remarked.

"Well, you would know that better than I."

Isaac scratched his head and smirked at Lacey.

"I don't know, Lace. He still would love to have his family there with him, but you made the rules and he's just playing the hand you dealt."

"I guess." Lacey mumbled. "But you do understand why I chose this don't you?"

"I know why you think you had to choose this, but I hope you've learned that you can't control people Lacey. And you can't plan their lives for them. Right?" He bent his head to meet her lowered eyes.

"He would have ended up resenting me and Luca if he had stayed here, in Atlanta. You know that France was what was best for him."

"I'd bet he feels differently," Isaac countered.

"Now, we'll never know. He loves Gigi, or whatever her name is. And she seems perfect for him. She doesn't try to change him. She thinks he's perfect just the way he is – although he has a real goals and ambitions now – none of which he had when he was with me!"

Isaac chuckled at Lacey's petulance.

"He had a goal to make you his wife and raise his family in one country, under one roof. But, you knew better than my aimless, runaway little brother. Right?"

"That's not fair, Izz." A tear rolled down Lacey's face. "I did what I thought was best for him. He deserved someone to think about what was best for him, for a change."

Her defense landed more like an accusation and Isaac sat up straighter in the little round metal seat and slowly rolled his strong, muscular neck. He didn't expect Lacey to understand his choices. She had had a very different childhood than he and his brothers had.

Isaac was a child when he found himself thrust into the role of breadwinner and caretaker of his two younger brothers. Growing up on Scovill Avenue in Cleveland was no easy feat for boys like the Barnetts. They were easy targets for the neighborhood hustlers and drug dealers. Everyone on the block knew that their mother was a crackhead, who disappeared for days on end, leaving them to fend for themselves. Isaac and Benjamin were threatened and propositioned everyday on their ways back and forth to school. With the limited options for a thirteen year old to feed and clothe his younger brothers, Isaac took to the drug trade. He was crafty and resourceful, qualities that catapulted him to the upper echelon of moneymakers around Scovill Avenue. They also made him a prime target for both law enforcement and rival dealers, numbering the days to his downfall.

Isaac vividly remembered the day he was busted. All he could think of while he lay face smashed against the hood of a City of Cleveland police cruiser, was would his younger brothers remember where he hid the emergency stash, in case he was ever taken away or killed. His mind raced with worry during the entire search of his home and person about them remembering everything he'd tried to teach them about surviving without him and about taking care of each other, and their mother. He never once thought of himself or of his own future. He only thought of his baby brothers and his mother. He couldn't hold Lacey's veiled accusation against her, because there was no way she could ever understand how much he'd prepared for and thought about what was best for Oliver. He shuddered slightly, but dismissed Lacey's perceived insult without further discussion.

"Look, Lace. If you feel like letting Oliver go to France without you and Luca was your best option, then that's that. You don't owe anyone any explanations for your choices, because you have to live with the consequences. Right?" Isaac conceded.

"So what are you going to do, at this point? Let him ride off into the sunset with that sexy ass Baby Melo?"

He managed a forced chuckle.

"Ride off into the sunset? Really? You're so lame! Enough about me," Lacey playfully slapped the stainless steel tabletop, lightening the mood. "How are you preparing for your release?"

"I'm *not* preparing," Isaac clasped his large hands together on the table. "I expected to be out of here before Luca was born," he raised his hands above his head, "but here I am three fucking years later. So forgive me for being pessimistic."

Lacey took his hands in hers and looked him deeply in the eyes. She smiled at him and patted his hands.

"Well forgive me for being cautiously optimistic. I can't wait to have you out and a regular part of Luca's and my life," Lacey beamed. "I have work ready for you; so that's something to look forward to. Right?" She nudged his knee with her own. "Do you know how many people in your position can't find a good paying job when they get out?"

"Yes, Lacey. I know." Isaac grumbled, but smiled a little. "I know how blessed I am to have you looking out for me."

"Yeah! You just remember that when you get out. You'll owe *me*, not Oliver! He'll try to get you to come to France, but I swear, if you leave me, I'll make you pay. And I'll make it hurt!"

"See! It's people like you who are the real criminal geniuses and you're just out in the world roaming around, voting and shit!"

Lacey and Isaac laughed. She always felt better after an hour or so with the oldest Barnett brother. The two hugged. Isaac's head swirled a bit from the scent of her perfume. They held onto one another until a guard loudly cleared his throat.

"Safe travels and don't forget to take lots of pictures," Isaac said and lightly kissed the backs of her hands. Lacey promised to send him pictures of their time in Marseille and made him promise to call Oliver during her visit to France.

CHAPTER TWENTY-FOUR

Bienvenue

The South of France was every bit as beautiful as it looked in books and on TV. The blues seemed bluer and the greens seemed greener, but nothing was more spectacular than the sparkle in her baby boy's eyes when he spotted her and raced towards her with his little arms stretched out to their full length.

"Mommy!"

Luca yelled as Lacey burst through the wrought iron gate that surrounded Oliver's two-story townhouse. Oliver and Farai stood arm in arm at the front door, waving them in. They looked very sophisticated. Oliver wore his hair in a short twisted Afro and had put on what looked like about ten pounds of what Mr. Robinson called, grown man weight. He looked mature and heartbreakingly handsome. He was in his standard khaki green cargo cut off shorts; Adidas flip flops and a faded black t-shirt, which read, "Don't remove the kinks from your hair. Remove them from your brain. - Marcus Garvey". Lacey was taken off guard by how much she'd missed him. Her heart sank into her gut and she swallowed hard against a large lump that setup in her throat. Farai's trademark curly mane was piled high atop her head and wrapped in what looked like one of Oliver's old gray t-shirts. She was wearing a body skimming, navy and gray striped cotton maxi dress. Her perfectly firm breast and shoulders shimmered beneath the spaghetti straps and the leather gladiator sandals she was wearing were stunningly chic. Though Lacey had watched hours of YouTube videos of Farai Sekibo, none of them did her cocoa colored freckles and striking Ethiopian features justice. She absolutely glowed. Her genuine warmth and openness drew Lacey and the others into her long outstretched arms. She greeted each of them with an embrace and a kiss on each cheek.

"Bienvenue! Come in. Come in. It's so hot this time of day. Oliver has prepared kir royales for aperitif and a very big meal for lunch. He's so excited to have you all here. So am I."

Oliver hugged his guests one at a time before scooping little Lena up into his arms and covering her chubby face in kisses, as she wriggled and giggled in his arms. Luca walked in last wrapped around his mother's legs with a smile as wide as the Marseille Bay. After washing up and settling in, they all gathered in Oliver's open air kitchen and sat on either side of his long kitchen table to Farai's favorite Ethiopian meal. She insisted on helping Oliver prepare lunch. She and Oliver prepared a traditional Doro wat - a chicken-based stew native to her parent's country. The stew was thick and rich, getting its intense shade of red from the dark red blend of sun-dried chiles, ginger, garlic, cardamom, nutmeg, cloves, cumin, and coriander. The chili flavored stew was chock full of dark meat chicken and a whole boiled egg. They served the wat with a vegetarian platter and Orange San Pellegrino for the kids. The afternoon was a success and Oliver eagerly awaited Mathilde and Henri's evening visit.

The adults lounged around the garden, watching the children play a game of tag and sharing bottles of white wine. Farai laid beside Oliver on the chaise lounge, Ali and Cami sat at the Oliver's tiny garden table while Lacey sat crisscross on a blanket in the grass in the shade of a lime tree.

"Oliver your backyard is beautiful. It's like you're all grown up now."

"I can't take credit for it, Lace. Mathilde is the gardener. You'll meet her tonight."

Lacey watched quietly as Oliver twirled locks of Farai's hair around his fingers. She was a beautiful young woman and her French-ness made Lacey crazy with jealousy. Every time she slipped between speaking English and French Lacey's top lip twitched. Or whenever Oliver touched her the way he used to touch her or called her Fifi, Lacey thought it just about all she could stand and she hadn't been under the same roof with them for four hours, yet!

"Oli-ver is being modest. He knows everything that's growing out here." She added in her singsong French accent. He smiled down at her and kissed her on the forehead.

"Enough you two! Jesus, Oliver. You're so French now. Gone is my little bro from Ohio." Cami teased him.

"Nah, I'm still the same old O. Just ask my momma!" He laughed easily.

"How is Ms. Valentina?" Ali asked.

"She's fine. She's the one that's so NON-Ohio these days." Oliver answered.

"Non- Ohio? I don't understand that." Farai said to Oli-ver.

He explained the phrase to her in a quiet side bar.

"Is the language barrier a challenge between you two?" Lacey asked.

"Not at all." Farai fired back. "He's learning French and I speak English fluently."

"She speaks four languages. Right, Babe?" Oliver gushed.

"Yes."

Ali kept a close eye on his baby sister. He knew that seeing Oliver in a serious relationship would be tough on her, despite her solid act.

"Really? Which languages are those?" Lacey asked.

"There's French and English, of course. And there's Oromo and Amharic, which are both dialects native to my parent's country of Ethiopia, so I count them as one and lastly I speak Italian, but not properly, I'm sure. I have several Band members who are either Italian or Corsican, and they're hardly proper." She laughed.

"That's impressive, Farai." Ali joined in. "I'm sure you travel a lot with your music."

"Yes. I enjoy travel though, so it doesn't feel like work to me."

"That can't leave a lot of time for you and Oliver. I mean between him running a kitchen and your world travels, how do you make it work?" Lacey probed.

"Love always finds a way." Mathilde's strong French accent chimed in as she and Henri came through the kitchen door. "Bon soir mes amis! Oh no! Valentina and Mix did not come? I was so looking forward to seeing them again." Mathilde breezed through the garden giving kisses and hugs to everyone. She reached out to Luca and he rushed into her arms.

"Bon soir, mon cheri!"

"Bon soir, Grandmere! Please meet my cousin, Lena."

Lacey was both shocked and impressed by her son's impeccable manners when greeting Madame Mathilde. Oliver picked up on her surprise.

"Mathilde insists on children being absolutely well behaved. It's the only way for the French." He chided Mathilde. Henri laughed heartily.

"Oui, Oli-ver! You have her pegged, indeed." He laughed again.

"Pssh, Henri!" She turned her sites to Lacey. "And you must be Lacey. You are a very lovely woman. A vision. It's truly a pleasure to finally meet your acquaintance. I've heard so much about you. Luca just goes on and on about his mother with the eyes like his."

Lacey smiled confidently and intuitively glanced at Oliver for his reaction.

"It's a pleasure to finally meet you, Madame Mathilde. I can't thank you enough for being so good to my little guy."

Luca wedged himself between the women and hugged them by their legs. He beamed like a ray of sunlight.

"Hush now. The pleasure is all mine. Luca is a very special little boy. No one can resist loving him!"

Mathilde swept Luca up into her arms and twirled the giggling and squirming child around.

"Breakfast is at the main house tomorrow morning! I insist! And I want you to bring the kids to the Ferris Wheel tomorrow, it's at Prado Beach in the Summertime. I'm sure Farai could bring you all. In the shed, we have more bicyclettes."

With her final instructions and a theatrical adieu, Madame Mathilde disappeared with her husband in tow.

Luca and Lena were pooped after their day at the beach. They'd frolicked along the sea and rode the Ferris wheel. Following a picnic lunch with Madame Mathilde Lacey, Cami and Farai carted them home and loaded them onto the daybed in Luca's bedroom. Cami was wiped, and excused herself for a little nap, too. Farai jumped in the shower, while Lacey checked her e-mails. The sun was relentless in the South of France and hung high in the sky for what seemed like forever. Lacey walked out of the bedroom to find Farai standing quietly on the second level overlook. She appeared to be listening to something downstairs. Farai pressed a finger to her full lips.

"I understand that you're with Farai now, and I'm happy that you're in a good place, Brother. Trust me. I am. All's I'm asking is that you, kind of tone down the PDA while Lacey's here."

Ali's voice was low and authoritative.

"Ali, you've grown on me. You're like one of my own brothers, but you can't come into my home and dictate how I act. You're a guest, my invited guest."

Farai and Lacey couldn't see the guys, and neither of them moved or made a sound.

"Look man, I promise you. I'm not trying to dictate anything," Ali said, with a chuckle. "But, I'm going to look out for my sister. She's been through enough and," Oliver cut him off.

"Whatever Lacey has been through has been of her own making. Lacey's not a victim. She's a goddamn puppet master."

"O, I know how hard you tried to do the right thing. I know how much you wanted your family to be together. Hell, I probably know better than anyone else. We were all rooting for you and Lacey to make it. But things didn't work out that way. and yes, she was the conductor. But I know my sister. She thought she was doing what was best for you."

"I didn't need her to!" Oliver exclaimed. "That's not what I needed from her. I needed her to be my wife. Or I thought I did." He briefly examined his past desires. "Ali look, I'm a grown ass man! I knew what I wanted. But of course, she knew better. She *always* knows better. I'm just a poor little runaway with no roots, no ambition and no prospects to her. I always was and I always will be." Oliver's voice broke a little.

Farai looked at Lacey, who in turn put her head down. Neither of them moved from their spots on the overlook.

"She loved you, Man. I think she still does. Back then she convinced herself that you would have resented her and Luca if she accepted your proposal and you stayed on in Atlanta. We all knew that France is where you wanted to be. And no one blames you for that. Man, you made yourself! And you are living out your passion. Not many people get that opportunity. Lacey knew that and didn't want to stand in your way." Ali explained.

"I made a home for her and Luca, here. She knew that. I waited for her to put our family first, but she's so damned prideful. She kept telling me to go on with my life. And then she goes and hooks up with Tobias!"

"That was all Mom. Mom orchestrated that whole mess."

"No! Lacey allowed it. She brought him into my son's life. Into my son's home. She did that. Not Ms. Tess." Oliver was yelling again.

There was a pause in the conversation. Lacey's eyes filled with tears and she put a hand over her mouth to muffle her sobs. Farai reached out and took her by the hand.

"I love Lacey. I probably always will."

Lacey gently squeezed Farai's hand.

"But, Farai is the woman I want now. I love her." Oliver considered his words. "She believes in me. She makes me believe in myself. She thinks I'm good enough, just the way I am.

Lacey saw me as a project - a fixer upper. She had to mold me to fit me into her life. Not, Farai. Farai and I just fit. I know you get that."

"I do. And I respect that."

"Well you have to respect that this is Farai's home too and I'm not going to ask her to alter herself in anyway, in her own space, to placate Lacey. Your sister made a choice, and her choice worked out for me. I'm not going to feel sorry about that. I hope Farai will be a part our lives for a long time. So she's going to have to get used to her." Oliver laughed a little. "Hell, I've actually enjoyed having us all together under one roof."

"Don't go all sister wives on us, now." Ali laughed.

"Hell naw! Lacey was more than I could handle one on one." Oliver fired back.

"I like Farai. I think Lacey does, too, but I know it stings to watch you love another woman. But, you're right. I overstepped and that's my bad. Are we cool?

"We're cool."

The men dapped each other and hugged.

Farai and Lacey stood glued to their spots on the overlook, understandingly staring at one another. Lacey nodded respectfully at Oliver's girlfriend and Farai responded in kind.

The visit went much too quickly for Oliver and his heart wrenched as he loaded Luca and Lena into the backseat of the driver's Range Rover. He took a deep breath and kissed his son lovingly.

"I love you, Little Dude."

Oliver fought back tears, as he mussed the kinky twists of his son's Mohawk.

"I know that, Daddy,"

Luca smiled, bobbing away from his father's roughhousing,

"You better know that."

With his pudgy little toddler hands, Luca took ahold of his father's hand.

"Don't cry, Daddy. Ms. Farai will take good care of you." He leaned forward, looking around Oliver to see Farai.

"Yes, I will." Farai affirmed with a smile. She leaned in and kissed Luca and then Lena.

"I'll see you soon. Okay?" Oliver said.

"I know. At Christmastime. Will you come too Ms. Farai?"

Oliver took Farai by the hand and looked to her for her answer to Luca's question. Her freckles darkened as she fought back tears, too.

"Of course," she managed. "I will block the entire month for you, mon petit amour."

Oliver turned to Lacey, who stood beside the car door watching the goodbyes. He hugged her.

"Thank you for coming. I think he needed to see us together, as friends - as family."

She breathed him in deeply. His scent painfully took her back to his hovel of a studio apartment in Little Five Points, where they first made love. She still loved him deeply. Her eyes filled with tears.

"You've done well for yourself, Oliver. And Farai is a very lucky and smart woman. I'm happy for you. I truly am." She whispered in his ear. "I love you."

"I love you too, Lace. Call me when you guys get home."

Lacey watched Oliver and Farai, wrapped in each other's

arms until they were out of sight. She sank into the back seat of the truck and surrendered to her broken heart's soul stirring cry.

CHAPTER TWENTY-FIVE

Homecoming

Lacey's heart raced as she turned into the Federal Prison. She recalled the first time she'd passed through the tall gray walls. She'd always found it odd that the prison looked more like a historic library than a penal institution that house hardened criminals. Moreover, she was going inside of a United States Federal Prison to visit her bohemian boyfriend's brother, something she could have never imagined for her life. The cold gray building that once terrified her had become a place of solace for her. It was where she turned to when she needed to alleviate the stresses she buried deep inside of herself. It was where she turned to, in order to make sense of her world when it was dismal and bleak. It housed one of her closest friends and her confidants, and today it would set him free.

Isaac's chiseled features and sparkling brown eyes seemed more pronounced seeing him in the light of day. He was wearing the dark jeans and gray V-neck merino wool sweater Lacey had brought him for his release. He lit up and waved excitedly once he recognized Lacey and his mother behind the tinted windows of the white Porsche. Valentina nearly jumped out of the car as Lacey drew closer to where Isaac was standing holding a clear plastic bag and a manila folder.

"My baby!" She cried wildly.

Her cries were almost primal. She held Isaac tightly and rocked his six-foot frame back and forth. The scene brought tears to Lacey's eyes behind her tortoise shell sunglasses. She stood back a ways allowing the mother – son reunion to play out in its own space and time. Isaac hugged her next, lifting her off her feet and kissed her on the cheek. Something shot through her, making her feel exposed and a little ashamed.

"I swear you two are the best thing these eyes have seen in twelve years!"

Valentina hugged her son again. The smile on her face illuminated the already stunning woman, making her beauty almost unbearable to the naked eye.

"Let's get you out of here!" She cheered. "Oliver and Benjamin are going to be so surprised!"

Valentina sat in the backseat and cried the whole ride to Lacey's house.

The townhouse was buzzing with activity. Lacey's parents and MJ were there along with Mix, Ali, Cami and Lena. Cami and MJ were in the kitchen slicing and dicing, while Ms. Tess busied herself rearranging Lacey's Christmas tree ornaments. The men were working through a tangled mess of Christmas lights and the children were sprawled across the blue vintage, Egyptian Kilim rug coloring in giant coloring books. Donnie Hathaway's, *This Christmas,* was playing over the sound system and the place smelled of smoked turkey and Ms. Tess's apple pie when Isaac walked through the door. He willfully fought back tears as he skimmed the room full of strangers. Mix walked over and embraced his stepson.

"Welcome back, Isaac. Merry Christmas, son."

Cami dried her hands on the apron she was wearing and introduced herself, Ali and Lena.

"It's truly a pleasure to finally meet you, Isaac." Cami held back tears and hugged Isaac as if she'd known him her en-

tire life. “Now. We’re complete.”
Isaac held on to her until she released him first.

“Benji was right. You are the consummate little sister, aren’t you?” he smiled. “Makes me want to thump O even more for keeping you hidden away.”

They all laughed. Arms intertwined, Lacey introduced Isaac to the rest of the family. Luca stood behind his grandfather’s legs peeping at the tall stranger.

“He looks like Daddy.” He whispered through a small smile.

Isaac smiled and kneeled to Luca’s eye level.

“You must be Luca.” He held out his large hand to Luca. ‘I’m your uncle, Ike. Your daddy is my little brother.”

“You know my daddy?” Luca’s big hazel eyes lit up.

“I do. I used to take care of him when he was your size. I’m his big brother.”

Everyone laughed at Luca’s obvious bewilderment.

“OK. OK. OK, everybody. Let’s let Isaac get settled. I’m sure he could use a moment to catch his breath,” Lacey ordered. “Let me show you to your room,” she almost whispered to him.

Isaac followed Lacey up the wrought iron staircase to his room, with Valentina tearfully looking on. He looked around the fine room Lacey had setup for him and sat on the edge of the bed.

“Lacey, I can’t thank you enough for everything you’ve done for me.”

Lacey stopped him. She sat on the bed beside him and put a hand on his muscular thigh, but quickly moved it away and smoothed a lock of her honey brown hair.

“You have no idea how much you’ve done for me over these past few years, Isaac. You’ve helped me through some really dark times and you've always been nothing but honest with me. That's hard to find in people. You know?" She looked him in the eyes and nervously pushed her glasses on her nose. "You never judged me for or treated me differently after the poor way I handled my relationship with Oliver. You never took sides and I appreciated that. So, you owe me no thanks. This is all my way of saying thanks to you. We're family and I've got you."

They sat in the bedroom shoulder to shoulder listening to all of the holiday cheer downstairs. Isaac looked into Lacey's eyes. Time seemed to stand still for him. He recalled the many times and ways he'd imagined being so close to Lacey, in her home. *In her room.* A knot formed in his throat. He tried to speak, but the crash of breaking glass cut through the uneasiness between them. Lacey jumped to her feet and scurried to the bedroom door.

"Well, you get settled or whatever and I'll see you downstairs," she said and darted out of the room. She stuck her head back through the door. "You really do look a lot like Oliver." And darted off again.

Lacey ran to her bedroom and closed the door behind her. She walked into her dressing area, removed her glasses and splashed cool water on her flushed face.

"What the hell is going on with you, Lacey Robinson?" she scorned her reflection in the lighted mirror. "That Oliver's brother! Luca's uncle! I know you're from Alabama, but damn girl. Pull yourself together!" She wiped at her face again and brushed a little loose powder under her eyes and across her nose. She held a cool wet towel to her neck and ran her fingers through her fluffy, blunt bangs. "Get it together, Lacey Robinson."

She stopped by Isaac's room and asked if he wanted to eat or take a nap before Benji and Oliver arrived. He declined both options, but followed her downstairs to join the others. Valentina signaled for Isaac to come sit beside her in the living area. Isaac sat beside his mother and began answering the barrage of questions tossed his way. His smile was enigmatic and he was as charming as Oliver had always warned. Lacey poured herself a glass of Pinot Grigio and took a slice of smoked turkey from the platter it was being piled up on. She bellied up to the kitchen island and watched her guest be beguiled by Isaac Barnett.

"What's that look in your eye?"

MJ cozied up to Lacey and whispered over her cousin's shoulder.

"You smell good. What's that you're wearing?"

"I don't know. Chanel Mademoiselle?" Lacey snapped.

"And lust!" MJ snapped back. "Whatever flighty notions are floating through your head—shake 'em! That's his brother. What the hell are you thinking?"

Lacey jumped up and snatched her cousin by the arm. She led MJ through the side door to the courtyard.

"What are you talking about, Mary – Anthony? You shut your mouth. Right now! Do you understand me?"

"No! I don't. Do you want to know what I'm talking about or do you want me to shut my mouth? You're all jacked up right now, Lacey Baby!" MJ shook her head disapprovingly. "I can't believe you."

"What! I'm not doing anything. Nor will I--ever!" she said, lowering her voice. "I'm just trying to help him get on his feet. He was so solid throughout everything. I just want to help him."

The chiming of the doorbell halted the conversation.

Laughter and cheers exploded inside, signaling Oliver and Benji's arrival. The brothers walked in to hugs and tears all around. The Barnetts were all together again.

Farai looked amazing with her famous mane coifed in larger than life curls. She was dressed in stylish black ankle length leather trousers with a black cashmere sweater layered over a crisp white button down and spiked pointy toe flats. She smiled graciously, as she was ushered from one embrace to another. Oliver, Isaac and Benjamin beamed and wrestled around like ten year olds. Cami rescued Farai and escorted to where MJ and Lacey were in the kitchen, Ms. Tess followed closely behind. Farai shyly greeted Lacey and asked for directions to the restroom. When Ms. Tess was sure Farai was out of earshot, she gasped,

"Oh my sweet Jesus, she looks like a movie star or model or something!"

"She is a looker," MJ chimed in. "And that accent!" It seemed as though Farai was the topic on everyone's lips.

"Little Bro, goddamn! Does she have specks of gold on her face?" Isaac laughed wildly.

"And she's a rapper!" Benjamin added.

"A sexy one! O, man how do you do what you do?"

"It's the food thing," Ali chimed in.

Lacey rolled her eyes, but couldn't stifle a giggle or two. Farai breezed back into the kitchen settling the hysterical laughter.

"They were talking about me. Weren't they?" she whispered to the circle of women in the kitchen, in her easy way.

"Yep!" MJ answered starting the uncontrollable laughter again. "No one's ever seen a star this up close and personal."

"And I didn't even know there were real Black French people." Isaac admitted.

"Or Black people with freckles." Mr. Robinson added nonchalantly.

"So I'm completely blowing your minds!" Farai retorted, good-naturedly.

The men all laughed and nodded wildly. Oliver reached out for her to join him and she did. They were a beautiful couple.

Oliver and Farai said bedtime prayers with Luca and snugly tucked him into his bed, before joining Lacey, MJ and Isaac downstairs.

"You've changed a lot of things around here, Lace. The place looks great."

Oliver sat on the floor at Farai's feet and rested his head on her thigh.

"Thanks," Lacey answered flatly.

"So what are your plans? Where are you staying Izz?"

"Here, for a while. Momma wants me to come back to Ohio for a visit, but I don't know about that." Isaac answered, with a quick glance at Lacey.

"Here? As in Atlanta? Or here; as in here at Lacey's?"

Oliver's tone and facial expression gave away his disapproval. He sat up.

"I don't know, man. I just got out this morning!" Isaac exclaimed.

Oliver squinted at his brother and then at Lacey who stood up under Oliver's gaze.

"Anybody want anything while I'm in here?" she asked casually.

Farai ran her hands over Oliver's shoulders and the back of his neck.

"No thank you, Lacey. I think we're all fine over here." Farai answered.

"Daddy and I want to give Isaac a shot at running our first cleaners here in Atlanta. He did run his own business in Ohio—essentially," Lacey said, defending her decision.

"That's great!" Oliver said. "I think he'll be great at it. But I'm sure Mix and Momma can set you up with a place here in Atlanta. They've wanted to buy something down here anyway."

MJ sat quietly watching and listening to what was being said and to what was not being said.

"Ok, Dude. I'll talk to them about it before they leave."

Satisfied with he and his brother's agreed upon arrangement, Oliver said his goodbyes.

"Alright, Babe. I think we'd better head over to the hotel." Oliver patted Farai's thigh and stood to his feet. "It's getting late and I want to be back over here before Luca wakes up."

Farai stood up and gathered her things. She hugged MJ, Isaac and Lacey.

"MJ. Are you staying here, too?" Oliver asked.

"I am, Sir." MJ answered cheerfully and kissed Oliver on the cheek. "It's good to see you, Brother."

"Same here. I've missed you," he said, hugging her once more.

"Well, we'll see you all in the a.m. Lace. Can I speak to you outside?" Oliver asked.

Lacey followed Oliver out to the courtyard and pulled the doors closed behind her.

"What's up?" she asked casually.

"Please don't be cavalier right now." Oliver warned her. "What the fuck was I sensing in there?"

Oliver looked sternly into Lacey's eyes. He recognized the glint of fire flash in them, but didn't back down.

"I don't know what you *sensed*, Oliver. Why don't you tell me what you *think* you sensed?" Lacey seethed over her crossed arms. She shifted her weight to one leg and defiantly glared back at Oliver.

"I hope I sensed nothing, Lacey."

"Me, too!" She fired back.

"Jesus, Lacey I don't want to fight with you. I just." He stopped short and raised his hand to her. "I don't know. Fuck it! Whatever, Lace. Do you." He threw both hands up and turned back to the house. "See you in the morning."

"See you then, Oliver!" Lacey hissed through clenched teeth.

Lacey tossed and turned all through the night. The nerve of Oliver to accuse her of some kind of impropriety enraged her. The nerve of him to bring *his* lover to *their* home for Christmas and flaunt her French-ness around *her* family was barely tolerable, but then to accuse her of something as distasteful as desiring his brother. She could hardly contain her outrage.

The sun hadn't broken the horizon before Lacey stomped downstairs to MJ's room to wake her.

"Can you believe the nerve of Oliver?" Lacey asked as she barged into MJ's bedroom.

MJ rubbed at her eyes and struggled to sit up.

"What did he say to you out there?"

"He asked if he *sensed* anything between his brother and

me?" She scoffed.

"Hell! He did. We all did, Lace."

"There is nothing! There is nothing to sense! Oh my God, MJ. What am I thinking?"

Lacey climbed into bed with her cousin.

"Did you know you had these feelings before he got out of prison? PRISON, Lace. Let me remind you—he just got out of *prison*!"

"There are no feelings. I don't know. Maybe," Lacey shrugged.

"You know that this all just crazy. And he can't live here with you and Luca." MJ leaned forward to look into her cousin's eyes. "You do know that. Right, Lace?"

"Yes. I know it, but I swear to you, I only want to help him out. Really. With no strings attached." Lacey insisted.

"OK. That's all fine and dandy, but keep it at that."

"I know. And I am so ashamed of myself. I don't know what has gotten into me."

"You lost Oliver. He looks like Oliver and he's been a captive audience for you over the past three or four years. That's all." MJ wrapped her chubby arm around Lacey's shoulder and Lacey cuddled up to her cousin. "You'll get all of this figured out. And everything will be just fine. I know they will."

Lacey watched her cousin peacefully drift off to sleep. She lay in the bed beside MJ with the covers pulled to her neck, inspecting the unexpected feelings she was experiencing for Isaac. Sure she thought he was attractive. He was undoubtedly the most handsome of Valentina's sons. And he had the whole "bad boy with a heart of gold" thing in spades. But he was Oliver's brother. Oliver practically worshipped Isaac, and Isaac loved Oliver. She was absolutely befuddled by the emotions that were swirling around inside of her. She quietly slid out of her cousin's bed and went to into the kitchen.

Isaac was sitting at the head of the giant dining table, and stood when she turned the corner. Lacey tightened the belt of her silk robe.

"You're up early." Lacey smiled.

"I'm trained." Isaac replied.

"Do you drink coffee? Oliver and Cami are total addicts," she giggled nervously.

"I do."

Isaac walked into the kitchen and hoisted his athletic figure onto a stool at the kitchen island. He pushed up the sleeves of his pajama shirt, exposing his toned forearms. Lacey pretended to not see them. She passed him brushing against his knees. She reached for the coffee beans on her tiptoes.

"I hate it when Lenny puts stuff up so high, in my house. He knows that I'm here alone," she argued.

Isaac jumped down to help her. She bristled at his closeness. She felt his thick crotch against her hip, and shuddered.

"I'm sorry," Isaac apologized.

"No. You're fine."

"Lacey, I don't know what's going on between us." He handed her the bag of beans. "But, I think we need to talk about it—if that's OK with you."

"There's nothing to talk about. There's nothing going on."

Lacey poured the roasted beans into the back of the coffee maker, and headed to the kitchen sink. Isaac took her by the hand—sending lusty waves shooting through the both of them—

and dropped it as quickly.

"You know this can't ever happen," Isaac whispered against Lacey's temple. The touch of his mouth on her skin made her weak. She closed her eyes against the sensation.

"I know."

"I spent most of my life trying to shield Oliver from hurt. I did twelve years in a federal prison because I wanted to make sure he never went without. I love my little brother."

"I know," she said, inhaling his masculine scent once more. Lacey tried to put a step or two between them, but Isaac reached out for her and held her by the belt loop of her robe.

"You're a beautiful woman, Lacey. And I'll never be able to repay you for everything you've done for me since we met. I'll never be able to repay you for everything you've been to me, but we can't do this." His lips were grazed against the soft fine hairs on her temple. He closed his eyes tightly and breathed her in deeply.

"He'd never forgive me or you," he said, almost whimpering.

Lacey stood frozen against Isaac. She took a step away, and looked into his steely brown eyes. "I know. I don't know what's happening; I'm sick about it. I really am."

She wrapped his hands around her waist and laid her head against his chest. They stood in the kitchen in each other's arms.

"Lacey, you can do so much better than me. You're accomplished and beautiful. You have all of the things a man wants going for you. Me. I'm just an ex-con, with a face like the man you love. You love Oliver. And you're reeling from losing him. It took you a long time to let Oliver in, and then you pushed him out. So now you're just reaching out for someone familiar, and I happen to fit the bill." He lightly kissed her on the side of her head again. "I care about you—a lot—so I won't complicate things for you. And I'd never be able to live with hurting my baby brother." He pressed his mouth against her forehead. "You have to know that, had I met you under other circumstances," he didn't finish his declaration.

"Mommy," Luca sleepily called out from the bottom of the staircase.

"I'm right here, Baby." Lacey rushed to her son's side and picked him up into a big hug.

"Let's wash up while Uncle Isaac calls Daddy and Ms. Farai! Okay?" Lacey looked back at Isaac and nodded knowingly, before disappearing behind her bedroom door with her baby boy.

Luca spent the day playing with the toys Santa brought him. His entire family was together under one roof, and he was the happiest little boy in the world.

Made in the USA
Lexington, KY
02 July 2016